9-15

W9-AFD-548

CRASH

THE GAME BOOK THREE

CRASH

THE GAME BOOK THREE

Eve Silver

 KATHERINE TEGEN BOOKS
An Imprint of HarperCollins Publishers

Katherine Tegen Books is an imprint of HarperCollins Publishers.

Crash: The Game Book Three

Copyright © 2015 by Eve Silver
All rights reserved. Printed in the United States of America.
No part of this book may be used or reproduced in any manner whatsoever
without written permission except in the case of brief quotations embodied
in critical articles and reviews. For information address HarperCollins
Children's Books, a division of HarperCollins Publishers,
195 Broadway, New York, NY 10007.
www.epicreads.com

Library of Congress Control Number: 2014952560
ISBN 978-0-06-219219-6 (trade bdg.)

Typography by Carla Weise
15 16 17 18 19   PC/RRDH   10 9 8 7 6 5 4 3 2 1
❖
First Edition

TO **MY READERS**

CHAPTER**ONE**

BEFORE MOM AND SOFU AND GRAM DIED, BEFORE GRIEF turned me into this needs-to-always-be-in-control kind of girl, I used to love roller coasters. There are those moments as the roller coaster climbs the hill, the ones that take forever, the ones where your heart beats and your breathing speeds up and that clump of snakes squirms around in your gut. Excitement wars with the urge to push up the safety bar and climb off, get off, save yourself before the car you're in crests and any hope you have of escape disappears.

Then the coaster hits the high point.

You can see for miles around.

You can lift your hands and touch the sky.

So you do. You lift your hands and as the coaster tips

over into the long, steep fall, you open your mouth and scream and scream. Half the fun is in the screaming, if you don't mind being out of control, if you're a roller coaster kind of person. But if you aren't, if you're just there because somehow you got caught up in the flow, by the time you realize that this is something you really don't want to do, it's too late, you're trapped, and then you drop.

Carly always hated the drop.

"I don't want to do this, Miki Jones," she'd say, using my full name, her tone mimicking the one Mom used when she was annoyed with me.

"It'll be fun, Carly Conner," I'd say, knowing it for a fact in the way that kids do when they aren't old enough, experienced enough, to realize that not everyone feels exactly the same way they do about the things they enjoy.

"For you, maybe."

"For both of us."

"I'll puke."

"You've never puked before."

"There's always a first time. And I'll probably do it in your lap. It would serve you right."

I'd laugh and grab her hand and drag her along. She never put up much of a fight once we were in line, maybe because she's always been middle-child-Carly-the-peacemaker, or maybe because once she was in line she knew the inevitable was at hand. She went on with me every time, eyes screwed shut, jaw clamped tight, a look of sheer terror on her face. I know that for certain because we'd always check the pictures they snap while you're on the ride, the ones they try to sell you for way more than they're worth. There I'd be, smile a mile wide, hands in the air. And there Carly'd be, face white, knuckles white against the black padded safety bar, stoically sitting beside me.

We laughed at those pictures.

I'm not laughing now. I may never get the chance to laugh with Carly again.

On my last mission, the game spilled over into my real life. I need to think about that, figure out how it happened and what it means, but not right now. Right now, there are too many other things crowding my mind. The Drau almost killed Carly at the Halloween dance, when the unimaginable happened and they crossed over from the game into the real world. My world. She survived, somehow waking up alive and unscathed on her bathroom floor, only to end up on the edge of death again a few hours later.

She and Dad were hit by a drunk driver.

They're both lying in the hospital, hurt, unconscious, maybe dying.

But I'm not allowed the luxury of focusing on them and willing them to be okay because the Committee chose this moment to pull me to a deserted factory on a mission to hunt the Drau, and I have to focus everything I have on finding them, killing them, and keeping my con from going red.

I glance at the black wristband with its rectangle of

color, swirling with variegated shades of green. My portable life bar. If my con hits red, if I die in the game, I die for real.

I don't want to die.

I don't want any of my teammates to die either, not Luka or Tyrone or Kendra or Lien. Not Jackson, the boy who pushed his way past the gray fog of my depression, made me feel again, made me care. I love him, in all his flawed glory. I just haven't found the right moment to remind him of that. He's hunkered down just ahead of me, knife in his left hand, weapon cylinder in his right as he leans forward and ducks his head around the corner, checking the wide hallway ahead. He's one hundred percent in the game.

From the second the rest of our team showed up in the lobby—the tree-lined clearing where we start each mission—Jackson locked away every emotion I know he has to be feeling and became the team leader he's been for the past five years. I followed his lead and gave nothing away while we all geared up and got our scores. None of the others have a clue that Jackson and I made an unexpected detour on our way from the real world to the lobby. That never happens. The routine is set: real lives, lobby, mission, back to the real world.

But this time was different.

This time Jackson and I came face-to-face with his sister, Lizzie, in a creepy control room crawling with tiny spiderlike nanoagents that swarmed over her fingers where they merged with the control panel. Lizzie, those nanoagents, and that control panel were able to pull us just like the Committee.

The thing is, Lizzie's been dead for five years.

So who was the girl wearing Lizzie's face, and what am I supposed to make of the warning she gave us?

The Committee, she said. *Don't trust them. . . . They aren't what you think. Neither are the Drau, the battles, the game.*

She talked about not trusting them, but how are we supposed to trust her?

More questions that have to wait for answers, because right now, the dim recesses of the deserted factory beckon and the Drau are out there, waiting for us. Waiting to kill us. I need—we all need—to focus on getting them first.

Jackson's expression is set, his attention focused. He's wearing his cool-calm-collected persona, but I can't imagine there isn't a whole lot of something else going on inside his head. He'll never let that show. His expression, his actions, the tone of his voice . . . nothing gives away the strain that has to be weighing on him. He's team leader, and he carries the responsibility of getting us all out alive.

I need to follow his lead, in more ways than one. I need to lock away my emotions in a box and keep my head in the game. No thinking about Dad and Carly. No thinking about the white room and Lizzie, up to her elbows in creepy nanoagents. No thinking about anything but the mission.

So who can I count on to have my back? I do a quick assessment of our team. Luka and Tyrone seem to have their heads in the game. Lien, too. Kendra, not so much. She's glued to Lien, their shoulders touching. She's not all here, her expression blank, her thoughts lost in the terrors that bite at her, both real and imaginary. Or maybe she's just shut down altogether, thinking about nothing at all. She's more a liability to this team than an asset.

We can't afford for me to be a liability, too, or we could all die here tonight.

No matter how much I want off this roller coaster, I'm about to tip over into the long, crazy drop.

Jackson leans close to me, his lips brushing my ear as he whispers, "Make it through this, Miki Jones." That's been his go-to line since the first time I got pulled, like he's giving me an order.

"Yes, sir," I whisper back past the lump in my throat, my mind dredging up memories of the mission in Detroit, the one where he almost died. "You, too."

"Yes, ma'am," he says, with a trademark Jackson smile—nine parts cocky and one part sweet. An irresistible combination. He uncurls his index and middle fingers from the hilt of his knife, spreads them into a vee, and points at Luka, then at the ever-present über-dark shades that hide his own eyes. Weapon drawn, Luka prowls forward and rounds the corner of the wall, Jackson covering him.

I force myself to be still as the seconds tick past, fighting the urge to move, to run, until Luka returns without a shot fired. That means the Drau aren't waiting around that corner. But I can feel them somewhere close, fear and disgust of them imprinted in my cells, a genetic memory.

I'm mostly human, but some part of my DNA—all my team's DNA—shares a genetic link with the aliens who fled a Drau attack on their planet thousands and thousands of years ago. They came to Earth and integrated, passing for human, marrying humans, raising families. The collective consciousness of those aliens now forms the Committee. And the Committee runs the game, pulling kids who are their hybrid progeny to fight against the Drau invasion.

Somewhere back in the family tree of every kid who's been recruited into the game are seeds belonging to an alien or two. Jackson and I just happen to have alien ancestors somewhere way back on *both* sides of our family tree, which means we have an extra dose of alien DNA and accompanying skill sets that qualify us as team leaders. Lucky us.

I check my con. No map. Which means I'm not team leader this time out, and I have no complaint about that. Jackson's the one with five years of experience, and right now he's the one the Committee's feeding information to.

"Wide open," Luka whispers.

Jackson jerks his head toward Kendra and Lien, and then gestures forward. The signal for go. I move up beside him. Tyrone takes my left flank, and the three of us cover the three of them as they run, the shadows of silent, looming machines falling over them as they pass. They duck around two massive wheeled garbage bins and a stack of gray metal boxes flagged with hazard stickers. Then, they take their turn covering us as we run to join them.

At least, Luka and Lien cover us. Kendra just leans her head back against the wall, eyes closed, her whole body shaking. Which I actually take as a good sign because fear's better than the near-catatonic state she's been in on the last couple of missions.

But there are no Drau to shoot at right now, so whether Kendra covers us or not is a moot point.

My muscles feel sluggish as I run, like in one of those cartoons where the character's legs spin but go nowhere. I push harder, trying to move faster. By the time I get to the stack of boxes, I swear I've slogged through a mile of quicksand.

"Something's off," Tyrone whispers as we all hunker down in a tight group. "It's like the game's lagging."

"Yeah. That's it exactly." Luka frowns. "You ever felt something like this before?"

"Nah." Tyrone exhales. "Nothing like this."

Everyone looks at Jackson.

"No," Jackson says, and then he lifts his chin in Lien's direction. "You?"

For a second I'm surprised he's asking her, then I realize it's because while Luka and Tyrone have been with Jackson from the start, Lien and Kendra came from a different team. Which means they might have experiences and information unique to that team.

Lien shakes her head. "No, and it's giving me the creeps."

"Amen," Tyrone says.

Jackson scans our surroundings, ever alert. I follow his lead, but see nothing. Whatever the Drau are planning, they don't seem to be ready to implement it yet. Which only amps up my anxiety.

"So now what?" Luka asks.

"We have a little talk," Jackson says. "Set our plan."

Tyrone snorts. Luka's brows shoot up. "Strategy meeting? Not really your style."

"Not a strategy meeting," Jackson says. "More of a strategy dictatorship."

"True to form," Tyrone says at the same time Luka says, "So what you meant to say is that you talk and we listen."

It's eerie the way Jackson stares them down even though his eyes are hidden behind his mirrored shades.

Tyrone glances at me. "You aren't saying much."

The urge is there to blurt it all out, to tell him about Dad and Carly and the accident. He'd get it. He'd understand. Tyrone knows all about heartbreak and loss. But it isn't just that. I want to tell him about Lizzie. About the white room and the nanoagents and the way she snatched us up before we could get to the lobby. I want to tell all of them.

But as the scenario plays out in my mind, the questions they'll ask, the amount of time it will take to lay out the whole story, I know this isn't the time or place. I doubt the Drau will be patient while I bring the rest of the team up to speed—plus, I don't want to be here for a second longer than I have to be. I need to get back to the hospital.

Maybe I'll save the story of Lizzie for the next time we're in the lobby waiting for scores, the moment of quiet between getting pulled and getting dumped into the battle zone. Not like we have a ton of other opportunities for earnest heart-to-hearts. I shrug and say, "Jackson talks and expects us to listen. New day, same old, same old."

Lien gives a short laugh.

Tyrone frowns but doesn't push me.

Luka's watching me, his expression weird—strained and puzzled and kind of vacant. In that second I realize he hasn't said a word to me about Dad or Carly. Not when he arrived in the lobby or while we grabbed our weapons or when the scores showed up. Not a word. He hasn't asked how they're doing. Hasn't mentioned the accident at all. But unlike the rest of the team who have no way to know what's happened, Luka does. He was with Jackson when they drove past Dad's totaled car. Jackson told me that at the hospital. He said it was Luka who recognized the Explorer.

His gaze slides away. It isn't the first time someone's been weird around me when it comes to stuff like this. When Mom was sick, half the kids at school pretended they didn't know because they had no idea what to say. Maybe Luka's feeling like that right now. But I sort of expected more from him.

"Kendra," Jackson says, and when she doesn't even look at him, he taps her cheek with the backs of his fingers.

Lien grabs his wrist. He turns his head toward her, away from me, and something she reads in his expression makes her let go.

"Kendra," he says again. "Listen to me. I know you're griefing—"

"Hey, we've already been over this," Lien interjects.

"Just listen," Jackson says, his tone hard enough that Lien snaps her mouth shut. "Here's the thing, Kendra. I want you to keep it up." He has her attention now. He has all our attention. "You and Lien keep going exactly as you have been. Steal as many points as you can without putting the rest of the team in danger—"

"What?" Luka interrupts, his voice a harsh whisper. "You *want* her to steal our points? Seriously?"

"In fact, you won't be stealing," Jackson continues, ignoring Luka for the moment. "We're giving them to you. I want you to up your score, stockpile as many points as you can. Get to a thousand." He turns to Luka then. "Yeah, that's exactly what I want her to do. And I want all of you to let her, even help her do it if it doesn't put you in danger. That's key, though. No one puts themselves at risk."

Lien's eyes narrow. "Why would you do this for us?" she asks at the same time Luka says, "I don't think this is a good idea."

"Not a democracy," Jackson says to Luka, then to Lien, "I'm not doing it for you. You know anyone who's earned the thousand points? Anyone who's hit the magic number? Made it out?"

"I—" She pauses. "No."

"Funny, neither do I," he says. "Luka? Tyrone?"

Luka doesn't answer, just stares at Jackson, expressionless.

"Almost," Tyrone whispers, and I know he's thinking of Richelle, of what an amazing fighter she was, of how her high score almost hit the mark right before she died.

I touch his shoulder, silent comfort, the same comfort Richelle offered me my first time in the game. He rests his hand on mine and squeezes and I see him consciously pull himself together.

"You got something in mind," he says.

"I do." Jackson offers a feral smile.

"You're thinking we let Kendra be the first." Tyrone catches on at exactly the same second I do. "We help her get the thousand points to test the truth in the rumor. To see if earning the magic number is the golden ticket out of the game. If it is, we help each other get out, one by one."

"Bingo," Jackson says, bumping my knee with his. Getting out one by one might be the plan for the rest of them, but not for us. Regardless of whether or not the thousand-points-and-you're-out rumor proves true, Jackson and I don't get to leave. We're in it for the long haul; we signed the devil's contract in a convoluted attempt to save each other.

Funny how we both pulled a life sentence. Like the Committee planned it that way. Which, of course, they did. They pretty much own our souls. But maybe we can save the others.

"I still don't like it, the whole stealing-points thing," Luka says.

"Why?" I ask.

"It's dangerous," he says, his tone flat. "Someone could get hurt."

I stare at him. "Being here is dangerous. Any one of us could get hurt." Living is dangerous. How can he not know that?

"And that's why Kendra only takes the points if it doesn't put anyone else at risk," Jackson says. "The usual rules apply. As soon as anyone's con goes orange, fall back. Defensive position only. And Kendra takes the kill only if it's workable. Got it?"

"Let's say this works, that we earn the thousand and get the hell out . . . there'll be new recruits." Tyrone bows his head and clenches his fists. "We'll all just be replaced by another team. Someone makes it out, someone new gets dragged in. They fight. They die."

A horrible truth. The game doesn't end until the Drau are defeated. When players die, they get replaced. I replaced a boy who died.

"But at least it won't be us anymore," Lien says.

Luka rolls his eyes. "Nice. Way to care about your fellow man."

"I care." Lien shrugs. "But in a case of them or me, I'd rather it not be me."

I wonder if she's always been this pragmatic, this hard, or if the game made her that way.

"I'd rather it not be anyone," Jackson says, the statement so out of character that everyone falls silent and just gapes at him.

After a few seconds, Luka says, "I thought you were all about every man for himself."

"Stop." Everyone looks at me. I guess I put more power behind that single word than they're used to hearing from me. "Stop bickering. We need unity to survive. One. Team." I turn my gaze to Jackson. "And stop pretending you don't care. Stop pretending you haven't put yourself in harm's way at some point for each and every one of us."

He doesn't say anything. He doesn't have to.

"We all know Jackson's been here the longest, survived the longest, kept the rest of us alive. Someone here think they can do a better job?" I look at each of them in turn. No one volunteers. "Then we do what he says."

I grab Jackson's wrist and turn it so I can see his con. There's a map and off to one side, six triangles in a clump. Us. "We're like sitting ducks. The Drau are getting closer. I feel it"—I press my closed fist against my abdomen— "here." I feel *something*, anyway. Snakes writhing. Bile burning the back of my throat.

I rise and straighten, flexing my fingers around my weapon cylinder, the shape conforming to my hand. Then I reach back and grab the hilt of my kendo sword, pulling it free of the sheath that rests between my shoulder blades, the black blade gleaming and deadly sharp. "Let's get this done. I have places I need to be."

Back at the hospital with Dad and Carly . . .

Thinking about them brings on a wave of anxiety.

I stare at the red stop sign that's painted on the concrete floor, counting the sides. Counting. Counting. The snakes in my gut twist tighter. The red octagon on the floor bursts apart into pixels then coalesces back to a single unit. I close my eyes tight, open them again. The stop sign just looks like a stop sign.

Tyrone's right. The game's doing something really weird.

"Miki," Lien says. I turn. "What you said about anyone thinking they can do a better job . . . I don't know if you can do a better job than Jackson, but when it was you at the helm, you kept us alive. We all made it back thanks to you."

"I almost got myself killed." Would have gotten myself killed if Lizzie hadn't intervened.

Lien grins at me. "But the rest of us were fine."

A return smile tugs at the corners of my mouth. "You're . . ." Words fail me.

She gives my hand a quick squeeze. I'm startled to realize that somewhere along the line, Lien and I have started to become friends. It's too late to stop myself from caring about her, to protect myself against the pain if I lose her.

CHAPTER**TWO**

"LUKA, TYRONE, TAKE POINT," JACKSON SAYS. "MIKI, WATCH our backs."

"Where will you be?" Lien asks.

Jackson snorts a dark laugh. "Helping you with protection duty." He dips his chin in Kendra's direction. "Let's go."

With that, we move, Luka and Tyrone leading us through unsecured territory, taking the most exposed position. Jackson and Lien flank Kendra. I'm behind, watching for an attack from the rear.

I feel them, the Drau, the awareness writhing inside me. They are the enemy. They're lying in wait somewhere in this massive factory, with its million places to hide. My skin crawls. They could be watching us right now.

Tipping my head back, I study the silent conveyor

belt overhead, suspended from the high ceiling by thick metal beams that have been painted a vibrant yellow. More yellow metal, this time a set of stairs marked by black-and-yellow-striped columns on either side. They lead to one of many overhead catwalks. Metal ladders climb the walls between tall stacks of wood crates.

I have no idea what they make in this factory, or even where in the world it is. I'm not sure I care. I turn, walking backward, studying the shadows in our wake.

Nothing.

No movement.

No sound.

Just the thud of my heart and the roar of my blood in my ears.

The creepy feeling intensifies. I start to turn.

"Sniper," Jackson yells, already firing at the overhead catwalk as burning flecks of light rain down on us. "Move!"

Kendra cries out and skitters to the right, the left, trying to find an escape route. Lien grabs her arm and drags her toward a stack of metal crates. The hazard stickers on the sides don't exactly give me a feeling of confidence, but at the moment, hiding behind them is the lesser of evils, so I keep my doubts to myself as I follow behind the others.

Jackson holds his position, right out in the open, covering the rest of us as we head for safety. Covering *me*. I want to hit him for that. Would it make us any less safe if he ran for cover while he fired?

My legs pump. The Drau aim for me, hit me. Tiny

droplets of blinding light sear through skin and muscle like acid. Their weapons incinerate us, little bits at a time; ours swallow them alive in a surge of oozing darkness. I shoot back, my attention on the catwalk.

My toes catch on a raised platform. I stumble, twisting as I fall, firing without precision or a sightline. Shooting blind. My butt slams hard on the ground, winding me. And then I'm sliding along the floor crazy fast and it clicks that I didn't hit the floor, I hit a low, wheeled trolley that carries me under a massive robot arm hanging suspended from the high ceiling.

My team—and the relative safety of the stack of crates—lies in the opposite direction.

I'm cut off from Jackson, cut off from the others. I'm completely on my own.

Jackson comes after me, maybe a dozen loping steps, only to stop short when enemy fire blocks his path. There are more snipers up there. At least three or four. Every time they fire, it gives their positions away. I try and offer him what cover I can.

My shots go wild, spurts of oily black death that don't quite hit the mark because the trolley underneath me is running its own marathon. And because there's something wrong with me. It's like I'm watching TV and the cable's on the fritz, images going pixelated or freezing altogether, then stuttering to life again. With a grunt, I twist to the side just enough to be able to reach my sheath and sink my kendo sword home, then I roll off the trolley and keep rolling until I'm sheltered beneath the comparative safety of a massive wheeled tool cart.

Jackson presses against a column under a barrage of Drau shots. Luka and Tyrone are with Lien and Kendra, pinned where we left them, fending off more Drau. Jackson points straight up. I follow his direction and see the steepled glass of a massive skylight and the stars beyond. The stars don't look like I've ever seen them. I get the feeling we're somewhere on the opposite side of the world. I glance at Jackson, trying to figure out what it is he wants me to see.

Again, he points up, then at the tool cart I'm hiding under, then mimes shooting at the ceiling. I roll to the far side of the cart, my sheath digging in against the bumpy bones of my spine, and duck my head out from underneath to see some sort of hydraulic nail gun with nails as long as my forearm and thick as my thumb.

I lie there, drawing shallow breaths and blowing them out in rapid puffs. Jackson holds up five fingers. Four. Three. Two. One.

I shove my weapon cylinder in its holster, roll out from under the cart, and surge to my feet while Jackson covers me. I flick the power switch, grab the nail gun two-handed, point straight up, and shoot.

Again.

Again.

I aim for the same spot in the glass because I need it to—

The glass roof shatters and comes down on me, Jackson, and the Drau. With a cry, I drop the nail gun and dive back under the cart as massive razor-sharp shards fall like hail.

I free my weapon cylinder and roll onto my stomach, using my elbows to drag myself forward as I try to spot Jackson. He presses up against a wall under some low-hanging ductwork. He must have found cover before the worst of the glass showered down because there's a cut on his forearm, blood welling in a thin line, but he looks otherwise unhurt.

On the metal grille above me, a Drau lies unmoving, its glowing upper body hanging over the edge of the catwalk, its lower body trapped by the railing. A shard of glass protrudes from its chest, jutting up like a shark's fin above the water.

The Drau's eyes are open. I'm careful not to meet its gaze just in case it's still alive. I know what those mercury eyes can do—drain me until I'm a dull husk, kind of like what happens to a car battery if the headlights are left on. The Drau can kill me with a look. I'm not going to give it that chance.

I aim and shoot, the faint hum of my weapon cylinder accompanying the black surge of death that swallows the Drau whole. I hate that part. I know it's them or me. I know they will kill my team, kill me. But that doesn't mean I don't feel a twinge every time I take one of them out.

Them or me. Them or me. My mantra pings around inside my head.

There's another Drau body up there. An arm overhangs the edge of the catwalk, gleaming bright. Jackson shoots. The arm doesn't even twitch as the Drau is destroyed. Maybe it was dead already, guillotined by the glass.

I'm more worried about the Drau that are still moving, firing down on us, zipping along the catwalk, so fast they're little more than blurs of light.

Firing in rapid succession, I take one of them out, miss a second and a third. Their aim's better than mine, their shots burning my arms as they hit their mark. My movements awkward thanks to the sword sheathed tight against my back, I scuttle all the way under the tool cart for cover, pinned in place by hostile fire. Jackson gets one on the opposite side of the catwalk, then another on the catwalk above me. I'm about to break cover and sprint toward him when he shakes his head and points directly up. Through the metal grating, I see the gleam of a Drau's feet.

My vision stutters, stalls, then starts up again, like someone pressed the Pause button. I drag the back of my hand across my eyes, wiping away sweat.

Jackson points up again, then at me. I nod, grip my weapon cylinder tight and slither out feet-first from under the tool cart. I circle the edge, aiming, shooting.

Got it. The Drau's light flickers out as it's sucked into the black ooze that erupts from my weapon.

Jackson signals back in the direction we left the rest of the team. We run, firing as we go, aiming for anything that glows. In my zeal, I take out an overhead lamp, tiny bits of glass from the broken bulb tinkling down on us. I hunch forward, shoulders high, as if that'll protect me from the fallout as we sprint to the far wall. The two of us collapse against it, listening for any threat.

The factory's quiet.

Jackson leans around the corner.

"Looks clear," he murmurs.

I reach up and pick a glittering bit of glass from his hair. From the skylight or the lamp I shattered? Silly to even wonder. Does it matter?

"Go," he says. "I'll cover you. Head for the stack of crates." Before I can protest, he continues, "I'll be right behind you."

I sidle past him and peer around the corner, catching Luka's eye. He gives me the thumbs-up, his weapon cylinder at the ready. Tyrone nods at me. They'll cover my front. Jackson'll cover my back.

Three. Two. One.

I run.

But I don't move. Not at all.

Seconds drag past and it's an eternity before I take a breath, filling my lungs on a sharp gasp, as if I've been underwater too long and my head's finally broken the surface.

I close my fingers around my weapon cylinder, but it isn't there.

I'm in the wrong place.

No factory.

No Drau.

We stand in the middle of the hospital waiting room, Jackson holding tight to my hand, exactly as we were when we got pulled hours and hours ago.

Or was it days ago? Seconds ago?

The time shift thing between the real world and the game makes me crazy. Makes me sick.

I stare straight ahead at the flu vaccine poster. The hard thud of my heart mingles with the hum of voices from people passing in the hallway and the distant mechanical hissing and beeping that filter in.

Bam, we're back. But we shouldn't be. Not yet.

I should be relieved we're back here, that I don't have to focus on fighting the Drau when I want to focus on Dad and Carly. But I'm not, because I've learned that when something unexpected happens in the game, it's never good.

"What are we doing here?" I ask, then louder, "We're not done yet. We didn't finish. We were just starting. The mission wasn't complete."

"Shh," Jackson glances at the open door and takes both my hands in his. Either my hands are really cold or his are really warm. He leads me to the far corner of the room.

I'm used to the routine now: get pulled, complete the mission, respawn in real life. Everything has to be in its place, neat and tidy. This is messy. Wrong. "It isn't happening in the right order," I whisper.

"No, it isn't." He doesn't sound happy about it.

"I can't think." I rip my hands from his and press the sides of my fists against my forehead. "The mission . . . it wasn't right. It felt off. Fractured. I felt like I wasn't a hundred percent there, right from the start. Like the mission was . . . I don't know . . . I guess the best way to describe it is that it felt like it was stuttering. Like someone kept hitting the Pause button."

I spin away, pace to the far end of the room, pace back. I'm jumping out of my skin, anxiety crawling through me.

"My vision kept doing this weird thing where it would dissociate into little spots or rectangles, then fix itself. Like the game froze. And now we're back here, out of order. Why?" When Jackson doesn't answer fast enough, I grab his forearms and demand, "Why? What's happening? What's going on?"

"It could have something to do with the way we were detoured." He's talking about Lizzie, about the way she managed to grab us somewhere between the real world and the lobby and bring us to the white room. He pauses, frowns, then says, "No. That can't be it. Because Luka and the others said they felt off, too."

And they didn't make the same stop on their way to the lobby. They didn't get pulled into yet another alien place to chat with a girl who's been dead for five years.

"Tell me what's going on. Jackson, don't mess with me. Just tell me!" Everything's out of control. The rules have changed and I need to know why. I need an answer. If I can just get an answer, everything will be—

"Miki," Jackson says. I'm still holding his forearms. I let go, and as he drops his arms to his sides, I glance down and see little half-moon marks on his skin where I dug my nails in deep.

He reaches for me but I jerk away and stumble back a few steps. "I'm sorry. I didn't mean to do that. I didn't realize—" I'm not in control, and I need to be because I can feel a full-blown panic attack body-slamming the edges of my failing defenses. I'm panting, my heart racing, sweat dampening my palms.

My chest feels like it's being crushed by a cement truck. There are a million centipedes crawling on my skin. I can't breathe. I can't think. Panic claws at me.

Miki, slow breaths. Just think about each breath.

Jackson eases his thoughts inside my mind, calm, comforting. I do what he says and add a few tricks of my own, imagining my hands are weightless, my forearms, my shoulders. I bring relaxation through my feet, my knees, my thighs. But I can't make it work. Anxiety scratches at the door.

"Look at me, Miki," Jackson says, his voice low. He flips his sunglasses up so I'm looking into his Drau-gray eyes, because, yeah, in addition to the alien DNA of the

Committee, Jackson's double blessed with a hit of Drau genes, too. "Breathe with me. Slow. Like this." He inhales. I shake my head back and forth. He cups my cheeks, holding me still, his eyes locked on mine. "Like this," he says again, and takes another slow breath.

I take three little gasps for his one.

"Slower."

Jackson's there, inside my head. I see the beach, the waves, feel the sun on my skin. He helps me see them.

Just think about each breath.

I nod and do better this time. I follow his rhythm, his pattern. I see nothing but his eyes, molten silver.

I don't know how long we stand like that. Long enough that my pulse slows, my breathing evens out.

Finally, I say, "Tell me what's going on," my voice calmer now.

"I would if I could."

"What does that mean? Are you still keeping secrets?"

He holds his hands out to his sides. "I don't have answers."

I stare at him, at the way he's standing, the first time in my recollection that he looks . . . indecisive. Or is that a ploy, a trick? That's the thing about Jackson, about the game, about everything . . . what am I supposed to trust? Are there things he knows that he won't—*can't*—tell me?

"Don't have the answers or don't want to share them?" That's the question. He's kept stuff from me before. We had a fight about it . . . God, was it just a few hours ago that I fought with Jackson about his penchant for keeping secrets? It feels like weeks ago.

"Don't have them," Jackson says. "I know what you know. That there was something really weird about being in that factory and that we're back here at the hospital and we shouldn't be. Not yet."

Back here at the hospital. My stomach turns. I'm fighting with Jackson about nothing when Dad and Carly are injured, maybe dying. The panic attack I staved off paces the confines of its cage, ready to pounce at the slightest opportunity. "You're supposed to have the answers. You're supposed to know everything about the game. You're—"

"Doing the best I can," he says, with a tight smile. "Just like you. If I knew anything else, I'd tell you, Miki."

"Would you?"

A flicker of hurt crosses his features. "Yeah, I would. But I get why you think I wouldn't. My track record isn't exactly stellar." He approaches me slowly, like I'm a feral cat that might lash out at any second. Maybe he isn't far from right. "I'm here. Lean on me." He holds up his hands, palms forward. "Or take a swing at me. Whatever you need. Just let me help you."

"How? How can you help me?" How can he take away the pain? The fear? The guilt? That's the thing. The guilt is chewing away at me. If only I'd hugged Carly one last time. If only I'd asked Dad to wait a minute while I found his cell phone. If only I'd made Carly sleep over, then they wouldn't have been in that intersection at exactly that moment.

If only.

I wish I could tell Jackson all that. Explain. Say it out loud. But the words choke me, refusing to come, even as I wonder why I'm holding back.

Finally, I say, "There's nothing you can do."

He looks like I just stabbed him through the heart, and I get it. As much as I need to be in control, so does Jackson. And part of his thing is being the caretaker, the strong one, the protector, even when he claims he isn't.

"I'm sorry. I'm scared." My voice catches. "I'm scared that we're back here even though we weren't finished there. That us being here means something terrible. Like in that movie, *Saving Private Ryan*. You know, the one where they wanted to bring the guy home from war to tell him all his brothers were dead. What if the Committee brought us back because Daddy . . . or Carly . . . What if they're . . ."

"They aren't. And what you just said about the Committee bringing us back because something's happened to your dad or Carly? They wouldn't bring us back because someone died. They don't care about two human lives in the grand scheme of things."

An ugly laugh escapes me. No, they don't. They care about one thing. Beating the Drau. And I guess I can stretch that and say they care about saving mankind by beating the Drau. But two individual human lives . . . Dad's and Carly's . . .

"You're right. They wouldn't care about that."

CHAPTER **THREE**

JACKSON REACHES FOR ME AND GATHERS ME CLOSE. I SLUMP against him. He holds me up, my torso resting against his, his arms solid and real. I wish I could stay here forever, grounded by the steady beat of his heart. But I can't.

I can't just stand here doing nothing, letting things unfold as they unfold. I need to do something, take action, make a choice. I start for the door. "I'm going to find a nurse, someone who can tell me something. It's been hours . . ."

"It hasn't," he says. "We respawned at the exact second we left here, so nothing terrible could have happened to your dad or Carly while we were gone. It's only been a few minutes."

I rest my palms on either side of the doorframe,

shoulders slumped, head bowed. "I wish I could run. Right now. Just my feet against the pavement. No thinking. Just moving. Hit the wall and crash through."

He rests his palm on the back of my neck. "There's nowhere to run."

A brutal truth.

I stiffen and push against him, then finally realize I'm fighting Jackson because I want to fight everything else. With a sigh, I turn and loop my arms around his waist and rest my forehead on his chest. But I can't stay still for long. If I stay still, if I don't do *something* with my hands—busy work—I'll implode. Jackson must sense that because he steps away, and as I bend over the low table and straighten the scattered magazines, I feel him watching me.

My jacket's on the chair where I left it before we got pulled. I snag it by the sleeve, fold it shoulder to shoulder, then in half. The sleeves slide free. I shake the jacket out then fold it again, careful to keep everything neat. But the seams don't line up. The folds aren't symmetrical. I shake it out and try again, finally getting it right on the third round.

Jackson walks over and takes the jacket from my hands. He sets it carefully on the chair, keeping all the seams lined up.

"So why do you think we're back here?" I ask. "What went wrong?"

"How do you know anything went wrong? Don't borrow trouble. We took out the threat on the catwalk. Maybe that was all we were supposed to do there."

He doesn't sound convinced. I don't feel convinced.

"What about Luka and the others? Do you think they're still there? Do you think we were the only ones who got pulled out?"

He fishes out his phone and types. He waits a few minutes and texts again, then waits. No response.

Phones don't work in the game.

That's why Luka isn't responding. Because he's still there.

I can't even consider any other explanation because the one that comes to mind is that Luka isn't answering because he *can't*, because he won't be answering his phone ever again. I swallow and pretend those thoughts aren't floating just beneath the surface.

Minutes drag past. I flop on a chair and watch the news station on the flat screen in the corner. Then I grab the stack of magazines, arrange them in alphabetical order, and then put the stack back down and tap the edges until everything's perfectly aligned. When I look up, Jackson's watching me, worry etched in his expression. Seeing that only amps up my anxiety.

Except, it isn't just anxiety. My skin prickles and the hairs at my nape rise.

"What?" Jackson asks, suddenly alert.

"Creepy feeling." One I recognize. "Like that day at school when I thought I was being watched."

Jackson's on his feet before I've even finished my

sentence, crossing to the door, checking the hallway. I'm a step behind him.

There's no one there watching us. Just a nurse walking along the corridor. She turns and waves at someone and I catch a glimpse of the sleeve of a green jacket as whoever it is rounds the corner.

"Excuse me . . . ," I say as the nurse turns back toward me.

"Yes?"

I study her face, thinking there's something familiar about her. But I can't place where I know her from and it really doesn't matter right now.

"My dad . . ." Jackson steps up behind me and rests his hand on my shoulder. I take a breath and continue. "He was in a car accident. He's in surgery. His last name is Jones . . . I was wondering if there's any news . . ."

Her expression is kind, sympathetic, but her answer holds no comfort. "I'll check for you, hon, and if there is, I'll let you know. But I don't think so. Not yet. The doctor'll come see you just as soon as he can."

Jackson and I stand in the doorway and watch her head down the hall. She doesn't come back, but a few minutes later, another nurse does. My anxious questions yield noncommittal answers. She really doesn't have anything to tell me yet. She asks me questions about Dad's general health. If he smokes. If he drinks. I answer as honestly as I can.

When she leaves, we retreat back into the waiting

room. I pace to the far end, flop forward and touch my toes, then straighten. The creepy feeling isn't quite gone. I turn and stare at the TV. What if the Drau are watching us right now? What if that's why the hairs on my forearms are standing on end and my skin feels tight, my scalp prickly? What if the Drau are piggybacking human satellites to watch us while we watch the news? I stalk over and turn off the TV. My gaze slides away, to the clock on the wall. It's three a.m.

"Do you need to go home?" I ask Jackson, hoping he doesn't, hoping he'll stay. "Your parents will be worried."

"I called them. Do you think I'd leave you?"

Everyone leaves. That's been my motto for a while. The seeds were planted when Gram and Sofu died, and certainty cemented two years ago when I held Mom's hand while she took her last breath. They all left me. And now Dad and Carly might leave me tonight.

No. *No.* I can't think that way.

"I won't," he says. I stare at him. He comes to me and hooks his index finger under my chin and lifts my face to his. "I won't leave you. I've spent my whole life traveling, never staying in one place more than a few months, and I liked it. Liked going from place to place, never being anchored. No tethers." He strokes the backs of his fingers along my cheek. "You aren't a tether, Miki. You're my lifeline. You're the best kind of anchor, keeping me from crashing on the rocks when a storm hits. And that's a two-way thing. I'm your anchor. I won't leave you."

I want to believe that so badly I feel it as a craving in my soul. "You can't promise that. You don't know what will happen. You could get—" My voice catches. I look away, stare at my feet, and keep talking. "You could get hit by a drunk driver. You could get cancer. You could get killed in the game."

"You're right. I could." I gasp. "I won't pretend otherwise," he continues. "But believe that I'll fight anyone and anything to be there when you need me. To keep you safe. And if I can't find a way to put myself between you and harm, I'll be there to help you bear it. You get that, right?"

I think of him standing out in the open at the factory, Drau fire raining down on him as he covered me so I could get to safety. He's done that since the beginning. On the very first mission, he jumped in front of me and took the full measure of a Drau hit.

I bump his shoulder with mine. "And you get how risky that is, right? You take too many chances, Jackson. I know that you want me safe, but does it occur to you that I need you safe, too?"

His lips curl in a dark smile. "You keep me safe, Miki. Who took out the Drau on the catwalk by bringing down the roof?"

We stare at each other. My heart hammers.

Then his mouth is on mine, hard, desperate. He kisses me with his lips, his heart, his soul, holding me so tight I can't tell where Jackson ends and I begin. I cling to him as he draws his lips from mine, our breath mingling in the inches that separate us.

I study his face. Purple crescents carve hollows under his eyes. There's a shadow of golden stubble on his jaw, and tension hardens his features.

"You look like hell," I whisper.

He tips his glasses back down. "So do you," he whispers with a little smile and somehow, I manage to smile back.

"I brought you something to drink."

Startled, I spin toward the door, one palm pressed to my chest, sorry we've been interrupted, sorry to be pulled back to a darker reality.

Mrs. Conner stands a few feet away with a couple of bottles of water and some packaged snack cakes in her hands.

She looks at Jackson. "It's good of you to be here."

"There's nowhere else I'd be." He edges a little closer so our shoulders touch, so I can feel his warmth and strength.

Mrs. Conner nods.

"Any news?" I ask.

"No. Nothing. Carly's still having tests. A CT of her brain and c-spine." She offers the items she brought. I take them, then stare at the bottles and packages, not really sure what to do with them. Jackson takes them and sets them on the table.

"What's a c-spine?" I ask.

"It's . . . Carly's neck."

I take a sharp breath. "Why? Is it . . . It's not . . ." I can't say the word *broken*. Carly's neck can't be broken.

"They said that evaluating the neck is routine." She doesn't sound convinced.

I sink into a chair. "Did she wake up yet?"

Carly's mom shakes her head, her eyes sad. Desperate. She looks away. "Your dad's still in surgery."

"I know. I asked a nurse. She said she'd come back if she heard anything . . ." I sigh. "Did the nurses tell you anything else?"

She scrubs her palm over her face. "Since I'm not family they won't tell me everything."

But I *am* family, and they've told me nothing.

Jackson's fingers thread through mine. I close my hand on his tight enough that it smarts, the pain grounding me. He doesn't complain.

"What about the driver?" I ask. "Of the car that hit them?"

She doesn't answer for so long that I figure she isn't going to answer. Then she whispers, "Not a scratch on him."

Jackson's breath hisses from between his teeth. I slam the side of my fist against my thigh, not even realizing that I've done it until the pain blossoms.

Mrs. Conner lays one hand on Jackson's forearm and one on mine. "He's been charged."

Does that make me feel better? Should it?

"And if he gets a good lawyer?" My head jerks up. Carly's dad stands in the doorway of the waiting room, his hand deep in his pocket, the sound of jingling change filling the silence. "A good lawyer and he'll walk while our baby's lying—" His voice cracks.

Carly's mom sighs and gets to her feet. She goes to her husband, slides her arm through his, and says, "Let's walk," and then they're gone and Jackson and I are alone in the waiting room once more.

I look up at the clock. Three o'clock. Still three o'clock. The hands haven't moved . . . aren't moving. No, wait . . . they are. The minute hand stutters forward, then freezes, then stutters. I look away, look back, and the hands are running smoothly and the time reads 3:27. Jackson watches me, frowning.

He picks up one of the water bottles, cracks it open, and hands it to me. He lifts the second one, opens it, and takes a long swallow. Then he drags the back of his hand across his lips. "They're going to be okay, Miki. Both of them."

My gaze flicks up. "False reassurances? From you, Jackson? Not really your style. Plus . . ."

"Plus?"

"The fact that you're offering them makes me even more afraid."

"Fair enough. I'll rephrase. They have a lot of reasons to be okay."

I take a drink. Then another. I didn't realize how thirsty I was. "Lien said something once. On a mission. About tasks left uncompleted. She said that if we left a task unfinished back home, we'd have to come back from the mission to finish it." Even as I say it, I realize how ridiculous it sounds. Mom had so many tasks left unfinished.

"Hey," Jackson says, and rests his palm against the back of my neck. "Your dad and Carly have a lot of stuff to finish still."

I nod, my teeth sinking into my lower lip. "Carly told me once that she wants to fill a mayonnaise jar with vanilla pudding and eat it in a crowded place."

"Why?"

"She said it would be hilarious. People would think she was eating mayo straight from the jar."

"Then she definitely has to get better," Jackson says, "because that's one hell of a worthy aspiration."

I choke on a watery laugh. "There were more. She has a list. She plans to wear a T-shirt that reads LIFE and hand out free lemons. And hire two private investigators to follow each other."

"She find that list online?"

"Probably." I swallow, then whisper, "And Daddy? What has he left unfinished?" I think how much he misses Mom, how sad he is. "What has he got to come back to?"

Jackson brushes the pad of his thumb along my cheekbone. "You, Miki. He's coming back to you."

At 4:44 the doctor steps through the door.

"Miss Jones?"

He's wearing scrubs and a white coat and a nametag that identifies him as Dr. Charles Lee. He looks like he's really young, maybe early twenties, but I figure that can't be right.

"I'm Miki. Miki Jones," I say, shoving my hair out of my face and scrambling to my feet. "Daddy? Is he okay?"

"Your father is out of surgery. We did an open splenectomy. In some situations, we can make small incisions and remove the spleen laparoscopically through one of those incisions." He pauses. "In your father's case, we had to make a larger incision."

I almost ask why. But I don't really care. There's only one question that matters, so that's the one I ask. "Is he okay?"

His mouth opens and shapes a letter, but no sound comes out.

Bright snakes slither across the edges of my vision. The world tips and sways.

Oh God. Not now. I can't do this now.

I grope for Jackson's hand and hold on, the tips of my fingers and toes gone numb. Dr. Lee keeps talking in slow motion. Sounds—not quite words—come at me from far away, echoing like they're traveling down a long tunnel. I know he's saying something, but I can't catch the meaning.

"What? I can't—"

My vision bursts in an explosion of color that makes no sense, frozen rectangles of blue partially overlying rectangles of red. Green. Orange.

The colors implode.

The floor drops away. I spin end over end, landing on

my feet, heart pounding as I run flat out, my weapon cylinder in my hand.

I skid and slam down on one knee, the pain shooting up my thigh through my hip to my spine. I swear it shakes my skull; I can feel it in my teeth. Disoriented, I look around, trying to get my bearings. I'm back in the game, but not at the point I left it. Last thing I remember I was running toward Luka and Tyrone, Jackson behind me, covering my back. Now I'm alone, between two machines that smell like oil, with a wall of Drau between me and where I last saw my team.

CHAPTER**FOUR**

MY BREATH COMES IN JAGGED RASPS AS I GET TO MY FEET,
babying my knee. I lean out from behind the machine just
enough to scope the spot where I expect Jackson to be.

He isn't where I left him. I try not to freak out because
I'm not where he left me, either.

The Drau are focused on Luka and the others and when
a lone Drau darts my way, it's picked off by a shot from
above before I can take it down. I exhale and sag against
the machine at my back, choosing to believe that was Jackson playing sniper, keeping me safe.

I shake my head to clear it.

The Committee's dumped me back in the game at the
worst possible moment. My focus needs to be here, in the

game, but it isn't. Not fully. It's back at the hospital with the people I love.

Daddy.

Carly.

I respawned in this pit before I could hear what Dr. Lee had to say. I don't know if Dad's okay, if he made it through the surgery . . . I picture the doctor's face, remember everything I can about his expression. Did he look regretful? Distressed? Did he look like a man about to tell a girl that her father didn't make it?

I don't want to be here, but I have no say, no choice, no control. Part of me wants to sink to the floor, wrap my arms around my knees and keen out loud while I rock. I don't let that part grab a handhold. I'm stronger than that. I will get this done, finish the mission and get back to where I need to be—with my father and my best friend.

A splatter of light burns through my sleeve and skin, digging deep into the muscle of my forearm.

My little pity party's out of time. It's either focus or die.

I lean out from behind the machine just enough that I have a clean shot, steady my weapon cylinder against my forearm, and start shooting. I aim at the clump of Drau that has my team pinned.

There are so many of them.

Three break off and come at me. I pick them off one by one with—I think—a little help from Jackson and his overhead vantage point.

More Drau break away from the group and head in my

direction. I take out one. Jackson takes out another. Someone from my team—I think it's Tyrone—takes out a third. Still more of them head for me. It's like they smell my isolation and plan to take full advantage of it.

I back up, firing, hitting one, missing another.

The Drau split their attention between me and the rest of my team. I catch glimpses of Lien's face, her expression hard and focused. Then Luka. Then Tyrone. I edge forward, firing on the enemy, picking them off. Others come at me.

Still shooting, I back into the narrow groove between the machines, using the metal to protect me from the Drau's weapons. Boots pound on the metal grate above me, then Jackson's there, taking them out, buying me a chance to catch my breath.

"Get out of here," he orders, yelling down to me through the metal grating of the catwalk.

"But Tyrone, and Luka—"

"Are holding their own. They have a better position than you. Go."

Four more Drau come at us. Jackson gets one. I get another, but not before its weapon discharges and sears my upper arm. I smell burning flesh. I hear a sharp feminine cry: Kendra or Lien.

I'm dividing Jackson's attention; if he's focused on keeping an eye on me, he isn't helping the rest of our team the way he could be. Just like that first time, the time he couldn't save both me and Richelle.

"Go," Jackson snarls. "I'll find you."

I peer around the front edge of the machine. Go where? There's a wall of Drau in front of me, so that's not an option. I glance back and see that there's just enough space to squeeze between the machines if I turn sideways.

Crazy as it seems, in the midst of mayhem I hear Mr. Shomper's reedy voice in my head, reading Shakespeare. *The better part of valor is discretion.* Valor would see me charging into the fray, but discretion would make me pick a spot where I can hold out longer and help my team.

"Discretion it is," I mutter as I wriggle through and bolt.

One of the Drau darts at me, then another, coming through the tiny opening single file. I jog backward, firing at them. My heels bump up against the metal stairs that lead to yet another one of the catwalks that stripe the ceiling at regular intervals. Perfect. I go up backward, keeping an eye on the battle below. The metal crates protect my team, and Jackson picking off Drau from above takes care of whatever threat Luka and Tyrone and Lien aren't managing very nicely on their own.

I hit the catwalk and find shelter behind a section of the massive robot arm that hangs from the ceiling. With my forearms resting on the rail, I pick off a Drau. Another. A third.

Luka looks up, spots me, taps his con, and grins. Then he disappears behind the crates, and a few seconds later I see Lien hustling Kendra down a hallway that juts off the main room, Tyrone covering their retreat.

I'm guessing the Committee's feeding location info to Luka's con, leaving him leading their little group and me with Jackson. Usually it's just team leaders who get maps, but I remember from the caves that sometimes the Committee varies that rule. I glance over to where I think Jackson's last shot came from. For a millisecond I'm confused; then I'm terrified because the spot I last saw him is now occupied by glowing Drau.

I follow instinct and fire three shots in rapid succession, then slam down the stairs, the metal shaking beneath my feet. As I reach the floor, I look up for a split second. One Drau is down but not dead and the others zip toward me, almost at the stairs.

There's no sign of Jackson.

I freeze, spin, try to catch a glimpse of him. Drau fire singes my shoulder, my back. I dive and roll behind a tool cart, then surge to my feet and move, ducking between stacks of crates. Panting, I press into the shadows, looking for Jackson.

He has to be okay. I didn't see him lying at their feet. Didn't hear him cry out. Maybe he'd already taken off by the time the Drau found his hiding spot.

Maybe he didn't have a chance to call out and warn me before he ran.

And maybe he's hurt.

Dead.

I can't let myself think it.

An image of Carly, her yellow spandex bodysuit wet with her own blood, flashes through my thoughts, followed by an image of my dad, bleeding, broken, trapped in the mangled remains of his car . . .

It didn't happen like that.

Dad isn't trapped in the wreckage. He's in the hospital. Dr. Lee said he's out of surgery. I have to believe he's going to be okay and Carly's going to be okay and Jackson's okay. Not everyone in my life dies; not everyone leaves. I have to try to believe that.

Jackson got away. The Drau didn't catch him.

And they won't catch me.

That's what I need to believe. But it's hard. Everything's unraveling and spinning out of control. Lights zip along the catwalks overhead, converging on me. They know where I am.

I cry out as droplets of agony rain down on my back, burning through cloth and skin. I skid around a column, press against cool plaster and stick my head out just enough to assess my situation. Too many Drau for me to handle on my own, coming in fast. I pull back. One hallway looks pretty much like the next. I choose one and run.

Veering to the right, I tear along another hallway that opens to a massive space with conveyor belts and more of the robot arms and massive wheeled tool carts like the one I hid under before. Yellow-and-black-striped caution markers stand sentinel at the base of more yellow metal stairs. They lead to another overhead catwalk.

Not going up there. Nowhere to hide.

Instead, I keep running, turn left and thunder up a set of concrete stairs. Gray stairs. Gray walls. My breath comes hard and rough as I hit the top.

Crap. More open space.

I chance a glance over my shoulder. No Drau there, not yet.

Panting, I look right, then left. Neither option is great. The one will have me running between rows of wooden crates. The other will take me to control central—a room with banks of TV monitors showing the silent robot arms throughout the factory. Problem is, that room's behind a wall of glass, which doesn't exactly offer ideal cover.

I choose, heading for the glass, but not the room behind it. Instead I take the corridor that leads past, hoping it isn't a dead end.

More stairs; these head back down. I freeze, hugging the wall, and look back. A flash of light zips across the far end of the factory floor. There's at least one Drau behind me, maybe more, weaving between the stacks of crates, searching for me.

I want to run. Instead, barely daring to breathe, I force myself to creep sideways along the wall, checking behind then in front of me, trying not to alert my enemy to my presence. I keep my sword at the ready, my weapon cylinder raised.

Slowly.

Slowly.

More stairs. I squelch the urge to lope down them two at a time and instead inch forward, taking care not to make a sound. A quick glance at my con reveals a swirling yellow screen. Not bad. At least it isn't orange. My health's sort of holding up, which is a definite check in the positive column.

On the negative side is the fact that the Committee isn't feeding me any information: no map of the surroundings and no green triangles to tell me where the rest of my team is.

Jackson and Luka, Tyrone, Lien, Kendra. I choose to believe they're okay. I can't add another layer of worry to the bubbling lasagna cooking in my brain, threatening to ooze over the sides if I loosen the reins of my control even a little. Those emotions won't do a damned thing to help me stay alive, so I lock them up tight and think only of putting one foot in front of the next.

I get to the bottom of the stairs. On the wall directly ahead of me is a massive whiteboard with the words *Problem Solving* centered at the top in bold black print and a grid underneath with about a third of the spaces filled in. A corridor extends to either side.

Without input from the Committee, I have no idea which way to turn in order to find Jackson or Luka and the others. I catch a flicker of light out of the corner of my right eye. Problem solved: That direction's out. I go left, crouching to avoid being seen through the square windows that cut the wall at three-foot intervals.

Already a half dozen steps past a door marked *Security*, I stop dead and backtrack. If the Committee won't help me find my team, I'll just have to come at the puzzle from a different angle and solve it on my own. Holding my breath, I turn the knob and exhale in a rush when the door opens. Perfect. I slide inside and close the door behind me. Lock it.

I examine the inside of the room and almost weep with relief. There are two office chairs, a long desk, and a ton of small security monitors showing various parts of the factory. I set my weapons on the desk and rest my hands on the edge, leaning close, my eyes flitting across the monitors.

At first, all I see are black-and-white images of rooms and corridors and stairs, nothing familiar, and no sign of my team. I look again, taking my time. There—a flash of light that marks a Drau speeding past a camera. And there, more flashes going up a set of stairs.

But no hint of any human movement.

I rub my palms together. They're damp and my hands are shaking.

It takes two more passes before I finally see Kendra and Lien and Luka, pinned in an open waiting room near a set of glass double doors. I wonder if Tyrone is still with them, just offscreen, if he got separated from the others by accident, or if the Committee sent him in a different direction.

Of course, there's one other option, but I don't let myself consider it.

And I try not to let myself worry about Jackson. Instead,

I try to focus on just this moment.

Luka and Lien turn one of the low chrome-and-cloth couches on its side. There's no sound with these monitors, but I can tell that they're being super careful to move in silence. They hunker down behind the couch, Kendra positioned between them.

It's weird watching the scene on the monitor rather than living in the thick of it, especially when I'm seeing things in black-and-white.

I'm a spectator watching the game unfold.

Powerless. Useless.

I want to tear out of this room and run to them, but I have no idea how to find them. Again, I check my con, hoping for a map.

Nothing.

I mentally give the Committee the finger, my gaze flicking across the screens. Rooms. Wide-open spaces filled with equipment. Robot arms. Catwalks. Stairs. Corridors. A couple of landmarks I think I recognize. I drag open desk drawers until I find a pen and paper. Then I start at the first monitor and try to create a map of the factory, filling in what I remember from the places I've been, rapidly sketching in the rest from the rooms and corridors the cameras reveal.

A small group of Drau, glowing and bright, methodically checks each room they come upon. Any minute, they're going to get to that waiting room and all hell will break loose. A leaden lump congeals in my throat. I stand there, impotent, fists clenched as the Drau creep closer to three people I care about. Three people I can't do a damned thing to help.

I'm helpless to help them.

All I can do is watch, pulse racing, anxiety gnawing at me as the Drau converge on Luka and Kendra and Lien.

CHAPTER**FIVE**

LIGHT EXPLODES LIKE A SHOWER OF FALLING STARS. THE DRAU move so fast. I lean close to the monitor, not wanting to look, not wanting to look away.

One word ricochets around my brain again and again. *Please.*

Black ooze disgorges from Lien's weapon, like a surge of inky water from the end of a fire hose.

Luka holds back as the Drau come at them. I lean close to the screen, willing him to fire. This is not the moment to let Kendra rack up points. Jackson was pretty clear in that regard; no one is supposed to put himself at risk, but here Luka's doing exactly that, waiting . . . waiting . . .

Finally, when it's practically on top of him, he takes out one of the Drau. Lien hits another. A third bypasses their defense and lands a direct hit to Lien's chest. I hear the sound of my voice before I realize I've cried out. With a gasp, I slap one hand over my mouth.

Have I given myself away?

I scan the monitors, looking for one that shows the hallway outside the security room. There. On the bottom right. There's nothing on the screen, which means there was no Drau outside to hear me.

I check the map I've drawn. There are too many blank places for me to be sure of the route. But I can't wait any longer. I need to get to them. I grab my sword and my weapon cylinder and take one last look at the screens.

Kendra's face is a mask of anguish as she checks Lien's con. I wish I knew what color her con is. But the screens are black-and-white and all I know is that she isn't dead because I can see her lips moving. She looks right at Kendra as she speaks, then takes her hand and presses a kiss to her palm.

The Drau move to one side of the room, then into the camera's blind spot. I can't see them, but I can see the rain of light from their weapons.

"Fire," I whisper, my grip tightening on my weapon cylinder as I will Luka to take the shot.

He doesn't.

I get one hell of a surprise as Kendra rises from behind the cover of the couch. She aims and fires, again and again, her expression twisted in rage and pain, her mouth open in a way that tells me she's yelling each time she wills her cylinder to fire.

Then she stops, just stops. They all stop. Luka's frozen in place, his face turned away from the camera toward Kendra. Lien's lying on the floor, propped on one elbow, her expression a motionless mask of surprise.

I figure my face probably looks pretty similar.

On each successive mission, Kendra's terror has escalated to the point that she wasn't just useless as a soldier; she was a danger to herself and the rest of us. But she just beat it, she overcame it. She stepped up.

Didn't expect that one.

Lien gets to her feet, Kendra supporting her elbow, and after a few woozy looking minutes, she straightens and pulls away to walk forward on her own steam. They pass into the camera's blind spot and disappear, leaving the map I've drawn useless to me for the moment.

I check the other monitors, hoping for a glimpse of Jackson and Tyrone. The first sweep reveals nothing, not even Drau teams. The second sweep leaves me sagging against the desk in relief. There's Jackson. He silently dispatches a lone Drau with his knife. I get a clear view of his face, his expression completely blank as he kills it. No pleasure, and in all honesty, I'm glad about that. No regret though, either. It's like he doesn't feel *anything*. Maybe I'll get to that point once I've been in the game for five years.

Five years.

Just the thought of that makes a shudder crawl across my skin.

Jackson continues on his way and I follow him from monitor to monitor, looking for a landmark that I recognize so I can head toward him. He stops and checks his con every once in a while and I realize he's looking for the rest of us, following the map on the tiny screen, moving toward the location of one of the triangles.

A few minutes later, Jackson backs along a hallway, keeping an eye out for a Drau patrol he passed—and evaded—a few minutes ago. I almost laugh when I see Tyrone doing the same, backing up the hall that intersects Jackson's at a ninety-degree angle. It's comical when they thump back-to-back, spin, weapons raised, and then grin, teeth flashing in the dimness.

They have a brief conversation. Jackson taps his con, points along the hallway then gestures to the left, the right. Tyrone nods. Then they split up and I'm guessing he's sending Tyrone to find the others while he comes after me.

I track Jackson's progress on the monitors until I see something that makes my heart stutter in my chest. Drau. A group of them, heading my way.

If I sit tight, hoping the Drau don't discover my position, and wait for Jackson, I'll let him walk right into their midst. Which means I can't stay here, locked in and relatively safe. I need to move, to lead Jackson away from here as he follows the little Miki triangle on his con.

I check the screens, plot my best options, and head out. I don't get far. Three Drau, a scouting party, practically bump noses with me as I round a corner. For some reason, we all freeze. I don't shoot. They don't shoot. We all just stand there.

Then instinct kicks in.

At the same second the lead Drau lifts its weapon, I hack with my *katana*, bringing the honed blade down on its forehead, splitting its head like a coconut. With my other hand, I shoot the next Drau. It makes that terrible high-pitched sound as it's swallowed whole. Something clatters to the floor behind me and I whirl to take out the third Drau, but it's gone, its weapon lying on the floor.

My heart beats too fast. Did it run away? Or did it go for reinforcements? Either way, getting myself out of here right now is a definite plan.

I have no need for its weapon, but I don't want to just leave the thing lying there, so I snatch it up, shove it in my holster, then run in the direction I came from earlier, along the hall, across the open space, staying close to the equipment and the crates, hugging the shadows.

A choice: up a set of metal stairs to the catwalk, across to the far end of the factory floor with the hope that it isn't a dead end, or up the back stairs to the second floor.

I decide on the factory floor, my kendo sword held ready, my weapon cylinder heavy in my hand. At the far end, there are two hallways. I take the one on the left, because based on my sketchy map, I think it'll lead me toward where I saw Jackson.

Bad choice.

There's a lone Drau pressed up against a closed door, staring at me. I tell myself not to look at its eyes, its mercury eyes. I know it can kill me.

It lifts its hand.

I almost shoot, but stop at the last second.

It has no weapon. Its hands are empty. It's lifting them in a gesture of surrender.

It must be the same Drau that ran away, the one that left its weapon on the floor.

Shaking, panting, I hold my weapons before me. I don't move. The Drau doesn't move. My arms start to feel the strain.

Please.

The plea slams through my mind, echoing on itself. It isn't a word. Not exactly. It's an emotion, or, actually, a mélange of emotions. Fear. Desperation. Hope.

Excitement. Because it knows I can hear it.

Please.

My breath comes in frantic little gasps.

It's talking to me. Inside my head. Sort of the way that Jackson and the Committee have talked inside my head, but different. There are no words here. There's just raw thought.

I take a step back, terrified, horrified.

Mercy. Please.

It lifts its hands a little higher. I stare at its fingers, long, elegant, glowing like hundred-watt bulbs. My hands tremble. My arms shake. But I don't lower my weapon cylinder or my sword.

I don't know what to do. Nothing in my experience of the game has prepared me for this. I've been told that the Drau are my enemy. That they're purely evil. That they want to annihilate mankind. That they want to *eat* us.

And it isn't just what I've been told. It's the bone-deep certainty I've felt since before I even saw one, the sensation of chilling fear that I first experienced outside the warehouse in Vegas right before I battled the Drau for the very first time.

But as this Drau pleads for mercy, I don't feel that chilling fear. Instead, I feel . . . pity.

So what am I supposed to do? Just kill it as it begs for its life? Turn and walk away? What?

Slowly, it continues raising its hands until its fingers are curled around the back of its head. Then it sinks to its knees in front of me and the inside of my skull reverberates with its renewed pleas.

PleasePleasePleasePleasePlease

I lower my sword.

I lower my weapon cylinder, an inch at a time, unsure.

It lifts its head and its eyes meet mine. Beautiful. Turbulent. Mercury bright. Swirling with a million shades of molten silver.

Like Jackson's eyes, except his pupils are round and human. The Drau's are slitted, reptilian.

Don't look at its eyes.

Too late.

They're poison. They will kill you.

Seconds eke past. I can't bring myself to look away.

Then realization dawns: we're looking at each other and it isn't doing anything to me. I've looked into a Drau's eyes before, and it felt like my entire insides were being pulled out through my pupils.

I don't feel that now.

It could kill me, and it isn't.

I lower my weapons the rest of the way to my sides. Since I don't know how to make my thoughts dance around in its head and I don't think it understands English, I gesture for it to get up, off its knees.

It starts to rise.

The sound of footsteps echoes from behind me, two sets, coming fast.

I turn.

Lien and Kendra run along the hall toward me.

Kendra lifts her weapon.

Wait. I almost get the word out—almost, but not quite—before an oily surge swallows the Drau, its terror echoing inside my head, terror so sharp it flays me alive.

The Drau's raw thought bombards me to the agonizing end; I feel it die.

I sag back against the wall, heart pounding, stomach churning.

"Are you okay?" Lien asks and darts to my side.

I press one hand to the wall and bend forward at the

waist, then sink down, knees bent, weight rocking back on my heels. Head bowed, I struggle to get the nausea under control.

"Where are you hit?" Lien asks, dropping to her haunches in front of me so our faces are level. "Where are you hurt?"

I shake my head.

Kendra comes up behind me and rubs circles on my back.

"I'm okay." I'm not. I push to my feet as Lien gets to hers. "How did you find me?"

She turns her wrist and shows me her con. There's a map and three triangles. Us. The Committee led her to me.

I should feel grateful that the Committee sent them, that they showed up to save the day.

But I don't. Because they didn't save me. I didn't need saving, not from a Drau that was begging for its life. A Drau that had the chance to kill me, and chose not to.

CHAPTER**SIX**

I RESPAWN IN THE HOSPITAL WAITING ROOM, FEELING WOOZY and disconnected. Mission complete.

"... we'll be moving him to the surgical ICU."

I stare at the doctor, trying to reorient back to the second I got pulled. To Dad, his surgery, Dr. Lee. It takes a few seconds before my brain manages to process what he just said. They're moving Dad to the surgical ICU. Which means he's *alive*. I can't think, can't breathe, the relief is so strong. I blurt, "Can I see him?"

"He's in recovery now, but we'll let you know once he's moved. You can see him for a few minutes then."

"You took out his spleen?"

Dr. Lee frowns. "Yes." He pauses and glances at Jackson.

"Miki, do you have anyone else you can call? Your mother? Another relative?"

I hear what he doesn't say: an adult. Someone who can hold it together better than a sixteen-year-old girl. I'm guessing he must think my parents are divorced and that's why my mother isn't here with me.

"Mom died two years ago. And my aunt Gale wouldn't be able to get here any time soon. She's in Korea. She's a management consultant." I have no idea why he might need that extra bit of info, but I tack it on without really thinking about it. I hold his gaze, trying to read what he isn't saying. "Why do I need to call someone, Dr. Lee? Is my dad going to . . ."

Jackson twines his fingers with mine.

"Your dad came through the surgery just fine, Miki. His spleen sustained significant damage and his splenic vein was ruptured. There was some blood in his abdomen—"

I gasp. Jackson's arm slides around my waist.

"—which is common with an emergent injury such as your father sustained. We gave him several units. He has a mild concussion, cuts and bruises, and three broken ribs on his left side."

"Units? Of blood?"

"That's correct."

"But he's going to be okay?"

"His condition is fair. His vital signs are stable. Indicators are favorable."

I'm familiar enough with doctor-speak to unravel the puzzle. That isn't an unqualified thumbs-up, but it's leaning toward the positive. If we were talking health bars, I'd peg Dad's somewhere between orange and yellow right now.

"As soon as your father's ready for transfer, we'll let you know. You can see him for a few minutes once he's settled." Dr. Lee pauses. "And then you should go home and get some rest. If you're here every second of every day until he's well, you'll burn out."

I know that already. I lived it with Mom, first in the hospital, then in hospice. But Dad and I took turns, and Aunt Gale only lived an hour away then. And there were a lot of nights I slept at Carly's . . .

"What about Carly? Can you tell me anything? Is she okay?" When he just looks at me, I clarify, "Carly Conner. She's my best friend. She was in the car with my dad."

"I'm afraid I don't know anything about her condition."

And then Dr. Lee is gone.

I turn to Jackson. "I didn't think to ask him where I should wait. Here . . . or if we should go to the ICU . . ."

"Here," Jackson says. "They'll come tell us when they're moving him."

"Should I go look for Carly's mom and dad? I really want to know . . ."

"How about we wait here till they tell us your dad's settled, then we find the Conners before we head to the ICU?"

I blow out a breath. "Always the man with the plan."

"Always," Jackson murmurs. Typical Jackson, having the last word, but at this moment I find it more reassuring than cocky.

I rub the back of my neck, my muscles aching. Jackson steps behind me, his strong hands kneading the tension from my shoulders. "What would I do if you weren't here?" I ask.

His hands still, then start moving again. "You'd be strong. And brave. Because that's who you are, Miki. You already dealt with a hell of a lot before I ever came along." From his tone, I can guess what he's thinking even though he doesn't say it. That thanks to him, I'm in the game and therefore have a whole lot more to deal with.

"Stop blaming yourself," I say.

Again, his hands still, then start up again, working their magic. "Reading my mind?"

"Isn't that supposed to be my line?" From the very beginning, he's been able to talk inside my head, and for a while I thought he could hear my thoughts the way I heard his. Might be nice if he could. Not all the time, just when we're on a mission. I look back at him over my shoulder. "I just know how you think."

"Do you, now?"

Sometimes I think so. Sometimes I don't.

"I told them about you, Miki," he says after a moment. I know he believes that. He believes that he found me and told the Committee about me so I could take his place as team leader. So he could trade me for his freedom and finally escape the game after five agonizing years.

But what if he's wrong?

"Did you? Did you really tell them about me? Or did they just let you believe that?"

I start to turn, but he doesn't let me. He just keeps massaging my shoulders. I lean back so my spine is against his body and tip my head back so it rests on his shoulder. "Did you ever think that the Committee let you take the blame for recruiting me, Jackson, but that they knew about me the whole time? Maybe even sent you to find me? Maybe all along they were moving us both like chess pieces on a board."

He turns me to face him. "Why the Committee-hate right now?"

I almost tell him about what just happened with the Drau, about the Committee sending Kendra to take it out before I could really communicate with it. But my brain can't follow that path right now. It's already too full.

"Later," I say.

For a second, I think he's going to press me. Then he nods.

I break away and pace the room.

He rests one shoulder against the doorframe, arms crossed over his chest.

I sit.

He sits beside me.

We wait for what feels like eternity, Jackson leaning back in his chair, legs splayed, his fingers linked behind his head, me leaning forward, forearms resting on my thighs.

Finally, I can't take it anymore. "What's taking them so long to get Dad ready for transfer?"

Jackson checks his phone. "It's been four and a half minutes."

I bound to my feet. I don't know what to do with my hands. I can't bear to talk. I can't bear the silence. My thoughts tangle and knot, so I pick a single thread and follow it.

"When we went back to the game, I didn't respawn where I should have. I should have been running toward Luka, but I wasn't."

Jackson lowers his hands and sits up straighter. "You want to talk about this now?"

"Yes. No." I shake my head. "I don't know."

"Okay," Jackson says, leaning back again. "Let me know when you figure it out."

"You're being amenable."

"Amenable's one way to describe it."

Seconds crawl past.

"I wish a nurse would come." I wish someone would take me to see Dad. Talk to him. Watch his chest move as he breathes. I just need proof he's alive.

I wish someone would come tell me that Carly's okay. That I can see her, hug her.

Mom always used to say, *If wishes were pennies . . .*

It hits me that I'm silently pleading for Dad to be okay, for Carly to be okay. *Wishing. Pleading. Begging.* Like the

Drau, begging for mercy. The image won't leave me alone. Maybe this *is* the time to talk about it.

"It wasn't just the weird respawn," I say, rubbing my forehead. "Something else happened. It might be important." I look up at Jackson's eyes, but all I see are reflections of myself in his mirrored shades.

"Important right this minute?" Jackson asks. "To the things happening right now?"

"No."

"Then you don't need to think about it. You don't need to talk about anything having to do with the game. It'll keep." He sits forward again. "Unless you want to talk about it. Then go right ahead, if it will help."

My gaze slides to the TV, and I remember the creepy feeling of being watched and my suspicion that the Drau were spying on us through the screen. Is that even possible, or am I being paranoid?

"I—" I choke on my words.

It's all too much. Thoughts bombard me and images flash behind my eyes like a strobe light: The Drau getting swallowed by the black ooze from Kendra's weapon. The image flickers and shifts to Daddy, covered in blood, trapped in crumpled metal. Daddy, cold and white and dead. Then Carly, lying dead on the floor of the school after the Drau crossed over into the Halloween dance, blood flowering on yellow spandex. Carly, dead on the cold ground in front of the twisted remains of the Explorer.

I wrap my arms around myself. I don't want these

images in my head. I shove them out but they bounce right back in.

Jackson rises and pulls me into his arms. "What is it?" he whispers against my hair.

"Overactive imagination. I keep picturing everything turning out bad, and not just here. *There*, too. I keep seeing possibilities, none of them good."

"The doctor was optimistic about your dad. Focus on that. Don't let yourself think about the game."

"That's just it. I'm not thinking about the game, but somehow, the game keeps pushing its way in."

"Push back."

As soon as he says that, it hits me that there's something off about the images in my head. It's like these thoughts aren't mine, like they're being forced into my brain.

"Do you think it's the Committee?" That's the Committee's mode of communication. They've placed thoughts in my head before, when I was team leader, and when I faced them in the amphitheater, when they pushed so hard it hurt. Maybe they're doing it right now, making me think these terrible things. Maybe this is the way they phrase a threat. They could be trying to distract me from telling Jackson about that Drau, or warning me off, showing me what they'll do if I tell Jackson everything.

I don't even know why I'm thinking along these lines, why I'm suspecting them, seeing threats everywhere.

"The Committee? What would be their purpose?" He doesn't sound convinced. But he doesn't sound dismissive, either. "What would they gain?"

"Control."

"They already have that."

That pretty much sums it up.

I sigh. "I'm not making much sense, am I?"

"Right now, you deserve to just live in this reality, Miki. You deserve to be able to focus on your dad and Carly. You *need* to do that. Put everything else away for now. It's too much. Psych overload. I know. I've been there."

He has. When Lizzie died. Lizzie, who's dead but isn't dead.

One more terrifying piece of the puzzle.

CHAPTER**SEVEN**

WE SIT SIDE BY SIDE OPPOSITE THE FLU VACCINE POSTER, minutes crawling past until I can't take the quiet anymore. I rise and pace, then spin back to face Jackson. "How did you cope?" I ask. "When everything felt like too much? After Lizzie died and the game and . . . When you thought you were going to crash?"

"I shut down. Built walls. Locked everyone out." Jackson huffs a soft laugh. "Became an asshole."

"Pretended to become an asshole," I say.

"Always seeing the good in me."

"Not always."

His brows rise above the frames of his glasses. "I closed down, Miki. Got numb. Emotions were messy. Ugly. I withdrew from my parents. I didn't feel a hell of a lot."

He pauses. "Didn't *let* myself feel a hell of a lot, except for crushing guilt. That leaked through just fine."

"But you aren't guilty. You—"

"Killed my sister, whether I meant to or not." He gets to his feet and closes the space between us. "My con was red. I was dying. She told me to make like a Drau, to borrow enough of her energy to stay alive. So that's what I did, except I didn't just borrow enough, I took it all. And I killed her." He touches my cheek with the backs of his fingers. "I felt guilty, inside the game and out. Like every loss after that, every death was on me. And let's not even talk about having any kind of true friendship or connection with someone, any kind of . . . intimacy."

"Did you see anyone? A therapist?"

He shrugs and after a couple of seconds I realize that's the only answer I'm going to get.

"Did you get a diagnosis?"

"Didn't ask for one."

Of course he didn't. Typical Jackson. "PTSD," I say.

He cocks a brow. "Your professional opinion, Dr. Jones?"

I shrug. "I read up on it. And pretty much every other anxiety disorder. Dr. Andrews said that's part of my need to be in control. I'm an information hoarder."

"The internet is a wonderful thing," he says dryly.

So much about him makes sense now. The way he was when I first met him in the game. The persona he shows the world. The way he got to know me and let me know him, like he didn't really want to let me in but couldn't seem to help himself.

"You're different now." Different than when I first met him.

"A little," he says, then goes quiet for so long that I think we're done here, that he's changed his mind about letting me take a peek at his soul. That he's said all he's going to say.

Jackson surprises me when he keeps going. "I've seen lots of people die in the game, their cons go red. I've felt it every time, like a punch to the gut. Loss. Guilt. I didn't mourn them. I didn't let myself mourn them. Didn't let myself have any vulnerability.

"But Richelle . . . she was different. Losing her was different. I respected her, liked her. Maybe even loved her a little." He pauses. "Not in a romantic way. But in a way I hadn't let myself feel in a long time, like I cared what happened to her. She *mattered*. And I didn't let myself recognize that until she was gone."

I nod, not daring to say anything, worried that even the sound of my voice might derail him, might stop him from talking, from telling me things I never, ever thought he'd share. It's like he's giving me a gift, giving me a tangible piece of himself to help me deal with what I'm going through.

"Her death was on me," he says. "My fault." I shake my head, but he doesn't let me protest. "But her fault, too. Her con went orange. She knew the routine. Fall back. Defense only. She made a bad choice."

"But if I hadn't been there," I say. "If you hadn't been watching my back—"

"No ifs, Miki. Chances are, even if you hadn't been there, I wouldn't have been able to save her, because I trusted Richelle to save herself. Sometimes nothing you do or say can change the outcome."

I sink down onto the couch. "Like Mom," I say. I'm too scared to say, *Like what happens to Dad and Carly tonight.*

Jackson settles down beside me. He leans forward so his elbows rest on his thighs, his hands hanging loose between his knees, his head bowed.

"Remember that mission where Tyrone was so messed up?"

The mission after Richelle died.

"I went to see him after. We talked." He turns his head toward me. "You're surprised."

"I am. Neither of you ever let on that you had any sort of connection outside the game."

"We didn't. Not till then. Tyrone said something that really clicked. That he was glad he knew her, glad he loved her, even glad for the pain of losing her because it meant he'd let himself experience loving her." He runs his fingers back through his hair in a totally un-Jackson gesture. "That made me think about Lizzie. About all my memories of her and how no matter how much it hurt when she died, I wouldn't trade those memories, wouldn't have traded having a sister, just to spare myself the pain."

"You can't recognize true joy if you've never known heartbreak," I say. "Pain makes you stronger. Fear makes you braver. Tears teach you to laugh. You can't know hope if you've never known despair. My friends sent me every inspirational cliché under the sun after Mom died." I pause. "I hated them at the time. They seemed like such bullshit."

"And now?"

"Now I think maybe there's some truth to them, if I let myself look for it." I nudge his knee with mine. "You?"

"Ever since Lizzie died, I believed that letting someone in, caring about them . . . it gives them power over you, whether they plan it that way or not. It gives them the power to leave, to hurt you. Why do that? Why give anyone that power? You open your heart and you're just begging for a beat down." He smiles a little. "Sound familiar?"

"Yes," I say, looking at the floor. It's like he's vocalizing all my fears.

"But living," he says, *"really* living is messy and sometimes ugly, and it hurts." He takes my hand and threads his fingers with mine. "The moments when it doesn't, the moments that shine, the ones where I get to hold you, kiss you, laugh with you, those are the ones that matter, Miki."

"Those are the ones that matter," I whisper, studying our linked hands. "It's so hard. Gram, Sofu . . . Mom . . . They were alive, and then they weren't. They didn't make it. I believed they would. With all my heart, I believed. Even when Mom was in palliative care, when the doctors told us there was nothing else they could do except make her as comfortable as possible, I couldn't stop believing. And it wasn't enough."

Jackson's quiet for a long time, then he says, "Your dad and Carly aren't going to die. They're going to pull through." He sounds so certain, and I don't get how he can be.

Then I think of him trying to save Carly after the Drau killed her, of him putting his life on the line to go against the orders of the Committee and use his Drau abilities. What if that's the reason he's so certain that Dad and Carly will make it? Because he plans to do that again? To save them . . .

If that's what he's thinking, I can't let him follow through. The Committee will kill him. But knowing Jackson, he'll do it in secret, keep it from me, not let the choice be mine. Because how am I supposed to choose between his life and Carly's and Dad's?

I almost say something to him. Almost. But just in case he hasn't been thinking along those lines, I don't—I don't want to put ideas in his head.

We sit there, the noises of the hospital filtering to us through the open door. After a few minutes, there's the sound of heels clicking on the hall tile and Carly's mom comes into the waiting room. Carly's dad stands in the doorway, both hands shoved deep in his pockets, his sandy hair standing up in all directions. He jingles his change and rocks from foot to foot. He can't bear to be still, either.

My full attention—along with all my hopes—turn to them. *Please let her have good news. Please.*

"Miki," Mrs. Conner says, and lays her hand on the top of my head. "I hear your dad's out of surgery."

I nod. "Dr. Lee came to talk with me. They're going to let me see him soon." My gut churns. "Carly?"

"They're moving her to the neuro-ICU. That's where we're going now." She glances back at her husband.

"Is she okay?" I ask, hoping, desperately hoping. "Did she wake up?"

"Not yet. She's in a medically induced coma. They want—" Her voice breaks and she swallows against her tears. Mr. Conner walks over and puts his arm around her shoulders.

"They want to keep her that way for a bit," he says. "They told us it can help minimize the damage to her brain."

I press my knuckles against my lips, feeling sick.

Tears track silver lines down Mrs. Conner's cheeks. She looks a million years old and so very tired. I remember Dad saying he was glad Sofu passed before Mom, that a parent should never have to bury a child.

My vision darkens at the edges, narrowing until all I see are those tracks of tears.

Mr. Conner looks at Jackson. "I feel like we're deserting Miki, but . . . we need to be there, be with Carly . . . Can I count on you, son?"

"I'm here," Jackson says at the same time I say, "You

aren't deserting me." I press my lips together. "After I see Daddy, is it okay if I come see Carly, just for a minute?"

Mrs. Conner cups my cheek and stares down into my face. Then she shakes her head. "Tomorrow, okay? You go see your father now and then you go home and get some sleep. You'll see Carly when you come back tomorrow and by then she'll be awake."

Mr. Conner swallows and looks away, and I'm pretty sure Carly won't be awake tomorrow.

CHAPTER**EIGHT**

I SIT BY DAD'S SIDE. HE'S HOOKED UP TO A TON OF TUBES AND machines, an IV dripping clear fluid into his vein. The sounds of the respirator and the beeps of the monitors, the antiseptic smell, it all reminds me of Mom, of the weeks it took her to die. I slump forward in the chair with my arms stretched out on his bed, my head on my forearms, my tears wetting the sheets.

I need to touch him. I'm scared to touch him. In the end, I press the tips of my fingers to the tips of his. They feel so cold.

The nurses move in and out, busy with the IV, with the machines, with administering meds.

"I'm Laila," one of them says after I've been there for a while.

I swipe my tears with the back of my hand. "Miki."

"It's time to go home, Miki." She's probably right. I'm not wearing a watch, but I figure it has to be close to dawn. Still I shake my head, but she takes my hand between both of hers and says, "You think you need to be here every second, that he won't get better if you leave. But he came through surgery with flying colors and he's stable now. He's been given some medication to make certain he sleeps. That's the best thing for his recovery. Sleep. And the best thing you can do to make sure you're there for him is get some sleep yourself. This is going to be a long haul for him, Miki, and if you burn yourself out now, who will be there for him later?"

She's the third person to tell me that—Dr. Lee, Carly's mom, and now Laila. If I hadn't already been through this with Gram and Sofu and then Mom, maybe I wouldn't believe her. But I have been through it. Three times before. And I know she's telling me the truth.

"Go home, Miki. Sleep. Eat something. Take a nice hot shower. Come back in a few hours." She pauses. "Do you have a ride home? Or money for a cab?"

Do I have a ride? I don't know how long I've been here. They wouldn't let Jackson into the ICU with me. The truth is, it's so late they didn't even want to let me in. But I was stubborn, even going so far as to have them call Dr. Lee and confirm that he said I could see Dad. They finally gave in.

"I have money," I say, thinking I'll take a cab if Jackson

79

isn't out there waiting for me. A part of me can't imagine he would be.

Laila smiles at me. "Come back after you get some sleep, okay?"

"Will you be here?"

She shakes her head. "No. Shift changes in about an hour, but there will be a lot of people here to take good care of him."

I give Dad one last kiss on his forehead and leave the ICU to find Jackson waiting for me in the hall, one shoulder propped against the wall, head bowed.

"You're still here," I say.

His head comes up; his brows rise. "Where else would I be?" His tone is gentle with just a hint of *silly girl*, which I kind of deserve. I wouldn't leave him if the tables were turned. Why would I think he'd leave me?

Because everyone leaves.

Not Jackson. Not if he can help it.

I'm a little surprised to realize I actually believe that.

Jackson drives me home. He opens two cans of soup. He makes me eat a bowl while he eats two. Then he rinses the bowls and puts them in the dishwasher and brings me upstairs.

"I hate the idea of waking up in the morning alone," I whisper.

"You won't. And it's already morning."

I look at him, startled. "Don't you have to go home? Your parents—"

"Dad's on an early flight out of town. Mom knows exactly where I am. You got a spare toothbrush?"

"Downstairs bathroom, the drawer under the sink. There's toothpaste there, too. And soap."

When I come out of the bathroom, teeth brushed, face washed, my clothes changed out for blue plaid flannel PJs, Jackson's in my room, wearing a pair of faded sweatpants and a loose T-shirt.

"That isn't what you were wearing before."

"I had extra stuff in the Jeep. Workout clothes."

I make a face.

"Clean workout clothes. I did laundry yesterday."

"You do your own laundry?"

He arches one brow. "You think I want my mom washing my boxers?"

I laugh, but the sound's thin and strained.

He pulls back the covers, pats the mattress, and says, "Into bed."

I walk to him, my feet leaden, my entire body sagging under the weight of my fatigue. I feel like I'm slogging through quicksand.

I sit on the edge of the bed. He sits beside me and our fingers intertwine. There's a slump in his posture I've never seen before.

"You okay?" I whisper.

He offers a shadow of his killer Jackson smile. "Sure." His fingers tighten a little on mine. I tighten mine right back.

It hits me that he isn't just comforting me; I'm comforting him, too. Because no matter how much he's trying to be here for me right now, *he* has to be thinking about the girl we saw in the white room. The girl who can't possibly be his sister. Because Lizzie is dead.

According to Jackson, he killed her.

But maybe he didn't. Maybe he's wrong. Maybe she's somehow trapped inside the game, has been all this time. Maybe—

"Do you want to talk about Lizzie?"

"Not right now." He draws his hand from mine, scoops my legs up, and stretches them out on the mattress. Then he drags the covers up over me and orders, "Sleep."

"I can't."

"Then just close your eyes." He lies down on top of the covers, his front against my back, his arms around me like a barrier against the world, against nightmares and the monsters under the bed.

Except they aren't under the bed. They're in the game and in my head and there are moments I'm not sure who the monsters are. The guy who got drunk and ran his car into Dad's?

The Drau? The Committee?

Kendra? Me?

I can't forget that Drau, begging for its life.

I close my eyes and see the white room, the nano-agents, Lizzie. "I think it's really her," I whisper. "Lizzie. I think she somehow got trapped in there, in the game, like the guy from that movie *Tron*."

He doesn't say anything. I feel his chest moving with each steady, slow breath.

"Jackson," I whisper.

"Sleep," he orders. Last word.

I open my eyes to sunlight peeking through the slats in my blinds, hitting me square in the face. There's a heavy weight across my shoulders. My first thought is that Carly slept over, got sick of the hard floor and crawled up on my bed. Wouldn't be the first time.

I blink against the light.

Carly.

Dad.

The hospital.

I jerk upright but don't get far. I'm trapped by Jackson's arm and the covers twisted around my calves. He groans and rolls onto his back, throwing his forearm across his eyes. His sunglasses are on my bedside table.

"Not exactly how I planned for us to spend our first full night together," he says, his voice raspy with sleep, his eyes still covered.

"That wasn't our first full night together. We slept together one night in the caves."

He drops his forearm and pins me with a look. "I think I'd remember if we slept together."

A flush heats my cheeks. I shove aside the covers and drop my legs over the side of the bed, scowling down at him. "I don't mean it that way."

He laughs softly. "I know. I'm teasing. And *you* slept that night. I didn't. I just held you." His expression sobers. "The caves don't count. Anything in the game doesn't count. This is the first time I got to hold you all night in the real world."

The way he's looking at me makes my throat feel tight.

My phone buzzes, giving me an excuse to look away. It's a text from Kelley. There are actually dozens of texts. Everyone must have heard about the crash. I hesitate, torn between wanting to text them all back and being daunted by the task.

"Give yourself a few minutes to wake up, get your thoughts together," Jackson says.

"And pee."

"TMI." He throws a pillow at me.

With a laugh, I catch it and throw it at his head. Then I sober, feeling guilty for laughing when Dad and Carly . . .

"Don't," Jackson says. "It's okay to give yourself a thirty-second break from worrying. Didn't you ever hear the old saying, 'laughter's the best medicine'?"

But I don't feel like laughing anymore.

After I grab a quick shower, I collect some clean towels from the linen closet and toss them to Jackson, then give him his privacy while I head down to the kitchen. My phone rings. It's Kelley.

"We drew straws for who would call you," she says, her voice strained. "I figured it would be tough on you to go through the details a million times with everyone who wants to know. I can call everyone if you want and keep them updated. Sort of act like a liaison."

"That would be great," I say, relieved by her offer, because the prospect of answering every text and call is just one more stress to pile on my growing mountain. I know everyone means well, everyone's worried, and I have to—*want* to—update them. But Kelley's offer takes the pressure off. It's a lot easier to have to just say it all once.

"I rigged it," Kelley says.

"What?"

"The straws. I was worried it would be Dee. And when I thought about all the things she might say . . . I mean, Dee's awesome and I love her, but if someone can pick the wrong thing to say at any given time . . . Remember what she said after you saved Janice's sister and almost got hit by that truck? She told that story about the guy who had a fractured bone in his neck and didn't know it and ended up dying, and then . . . I mean . . . Shit. I just did it, too, didn't I?"

"Nope. Not at all," I deadpan as I wander to the fridge and pull open the door.

"So . . . how are they, your dad and Carly? Can you tell me anything?"

I take out the milk and set it on the counter, then just stand there as I tell her what I know, how little I know, about Dad, about Carly and the induced coma. I can hear her crying and trying to hide it.

"Can we come to the hospital to see her?" she asks.

I put the milk back in the fridge, forgetting why I took it out in the first place. "I honestly don't know. I'll check with her mom and call you later. Probably not everyone all at once, but maybe one or two at a time."

The sound of another voice carries through the phone, then Kelley says, "My mom wants to make you a tuna casserole. I'll leave it on your porch if you aren't home. It's cold enough outside that it should be okay, right?"

"No!" Oh God. Not the dreaded casserole. When Mom died it felt like all the neighbors and Dad's coworkers and maybe even some relatives of relatives brought tuna casserole. We had casseroles piled so high in the freezer at one point that we couldn't even get the door closed. We probably still have a stray casserole covered in frost somewhere in the back, behind the ice cream and the frozen peas. "I mean, thanks, Kelley. Really. And thank your mom. But no. I'm good. I'll be at the hospital most of the time. I'll just grab stuff there in the cafeteria. I wouldn't want her to go to the trouble and then I don't even get to eat it."

"You could freeze it."

I close my eyes. "I'm good. Really. But thanks."

"You sure?"

"A hundred percent sure."

"Okay." She pauses. "Just know we all love you. Do you want to stay here? Till your dad's better? Mom says you can have your own key and come and go as you need to. And Dee said you can stay at her house. And Sarah said they have a spare room so you wouldn't need to share. Do you want to? So you're not alone?"

The shower turns off upstairs.

"I'm not alone."

"Oh." There are a few seconds of silence. "Good. That's good." I know she wants to ask if Jackson's staying with me. Instead she says, "Call me as soon as you know anything about Carly or your dad, or if I can do anything for you. Drive you. Pick you up. Feed you. Sleep over. Bring you to sleep here. Do your homework. Anything."

I can hear the love in her voice. I can feel it through the phone. I can feel it in my heart and all around me like a hug.

We end the call and I skim through my texts, finding lots of love from Dee and Sarah and Maylene, Shareese, Aaron, even Marcy and Kathy, which is kind of a surprise. Only when I scroll through a second time do I realize there's no text from Luka, which is also kind of a surprise—a not-so-nice one.

"Hey," Jackson says as he pads barefoot into the kitchen. His hair's wet, slicked back off his face, a few stray strands falling across his forehead. He's wearing his jeans and a faded T-shirt that's all stretched out, clinging to his broad shoulders and the muscles of his arms and chest, loose around his waist. His glasses hang from the neck of the T-shirt.

"Ready to go?" I ask.

"Just as soon as you have some breakfast." His tone

vetoes any possibility of argument.

Right. Breakfast. That was why I took out the milk. "You have control issues," I say.

"So do you. We've already established that. Yet another thing we have in common." He comes to me and presses a kiss to my lips. He smells like mint toothpaste and my shampoo. "Let me take care of you, Miki. I can't fix this, can't make it go away, can't protect you. At least let me feed you."

That's everything in a nutshell, and I get it. If the situation were reversed, I'd want to do the same, take care of him.

He weaves his fingers with mine and I stare at our hands. I see them, but I don't feel his touch. My fingers and toes are cold, numb, pins and needles spreading along my palms to my wrists and my feet to my ankles.

Jackson frowns and glances down.

When he looks back up, his face goes kind of weird, pixelated, like when I need to reset the digital cable box. Like my real world is lagging, just like in the game.

His eyes widen. He feels it, too.

I try to speak, my mouth refusing to shape the words that form in my brain. I'm caught somewhere between being tethered to this world and pulled into a different one. Not now. Not again.

There's no way to fight it, but I want to. I want to force my body, my consciousness, my reality to stay firmly rooted right here.

When sensation surges back to my fingertips, I sag in relief. Jackson's hand is warm, his hold a little too tight.

"Whoa," he says softly, and loosens his grip. "Thought we were getting pulled for a second there."

So did I, at first. But . . . "No." I shake my head. "It felt different than that. Weirder. If that's possible."

The corners of his mouth pull to the sides, tension hardening his features. Then he says, "Food," as if that's a solution, and starts opening cupboards, stopping when he finds the bowls.

I move to his side and rest my hand on his. "Thanks," I say, the word coming out raspy and thick. Insignificant. How can such a small word convey what I feel? "I mean it. Thank you. For being here. For caring about me."

"Caring about you," he says, staring at the bowls. Then he turns his head and his mercury eyes lock on mine, pupils wide and dark. "You have no idea."

But I think that maybe I do. Maybe all the doubts I had while we were arguing, all the worries about how we could make this work, about how he hides things from me and keeps secrets . . . Maybe I get that no relationship's ever perfect, that we'll fight, we'll disagree, we'll be very different people. But in the end, we can make it work if we both try, if it matters enough, if we're both willing to compromise and meet each other halfway.

There are so many things I need to say to him. My lips part.

"Wait," he says, and rests his fingers against my lips.

"Wait until your dad and Carly come home. Until you can think straight."

He stares at me a moment longer, then unclips his sunglasses from the neck of his T-shirt and slips them on. Shields back in place.

He taps one of the empty bowls. "I don't suppose I dare hope for Lucky Charms."

I snort and open a cupboard. "Will you settle for organic quinoa cereal?"

He grabs the box from my hand and checks the label. "There are no marshmallows." He shakes his head and pours some cereal into my bowl, filling his with a serving three sizes bigger.

We're about to start eating when I say, "Wait!" I drag my chair to the counter and climb up to rummage through the stuff at the back of the top shelf. Triumphant, I pull out a bag of colored mini marshmallows. "Carly brought these over last summer so we could make these chocolate-coconut-marshmallow roll things. They were gross."

I dump a whole bunch of marshmallows into his bowl.

"Last summer, huh?" He gets a funny look on his face when he takes the first mouthful, but I can't be sure if the problem is the unfamiliar taste of quinoa or the stale marshmallows. Either way, he eats the whole bowl.

CHAPTER**NINE**

WE HEAD TO THE ICU. DAD'S STILL SLEEPING, SO AFTER I watch him breathe for a few minutes and then press a kiss to his cheek, Jackson and I go to see Carly. As we pass the waiting room, two of her brothers, Mike and Scott, call out to me. They do the guy-nod to Jackson, then Scott hugs me. His and Mike's eyes are red.

"Tell me," I say.

"No change since last night." Mike swipes the back of his hand across his eyes. "They're still keeping her in a coma."

"They only let in two people at a time," Scott says. "Mom and Dad are in there now. We take turns. How's your father?"

"He's in surgical ICU. They took out his spleen and

they had to give him blood. His ribs are broken." I wet my lips. "He hasn't woken up yet."

"Bastard," Mike snarls, slamming the side of his fist against his thigh. I gasp, thinking he's talking about my father. "That bastard hit them and walked away without a scratch."

I blow out a breath.

"Michael. Language." Carly's mom comes into the waiting room, arms crossed over her abdomen, shoulders sagging. "I came out to let one of the boys go in, but I'm glad you're here, Miki. You go on in now." She smiles at Jackson. "You, too. Send my husband out. He could use a coffee."

We go in. It's horrible seeing Carly like this, pale and still, a tube in her nose, another down her throat, ventilator pulsating, monitors beeping. People buzz in and out, the low drone of their conversations offering us snippets of overheard information that sounds foreign and scary. Intracranial pressure. Subarachnoid bleed. Lots of words.

I sit in the chair beside the bed, the one Carly's dad vacated when we came in, and hold Carly's hand between both of mine—her right one because there's an IV in the left—my head bowed low, my forehead against her wrist. Jackson stands beside me, one hand on my shoulder, the other resting on Carly's forearm.

"Remember when you were ten and you thought you wanted to be a doctor?" I ask Carly, lifting my head. "You were going to be a pediatrician and you were going to live in New York and be a runway model on the side." Jackson huffs a soft laugh. I stroke Carly's hand. "Remember when you changed your mind?"

She doesn't answer. She just lies there with the machine breathing for her, other machines beeping and flashing and doing their thing. I hate hospitals. If I never have to see a hospital room again in my entire life, it'll be a lifetime too soon.

"Why?" Jackson asks, and when I look up at him, he clarifies, "Why did she change her mind?"

"We were at my house after school. Mom was doing laundry in the basement. We wanted apples and peanut butter and we didn't want to wait till she came up. So we got the apples and the knives and next thing I knew there was blood all over the floor and the counter." I trace the scar at the base of my thumb. It's a fine white line now, but I remember when it wasn't. "Carly looked at me, calm as can be, threw a dishtowel over my head, and told me not to look because I'd faint. Then she fainted."

Jackson grins.

"Mom came running when I started screaming. She found Carly on the floor, me squatting beside her pressing the dishtowel to my thumb and holding an ice pack to Carly's forehead with my elbow." I hold up my hand. "Four stitches."

He touches his eyebrow, the one that's bisected by the scar. "Jungle gym, meet skull. Four stitches. I was ten." He strokes my cheek. "Did Carly ever need stitches?"

"No. She—" She didn't have any. But she's going to

have some now. I had heard the nurses say something about surgery for her knee. I push to my feet and stand facing him, fighting tears. "I just need her to be okay." I turn back toward her and whisper, "I just need you to be okay."

Jackson and I split our day between Dad's room and Carly's—mostly Dad's. He talks under his breath, but nothing coherent. And he doesn't really wake up. Sometimes he moans and his face settles into a grimace, which tells me he's in pain, but when I ask the nurse about it, she says there's a limit to the amount of morphine they can give him, that it might dampen his breathing. Then she goes into a really detailed explanation about how removal of his spleen means he might not inflate his lungs properly with every breath, and the broken ribs just make that worse and how all of that might cause an infection that could turn into pneumonia, and how dangerous that is. All of which doesn't exactly endear her to me because I'd really like to wear my optimist panties right now.

And I pretty much hate her when she kicks us out at eight p.m. with a firm "Visiting hours are over."

"I need to go home for a bit," Jackson says as we walk to the Jeep.

"For how long?" I blurt.

He stops and turns to face me, tipping his glasses up so I can see his eyes. There's no mistaking the worry there.

"I didn't mean that the way it sounded," I say, feeling incredibly selfish. His parents haven't seen him in two days. He hasn't left my side since the accident. He still has to be reeling after facing Lizzie in the white room, and with all his energy funneling to me, he hasn't had time to process that. Maybe he just wants some alone time. I hold up my hand, palm forward. "Sorry. I just . . ." I go up on my toes and press a kiss to his cheek, the stubble along his jaw scratchy against my skin. "Thank you. For everything. Go home after you drop me off. I'll be fine."

"You can either come with me," he says, as if I never spoke, "or I can drop you at home while I go see my parents for a few minutes and grab some clothes." He strokes his knuckles along my jaw. "And I figure I better shave before I rub you raw."

He flips his glasses down and starts for the Jeep again. I take a couple of quick steps to catch up. "Oh. I thought—"

"I know what you thought."

I reach for the handle. Jackson reaches for the handle. His skin feels warm against mine. Then he loops his arm around my waist and spins me so I'm sandwiched between cold metal at my back, and Jackson's solid warmth at my front. He leans in and rests his forehead on mine, our breath puffing little white clouds between us. "When are you going to get it, Miki?" he whispers. "I won't leave."

I want to tell him I believe him, but actions speak louder than words and I'm not sure my actions are saying what I want them to.

I want to tell him I love him, but this isn't the right time.

We both already made those declarations under duress, and I don't want to do that again. I don't want to say the words now, when it's all about me, him being here for me. I don't want to say it when people I love are in danger of dying. It seems that I'm always saying *I love you* to people who die.

The next time I say *I love you* to Jackson, I want it to be in a moment that's just about us—me and him—and just about joy.

I climb into the Jeep as he rounds the hood. Before he gets in, he sends a text. I assume it's to his mom.

When we pull up to my house, Luka's sitting on the front step.

"Cold ass?" Jackson asks as we get out.

"So cold it's blue. Wanna see?" Luka rises, turns and hooks his thumb in the waistband of his jeans, dragging them down.

Jackson cuffs him on the back of the head. "Funny guy."

Luka turns to me and his humor fades. "Hey," he says, his dark eyes shadowed.

"Hey, yourself." I manage a weak smile.

I think he's going to say something more, about Dad, about Carly. Instead, he says, "Okay if I hang with you for a bit?"

I stare at him, confused, and then I get it. "Did Jackson call you to babysit me while he goes home?"

"I did not call him," Jackson says.

Luka grins. "He texted."

I laugh, exasperated. "Awesome." But it is kind of awesome, because Luka dropping everything to rush over and be here for me means a lot. I'm really happy to see him even though he's too freaked out to even ask how Dad and Carly are doing.

Maybe my expression gives me away, or maybe he realizes how weird it is that he hasn't asked anything and he wants to offer some kind of explanation, because he says, "No news is good news, right? Plus, Jackson's been texting updates. You text Kelley, he texts me, and between us we keep everyone else in the loop." His expression turns serious and he rakes his fingers back through his hair. "I'm sorry, Miki. I'm not good at this."

"No one is," Jackson says.

"Truth." I study Luka's face. He seems different than he was in the game on the last mission. I've kind of always thought of Luka as an open book, easy to read, but he's been odd lately in a way I can't exactly put my finger on. But right now, he seems like his usual self.

Jackson tries to hand Luka something, but Luka shakes his head in disgust and pulls back. "You're kidding, right?"

"What'd he try and give you?" I ask Luka as the two of us head inside.

"Nothing."

I cut him a look.

"Money," he says.

"Why?"

Luka hefts a white plastic bag I hadn't even noticed he

was holding. "Food," he says.

"You brought dinner?"

He looks sheepish. "Jackson might have made the suggestion. But I would have figured it out if I got here and found zero food."

"Which is what you would have found. I don't think we have much in the fridge. And it doesn't matter who suggested it, thanks for bringing"—I gesture at the bag—"whatever you brought."

"Kelley's mom wants to make you a tuna casserole."

I shudder. "I, uh, have this thing about tuna casserole . . ."

"So do I. Ever since fourth grade."

His mom died in fourth grade. "You had enough casseroles in your freezer to last months?"

He grimaces. "Maybe years."

"Us, too. Been there, done that. But today, I think my freezer's about to yield something you'll like." I dig out the container of butter tarts that Dad bought last week and set four out on a plate to defrost. "At least I can supply dessert. Two for you and two for Jackson when he gets back."

Luka studies the tarts. "You're not having one?"

I almost say no. It isn't Saturday. That's the only day I stray from my healthy eating rule.

Except . . . that isn't a hundred percent true anymore. I had cupcakes with Carly and Kelley and Dee and Sarah. That was one tiny step toward loosening the reins of my control. I stare at the plate and finally add a fifth tart before pushing the plastic container back into the freezer.

"I'm guessing Jackson told you what to order." I unload the plastic bag Luka brought.

"Sort of."

Steamed rice. Steamed veggies. Cashew chicken. Greasy spring rolls.

"Those are for me," Luka says. "I needed to add something edible to this pile of disgustingly healthy. Unless you want one. I mean, you can have one if you want."

"Definitely do not want." I load up a plate for each of us, putting all the spring rolls on his.

He talks as we eat, mostly about this new game he just bought.

"RPG," he says. "Love those. It's like you're helping tell the story. You ever play D&D? *Dungeons and Dragons*. It's like that." He stares at me for a long moment and leans closer. For a second, he almost doesn't look like Luka, his expression's so focused, so intent. "You play a specific character in the game and you go on all these adventures. Missions. There's a Dungeon Master who's the mastermind behind it all . . . the storyteller. The rulemaker. And you gain experience points while you play."

He stares at me, like he wants me to say something, so I do. "Dungeon Master. Mastermind. Got it."

His expression doesn't change and I start to feel like maybe I didn't get it. After a few seconds, he sits back in his chair, grins, and waves his fork at my plate. "Sorry, I get carried away. Eat."

I eat. He eats and talks between mouthfuls, telling me about his new game. It's comfortable. Comforting. Almost normal. Except my mind keeps wandering into worry territory and I have to make a conscious effort to haul it back.

" . . . and I want to go in with a fresh perspective so I never check out reviews or cheat codes before the first time I play," he says. "I don't want any preconceptions to influence my experience. I just want that first time to be with a fresh eye, you know?"

I nod and chew.

"So when I'm playing," he continues, "it's trial and error. I fail and fail a bunch of times and I get stuck on a level until finally I figure it out, take a different approach, and get to the next level. It's about a clean slate, like if I knew stuff about the game beforehand, if I looked it up or asked people about it, I'd have all these biased notions going in and that could blind me to opportunities. My mind wouldn't be open."

"Interesting philosophy."

Luka shrugs. "I can't claim it. It's something Jackson told me when we first met. But I agree with it."

I chew another mouthful and nod again.

Then I pause. Rewind.

"Wait, Jackson told you that when you first met him? Like the very first time you met? In the game?"

"Yeah, it was in the game." Luka frowns. "We were in the lobby. Maybe the second or third mission. So no, he didn't tell me that the first time we met. He was being

his usual self." He grins at me. "Cocky. Abrasive. Refusing to answer questions or answering with these cryptic
non-answers. Then he starts talking about video games. To
break the ice, I guess."

"What sort of questions were you asking him when he
burst into gaming verbosity?" I don't know why I think
this is important, but it is. I feel like there's some sort of
aha-with-harps-and-choirs moment here if I can just find it.

"Verbosity? Is that a word?"

"Google it."

Luka snorts. "I was asking him about the"—he lowers
his voice—"Drau. And about how we get pulled." Again,
he frowns. "I think the scores had shown up and I was asking about that. So instead of answering, he starts telling me
about moving to different campaign levels in *Call of Duty*,
saying that failure leads to knowledge by experience and
seeing it from a different angle and a whole bunch of stuff
like that."

I stare at him. "It wasn't to break the ice," I say slowly.
"It was to explain himself."

"What?"

"The way he never answers questions, never tells new
recruits much about the game . . ." I exhale on an incredu-
lous laugh. "He does it on purpose."

"Of course he does it on purpose." Luka holds his
hands out to the sides. "He purposely doesn't tell anyone
anything. Ever."

"But not because of the reasons we thought." When

we were in the caves and I didn't want our team to split up, Jackson made me think about strategy and see all the angles. I remember the way he looked at me, hung on my every word, like my decision, my *perception* mattered. Once I found out he meant to trade me into the game for his own freedom, I thought my decisions mattered that day because he was seeing what kind of leader I'd be. Now, I think maybe it wasn't that at all, or maybe not solely that. . . . The times he didn't tell me things and then watched my reactions, he was learning from them, using me to give him a new perspective, a fresh set of eyes.

I pick something up and absently nibble the edge. Luka makes this sound that's half growl, half laugh. I realize what I'm doing and gently place the spring roll back on his plate. "Sorry."

"*No hay problema.*" He bites off half the spring roll, dumps a packet of plum sauce in the other half, swallows.

"The first time I got pulled, you never explained that much, either," I point out.

"There's never much time to explain a whole heck of a lot when someone new gets dropped into the lobby," he says. "And Tyrone told you stuff. He gave you the rundown of the whole scoring system."

"Okay. That's true. But back to Jackson—"

"It's always back to Jackson." Luka's tone is teasing, but I can't help thinking back to right after the first time I got pulled when I thought Luka might like me. He and Jackson had this weird exchange where it was like Luka was warning him off, or maybe he was just being protective of me. I ended up thinking he might like Carly, then decided he liked both of us as friends and nothing more. I chalked up my confusion to being lousy at reading romantic signs since I was mourning while everyone else was learning the dating game.

But for a second, looking at him now, I feel like there's something else here that has nothing to do with who he's crushing on, something I ought to be able to see.

"So . . . back to Jackson," Luka prods.

"It's always back to Jackson," I mimic, bumping Luka's shoulder with mine. "So here's what I'm thinking . . . what if he didn't explain stuff because he wanted us to go in clueless, to discover things for ourselves. To *watch* us discover those things. You only get to go through the game for the first time once. Do you see?"

He gives me a look. "I'm the one who just told you that."

"I'm not talking about a video game. I'm talking about the *game* game. You only get to experience that first exposure once. Jackson's been in it forever. He sees it all through jaded eyes. He might be missing stuff because he has all these expectations based on what he knows and what he's already experienced. But a new recruit is going to go through it for the very first time, and if Jackson tells them nothing, then their experience isn't tainted by preconceptions." I pause. "Except one. The preconception that the Drau are evil."

A frown flickers across Luka's features, followed by something else I can't quite name. Wariness, maybe. "Well, that's kind of the whole point of the game, isn't it?"

"Except it isn't a game," I say softly.

"Isn't it?" He stares at me for a long moment. He opens his mouth and I think he's going to say something else. His look is so intense I start to worry. Then he just shrugs and grins and shovels in another forkful of food.

Because to him, these conjectures don't matter. To him, they aren't earthshattering revelations. But I'm the girl whose Sofu collected Japanese puzzle boxes, the girl who grew up solving them, and to me, this is another precious piece in the puzzle that is Jackson Tate.

"Hey, I'm curious," Luka says, eyes on his plate. "Did you and Jackson ever figure out why the game was lagging on the last mission?"

"No, why?"

His eyes meet mine and something in his expression reminds me of the day he tackled Carly on the field. When he caught me watching, he looked guilty. I thought it was because he felt awkward for having fun when the fate of the world was at stake. But his expression now is exactly the same, and I don't know what to make of that.

He shrugs and pushes some veggies over to bump up against his rice. "Just curious."

CHAPTER **TEN**

THE NEXT MORNING, JACKSON DROPS ME OFF AT THE HOSPI-tal's front doors and heads off to park the Jeep. I wait for him by the bank of elevators.

I've been there maybe two minutes when I get this weird sensation crawling along the back of my neck. The lobby's warm, and I'm wearing my down coat, but I shiver anyway. For a second, I think the creepy feeling is just because I'm back in the hospital, which isn't exactly my happy, happy place. But it's more than that. It's the shiver-up-my-spine feeling I get when someone's watching me, the same feeling I had in the hall at school the day Marcy tried to pass Jackson her number.

I turn. There are people everywhere. No one looks like they're paying attention to me.

Still, I can't shake the feeling that unseen eyes are locked on me.

I shift so my back's against the wall and there's no one behind me, then I scan the lobby. There's no one watching me, not that I can see. I wait for the creepy feeling to pass. But it doesn't. It amps up until I feel like a million centipedes are skittering over my skin. I rub the back of my neck just to prove to myself there's nothing there.

"Miki!" The Queen Bee, Marcy Kern, and her head lady-in-waiting, Kathy Wynn, stand in front of me wearing matching hunter green jackets. Cute. There's a part of me that isn't even surprised. At school lately, it's seemed like they've been following me, watching me. Everywhere I turned, there they were. In the halls, the caf, out behind the school under the giant oak my friends and I claim as our own. It got bad enough that I actually had this crazy down-the-rabbit-hole kind of nightmare. Lizzie was there, telling me *they* were watching, but she never said who they were, and then Marcy grew to gigantic proportions and Kathy shrank and shrank to the size of a thimble.

I told Luka I suspected Marcy was a shell.

Luka countered that her eyes aren't Drau gray and that I was having nightmares about her because she wanted to get into Jackson's pants.

Maybe he was right. But the last time I had this creepy vibe at school, I looked up to find Marcy right there, watching me.

And now she's right here.

Either way, Marcy and Kathy are among the last people I want to see right now.

"I'm sorry to hear about your dad," Marcy says, actually sounding like she means it. "And Carly . . . Oh my God, so terrible." I'm startled to see tears shimmering in her eyes. "Is there any change?"

"She's still in a medically induced coma."

"That's what Kelley posted this morning." She pauses. "And your dad? How's he doing?"

Again, I'm startled. She sounds like she actually cares. I glance at Kathy. She stands in Marcy's shadow, head down.

"I don't know yet. I'm on my way up to see him."

Marcy touches my arm. "I hope you have good news."

"Thanks." An awkward silence hangs between us, then I ask, "So what are you two doing here?"

"We're picking up Kathy's mom."

I glance at Kathy. "She was in the hospital? Is she okay?"

"She's a surgical nurse," Marcy says.

"Right." I sort of remember that from when we had career day a couple of years ago. I try to remember if Kathy told us about her mom, or if Marcy did the talking for her that day, too.

The elevator doors slide open.

"Hi, Mrs. Wynn," Marcy says with a smile.

I turn. Mrs. Wynn steps off the elevator. She's the nurse I spoke to outside the waiting room the night of the accident. I stare at her, suddenly remembering that I had the creepy being-watched vibe that night, too. Was it before I spoke to Mrs. Wynn, or after?

"Hey, look who I found," Jackson says, striding toward me. Beside him is Luka.

"Thought I should come by and see Carly," he says to the ground, hands shoved deep in his pockets, shoulders hunched. It's no stretch to figure out that Luka isn't exactly comfortable with this plan.

With a quick good-bye to Marcy, Kathy, and Kathy's mom, the three of us get in the elevator. As the doors slide closed I look up to see Marcy and then Kathy glance back over their shoulders as they walk away.

I'm up before dawn the next morning, donning my running gear, tying my shoes with meticulous care by the light of my bedside lamp. The house is silent. There's no one here. I didn't let Jackson sleep over last night even though he wanted to. Even though I wanted him to.

I need to be strong. I need to cope.

My life hasn't been this out of control since Mom died, and the anxiety and misery that haunted me for the past two years are right there beneath the surface, ready to leap if I give them the slightest opportunity. So I have a choice to make: I can wait for the beast to pounce, or I can head it off before it has the chance. I choose the latter and let myself out the front door, the wind slapping my cheeks, my breath puffing little clouds.

The sky's dark, the air frigid. Doesn't matter. I run my favorite route, my tunes playing, keeping me going, my thoughts focused wholly on putting one foot in front of the other. Nothing else exists for me, not right now. I'm in the moment, *this* moment. And it's this break from everything else in my life that's going to keep me sane.

I run until I hit the wall, the bonk, the moment when I know I can't run any more, exhaustion taking hold, legs burning, lungs craving oxygen that doesn't seem to reach them. Stopping isn't an option. Giving up isn't an option. I push through, using the techniques I've honed over two years, telling my body it isn't feeling what it thinks it's feeling, somehow making it all the way back to the house . . .

. . . to find Jackson sitting on the front step, two steaming cups of coffee beside him.

"You wouldn't let me sleep over. You wouldn't let me run with you—" When I start to interrupt, to explain yet again, he shakes his head and keeps talking. "No explanation needed, Miki. You need to be able to trust that whatever gets thrown at you, you're strong enough to deal. I get it. I don't agree with it. I don't like it. But I get it."

There isn't much I can say to that. I'm not sure if I love it or hate it, the way he reads me so well.

"So what I was going to say is, you wouldn't let me do anything else for you, but you can't turn down coffee." He gets to his feet and hands me a cup. "Skinny latte."

"Thank you." I lead him inside.

"So here's the thing," he says when we get to the kitchen. He leans one hip against the counter and sips his coffee. "I gave you what you need. Independence. Your turn to give me what I need."

I watch him warily over the rim of my coffee cup as I take a sip. "Depends on what you need."

His mouth curves in a slow, sexy smile. He takes a step closer and curls his free hand around my waist, drawing me in until I'm flush against him. "A whole lot of things, Miki Jones. But most of them will have to wait for another time."

I push against his chest. "Um . . . Does the word *disgusting* mean anything to you? I've just been running for an hour and have yet to shower."

"Don't care," he says, refusing to let me go. "Unless you mean that as an offer to let me watch."

"Watch me run?"

"I want to watch you shower," he whispers in my ear, then nips the lobe lightly.

"Do you, now?" I whisper back, borrowing one of his favorite phrases.

He's too close, too warm, too real, too safe.

I pull away and can't miss his reluctance as he lets me. I set my coffee down, busy myself pouring bowls of quinoa cereal, and say over my shoulder, "So you were telling me that it's my turn to give you what you need . . ."

He goes to the fridge, pulls out the carton of milk, sets it on the counter, and lifts his glasses so I can see his eyes.

"I need to feel like I'm doing something to help. I'm not great at standing on the sidelines." He pours the milk into the bowls. I grab the bag of marshmallows, but he pulls it from my hands before I can get it open and lobs it into the trash. "Never again," he says. "Eating those was right up there with oysters."

"You don't like oysters?"

"Or stale marshmallows."

"Duly noted."

He carries the bowls to the table while I get spoons.

"Here's how today's going to work," he says. "I'm going to drive you to the hospital before I head to school. Though I'd prefer to miss school altogether and stay with you."

"We've been through this. I don't want you falling behind on my account."

I poke at the cereal in my bowl. I know that at some point I'll need to go back to school, too, even if Dad and Carly are still in the hospital. But this isn't that point. Not yet.

"Eat," Jackson says.

Easier to do what he says than argue. Pick your battles. So I take a spoonful and chew.

He waits until my mouth's full before he continues. "I'll come by the hospital after with your homework. We'll stay till they kick us out, and I'll bring you home after." I watch him, wary. Everything he's saying sounds too reasonable, which is exactly why I'm on high alert. Jackson isn't usually a reasonable kind of guy. "And, uh, on the way back here we need to make a stop," he says.

"A stop?"

"My mother's making you dinner." Before I can protest,

he says, "It was dinner or you moving into the spare room until your dad comes home. I've put her off as long as I can. Take your pick. Dinner or spare room?"

Jackson with a slightly sheepish expression is hard to resist.

There's a certain appeal to the thought of moving in to the room next to Jackson's, but I shake my head and say, "Dinner. If I move in to your place and not Dee's or Kelley's or Sarah's, I'm going to have a riot on my hands." That isn't the reason and we both know it. It's more like: If I let myself drop my guard, drop my walls, let myself move in where someone's parents can take care of me, watch out for me, I'll stumble. I'll fall. I'll lose my hard-won ability to face whatever the day throws at me.

My friends don't get that at all.

But Jackson does.

CHAPTER**ELEVEN**

I SIT IN THE FAMILIAR PLEATHER CHAIR, PULL OUT MY MATH textbook, and work on some questions. I'm about halfway through when Dad whispers my name. My head jerks up and I study his face.

When I got here, the nurses said he had a good night last night, that he woke up and was coherent. It's one thing to be told he's improving. It's another thing entirely to hear him say my name like that. And then he opens his eyes and he looks right at me.

"Daddy." That one word comes out sounding like sunshine. I jump up, textbook and notebook falling unheeded to the floor, and lean over to carefully work one arm around his shoulder—the right one because his broken ribs and the incision from his splenectomy are on the left—and give him a hug. He tries to lift an arm to hug me back, but he's so weak he does little more than graze my hip before he drops his hand back on the bed. "The nurses said you're doing better, that you even had something to eat last night."

"Not sure . . . I'd call . . . three sips of juice . . . something to eat," Dad says, his voice raspy with disuse.

"Better than nothing, huh?"

"You think?" He offers a weak impression of a smile. He's pale, his hair disheveled, features drawn, eyes glassy from the pain meds. It doesn't matter. He's Dad and I'm so happy he's back.

I can't stop smiling. "You're going to be okay." I've said that so many times, sitting beside his bed while he was unconscious, willing it to be true. Saying it now, I finally believe it.

He starts to speak again, but his voice cracks. He runs the tip of his tongue over his lower lip. I pour some water from the blue pitcher on the bedside table into a Styrofoam cup and hold the straw while he takes a couple of sips.

"Not too fast. The nurse told me you shouldn't gulp a lot all at once."

"I should be the one taking care of *you*," he says, holding my gaze. "I think I've been falling down on that job for a while."

"I don't need to be taken care of." I set the cup down on the table. "I just need you to get better and come home."

"Working on it." He winces as he takes a breath.

"Hurts to breathe?"

"Nope."

"Bullsh—" He gives me that Dad look, the one where he lowers his head and lifts his eyebrows. "Bullcookies," I improvise.

He studies me for a long minute. "You getting enough rest?"

"Yes." That's the way Dad and I have communicated for a while. Mostly honest, but sometimes not.

He stares at me. The Dad stare.

I sigh. "No."

He nods. "You'll start tonight."

I want to tell him that I'll tuck myself in at nine p.m. sharp and sleep like a baby, that now that he's awake everything's great. But that would be a lie because Carly hasn't woken up yet and I don't know when she will. I don't dare let myself wonder *if* she will.

"Carly?" he asks, like he knows exactly what I'm thinking. "No one here would tell me anything last night. Just that she's getting the best possible care." He tries to lift his hand again, but he can only hold it up for a couple of seconds before it flops back on the bed. "Weak as a kitten," he mutters.

The nurses told me that if he woke up, I should keep things light. They told me not to upset him. I'm pretty certain that telling him Carly still hasn't regained consciousness and that she's in the neuro-ICU is going to upset him. So do I pull a Jackson and lie by omission? Or do I tell him the truth?

I'm saved from making that decision when Dr. Lee walks in. He nods at me, then starts talking to Dad, asking him questions. I can tell by his tone of voice that he's pleased with Dad's replies, and when he says, "We'll be transferring you later today," I get my confirmation. Dad's on the mend and they're letting him out of the ICU. Which doesn't mean he's a hundred percent yet or that he gets to come home, but moving him to the regular floor means he's one step closer.

Those bits of conversation with me and the visit from Dr. Lee wore Dad out; he nods off within seconds of Dr. Lee leaving. I head to the neuro-ICU and sit with Carly for a while. Her head's wrapped in white bandages. There's a tube in her nose and another in her mouth. The respirator hisses and other machines beep.

I get flashbacks of the rows of shells in the cave, dozens of bodies that all looked just like Lizzie lying there, hooked up to machines. Clones created from Lizzie's DNA. Empty shells created to house alien consciousness and allow the Drau to hide in plain sight. I think of Jackson and Luka turning off the machines, and me freaking out because they were killing people. Who turned out not to be people at all.

I scrub both palms over my face, then take Carly's hand in mine. I talk to her, telling her about all the texts and posts from all our friends. About Marcy asking after her. I talk until I'm hoarse, until Carly's parents come back.

"We went to see your father," Mrs. Conner says. "He was sleeping, but the nurse told us he's doing better." She sounds hopeful, like maybe if Dad's doing better, if he's going to be okay, Carly will, too.

I nod and hug her and we just hold on to each other for the longest time.

But what terrifies me is the way Carly's dad, a man I've known my whole life, who in all that time has never hugged me, not even when Mom died, steps over and wraps his arms around us both. I'm crying again. I dash the tears away with the back of my hand, angry to be this girl, this weeping, desperate girl.

I just feel so out of control. There's nothing I can do to help Carly, and that's killing me.

"I'll walk with you to the elevator," Mr. Conner says when I start to leave. "I'm going to get some coffee for the Becks."

"The Becks?"

"Their daughter's here, too. Has been for more than two weeks," Carly's mom explains. "Kristin Beck. She's the same age as Carly." She looks away and whispers, "She hasn't woken up yet, either."

I don't know what to say, so I just squeeze Mrs. Conner's hand and then hug her one more time.

When I get to Dad's room, he's awake again.

I lean over and kiss his cheek. "Aunt Gale?" he asks.

"She calls at least once a day. And I text her in between.

She has a flight home booked for tonight, but we agreed she'd cancel it if you woke up." I smile at him. "Guess she's staying in Korea, huh?"

"Looks like." He tips his head to the side. "Have you been staying at Kelley's?" I shake my head. "Dee's?"

"I've been staying at home. It's better, sleeping in my own bed, in my own house."

He doesn't say anything for a second, then, "Who's been staying with you?"

"Sometimes no one." I take a deep breath. "And sometimes Jackson."

Dad's eyebrows shoot so high they practically disappear into his hair.

"Trust me, Dad, I haven't exactly been in the frame of mind for anything you might be worrying about to have actually happened. I slept. He slept. End of story." I smile a little. "Besides, you told me I have to wait until I'm fifty," I say, reminding him about the crazy awkward conversation we had about boys the day my neighbor Mrs. Gertner regaled me with her hemorrhoid surgery stories.

Dad laughs, then groans and touches his broken ribs. "Don't make me laugh. Hurts." He sobers and gestures at the brownish-orange pleather chair that I've come to know far too well. "Sit. I want to talk to you."

I sit.

"I want to tell you where I was. All those nights, I want to—"

"I already know," I say, not wanting to talk about this,

but knowing I have to at some point. No sense putting it off, not if Dad's open to the topic right now. Who knows what later will bring. "I found your matchbooks. In the bowl in your bedroom. The one Mom used to keep potpourri in." I take a deep breath. "The Elk Bar, huh? I guess you really like that one because you have a ton of their matchbooks."

He just watches me and I keep talking, telling him everything that's been in my heart. Maybe he's finally ready to hear it, or maybe he's just my captive audience. I know I'm not supposed to upset him, so I try to keep my tone even and choose my words with care.

"Remember when you said you had it all under control?" I ask, my voice gentle. "I don't think you do, Daddy, and I can't just keep quiet anymore and wipe the counter and put away the empties. I need you."

He nods. "I know, baby. And I lost sight of that. But then I got it back." He swallows and I can tell this is hard for him.

I get up and offer him the Styrofoam cup. "We can talk about this later. We—"

"No." He takes another sip of water and gestures me away. "Now. You're right. I was going to bars, every night."

I look away, not sure I can keep my expression neutral.

"But not to drink. Well, that's not completely true. Some nights it was, but most nights it wasn't."

I set the cup down and turn to him. "What do you mean?"

"I started out by going to that AA meeting. The one

you told me about. But it wasn't for me." He holds up his hand before I can cut him off. "Some people say that if AA doesn't do it for you, if you say it isn't for you, then you're lying. To yourself. To everyone else. But just hear me out.

"I went. But I just couldn't talk there. Talking doesn't help me. It makes it worse. And hearing everyone else's sad story just makes me feel worse about my own. I went every day for a week. When I got home from those meetings, first thing I did was grab a beer. Or two. Or three. But I knew it had to stop. I had to make a choice. So I decided that I'd go to a bar every night until I could sit there and sip my soda water and not crave something harder."

I shake my head, not seeing how that would work.

He sees my expression and makes a rueful sound. "First night, it was agony. I just wanted a drink. I left after six minutes. I know it was exactly six minutes because when I hit five minutes I forced myself to sit there for another sixty seconds. I watched the clock and as soon as the second hand cleared, I bolted.

"When I got home, first thing I did was open a beer. But I didn't drink it. I just sat there in the dark kitchen thinking about your mom and how sick she'd be to see me like this. Thinking about you, how I was letting you down. Letting myself down. Thinking about how much I wanted to drink that beer.

"I got it then. I really understood." He holds my gaze, his voice steady as he says, "I'm an alcoholic and I could sit in a bar for a million hours, sip my soda water till I float away, and I will never stop craving something harder. Sitting there in the dark in the kitchen, wanting that beer more than I wanted to breathe, it hit me that the trick was going to be to learn how to be stronger than that craving because it isn't going to go away. Not ever. I will never sit in a bar and not want a drink and I have to learn to live with that."

I sink into the chair and take his hand, a tiny flicker of hope igniting inside me.

"I—" His voice cracks and he gives a pained cough, wincing as he touches his fingertips to his ribs. I lean forward and hand him the water, waiting while he takes a couple of sips. With a nod he hands it back to me and I set the cup on the table.

"I kept going back over the next few weeks," he says. "Different bars. But I liked the Elk. Not too crowded. Not too empty. No one gave me grief about just wanting soda.

"I worked my way up to three hours. Three hours, drinking nothing but soda water with lime, the booze all around me calling my name."

He looks down and smoothes his fingertips along the thin blue sheet stamped with the hospital logo. Then he looks up at me. "In the first weeks, I slipped a couple of times, Miki. Had a drink. But I never had more than one because of that promise I made you, the one about not driving if I drink. The thing is, it should have been me getting that promise out of you. It should have been me being the parent."

I lean over and rest my forehead on the back of his hand. We sit there like that for a long time, neither of us saying anything else.

Finally, I whisper, "I thought it was your fault. I thought you were drinking that night. I thought you almost killed yourself and Carly. I'm sorry."

I raise my head and look at him. His eyes are closed, his breathing slow and even. I don't know if he was awake to hear what I said. I don't know if I'll ever have the guts to say it to him again.

CHAPTER **TWELVE**

JACKSON SHOWS UP AFTER SCHOOL. HE BRINGS ME A PACK-age of work each of my teachers put together for me and a huge, handmade card for Dad signed by pretty much the whole school.

"The brainchild of Kelley and Dee," he says. "They said they'll be by later with the card for Carly."

If they were here in front of me right now, I think I'd cry. I stand the card where Dad'll see it when he wakes up.

"Did you see her?" I ask.

"Carly? Yeah. I stopped there for a couple of minutes on my way up. You?"

I nod. "I sat with her while her parents went to grab something to eat."

Neither of us says the obvious out loud. That Carly's status hasn't changed.

"There's another girl in the ICU. Kristin Beck. She was in a car accident, too. She hasn't woken up yet, either." I remind myself of my resolution to wear my optimist panties. Focus on the positive. "Dr. Lee was here. He said they're going to move Dad to the regular floor."

"Whennnnnnn?" The word stretches like pulled taffy. Jackson asks me something else, but it's just a jumble of nonsensical sounds.

The room around me explodes into a kaleidoscope of color and shape.

"Jackson!" I reach for his hand, our fingers connecting. "They can't do this. Not now. It's too much. I can't!" The world snaps back into focus.

I'm breathing too fast, the sounds jagged and panicked. Jackson wraps his arms around me.

"I can't," I say again. "I can't do another mission. Not now. What you said outside Carly's house, about buildings that sway when an earthquake hits and buildings that snap because they're too rigid? About me getting to choose what sort of building I'm going to be? I'm trying to sway, Jackson. I swear I am. But I'm breaking. I can't—"

"You bend, Miki. You do not break. I will not let you break."

"What makes you think you get a choice?" I whisper, and only when they're out there, hanging in the silence, do I realize the words echo one of Jackson's standard phrases.

The moment stretches like an elastic band then snaps back into place.

Jackson's lips move. I know he's answering me, but I can't hear the words. My ears ring. My vision spangles with flares of color.

"Jackson?"

"I'm here, Miki."

But he isn't. He's fading, the sound of his voice far, far away.

"I've got you," he says. "And you've got me. We've got each other, Miki. Don't forget it."

But we don't have each other.

We reach, stretch, trying to hold the failing connection.

The floor drops. And drops. And drops. I try to cling to Jackson's hand, but it's gone, he's gone, and I'm alone, spinning out of control.

I fall, hitting cold ground in a sprawl. The impact jolts through my thigh and one side of my butt, but my hands, my feet . . . I can't feel them at all. It's like an injection of novocaine before I get a filling, except this injection has numbed my limbs.

Resentment fills me as I force myself to my feet and stand at the bottom of the amphitheater in this place that exists but doesn't, this place where infinite years of alien consciousness unite.

Tiers upon tiers of seats rise all around me, filled by shadowy, wraithlike shapes. Before me is a floating platform occupied by three cloaked figures. The Committee. The first time they brought me here, they appeared as a Cleopatra look-alike, a brawny guy modeled on a combo of Odin and Thor, and a cowled grim reaper. But they don't actually look like that; they showed me something I expected to see. They don't plant the images; they just let the viewer play out their own mental video. It wasn't real.

So is any of this real, or is it a construct in my thoughts? Is there really an amphitheater and a floating platform, or is the Committee still just letting me conjure up something I expect to see?

Truth is, it doesn't matter. What matters right now are Dad and Carly and me getting back to the hospital. That's what matters to me.

But I'm sure the Committee has its own, very different opinion on that.

Forcing my voice to stay low and steady, I ask, "Is a mission imminent?"

"No." Their reply dances across my nerve endings like an elephant in army boots. With metal cleats.

I'm not surprised by their answer. If they'd pulled me for a mission, I would have respawned in the lobby and Jackson would be with me.

"We wish to converse."

"Converse," I echo. "As in, have a conversation." Anger surges. I get why we're pulled on missions to fight the Drau without warning, any time, night or day, without consideration for the pressures of our other lives: friends, school, family. People we love at the edge of death.

The Committee doesn't get to pick when the Drau invade. So we don't get to pick when we're pulled. The enemy comes. We fight them off, small battles in the grand war for the continued existence of mankind.

So, yeah, I get that we aren't in control. And I've come to accept it even though it sucks.

What I don't get, what I don't accept, is the Committee pulling me for a little meet and greet when they know what's going on in my real world life. My resentment crackles and sparks, my skin tingling.

There's no sense asking them to send me back. They work from their own twisted agenda. Instead, I go on the offensive and say, "So let's converse. You answer my questions and I'll answer yours." I don't give them a chance to decline my offer. "What happened? How did the Drau end up at my high school during the Halloween dance? How did Carly end up in the game?"

"The Drau altered expectations. They were not to be at your high school at all. They were expected in a different place."

I remember how my team originally respawned in a different high school, then somehow ended up at Glenbrook, so the Committee's assertion that the Drau were supposed to be somewhere else makes sense, but it doesn't really explain anything.

"We believe the Drau chose to threaten you by arriving in your alternate reality."

I have to choke back a sarcastic laugh at that. My alternate reality? As if the game is my real life?

"Wait . . . how does that make sense? Are you saying that the Drau just targeted me and my team? That they targeted my high school because of me? Or that they attacked every team out there on their home turf?" That's a terrible possibility. The Drau crashing through the boundaries between dimensions in a single place is horrific enough; the thought that they did it in multiple locations as a concentrated attack is beyond terrifying.

I wait for their answer, but it doesn't come.

Electric shocks erupt on my scalp, my palms, my soles, then reach for my wrists, my ankles as the silence stretches to infinity.

The sparking on my skin morphs into painful prickling. My vision flickers and vibrates. Blue rectangles over green over yellow in ragged patterns.

I blink and the world freezes, shadowy figures locked in place.

I blink and the world moves too fast, the amphitheater going round and round like a crazy carousel.

I blink and I'm in a blinding white room. The air smells artificial, like it's recycled and laced with air freshener. A dark rectangle appears, marking a doorway, one I've passed through before. I stumble through now and find the same curved hallway I saw last time I was here.

I start along the corridor but I don't get far. A girl with honey-gold hair rounds the curve and throws herself at me, enveloping me in a tight hug. Lizzie.

"Miki, I'm so sorry about your dad and Carly."

I'm startled enough that I hug her back. Or maybe I hug her because I remember the way she's saved my life more than once, and because her tone, her expression, they seem so sincere. "How do you know? About them? About the accident?"

She steps back and looks me over. "Are you okay?"

"Physically? I'm fine. Mentally? Not so much." I pause. "How do you know about the accident?" I ask again.

"I try to keep tabs on you. It isn't always easy."

"Keep tabs . . . Is that a euphemism for spying on me?"

She studies me for a second and then says, "You could say that."

Give the girl points for honesty.

"We don't have much time, Miki. We can't hold you here for long."

A million questions dance through my mind. *Where is here? What do you want? Who are you really? How did you manage to bring me here? Who is the "we" you're talking about? I only see you. I've only ever seen you.*

Before I can decide which question to ask, Lizzie says, "You need to learn how to keep them out. The Committee. They know. Do you understand? They *know*. And that's dangerous."

"Know what?"

"That you spoke with the Drau. That she communicated with you."

"She?"

Lizzie makes an impatient gesture. "That doesn't matter. Not right now."

"It's no stretch to believe you're Jackson's sister. He never answers my questions, either."

She laughs softly. "I know. I'm sorry. Yes, the Drau you communicated with was female. Now listen. Let me tell you what I need to tell you and then if we can still maintain the link after that, I'll answer your questions until I lose you."

Which only makes me want to ask a ton more questions. But I don't. Instead, I summon the patience and control I learned during hour after hour of repetitive kendo exercises in Sofu's dojo and say, "Okay. Talk."

CHAPTER**THIRTEEN**

"THE COMMITTEE SUSPECTS YOU MAY HAVE COMMUNICATED with the Drau, but at this point they have no proof," Lizzie says. "They're going to try to find out for certain, to find out what she said to you. They're going to try to invade your thoughts and poke around inside your head. Do you understand?"

"I understand." The possibility of them climbing inside my mind sickens me. I don't want them pawing through my memories, the precious moments I've folded away, memories of Mom, memories of my childhood. The first time I saw Jackson. The way I felt the first time he kissed me. They have no right to those.

But the Committee doesn't much care about rights.

I remember Jackson's screams carrying all the way

into the game and reverberating inside my head when the Committee tried to force its way inside his mind. He didn't let them in. He fought them. He won.

Would I win? I don't want to be in a position to find out.

"But why would they invade my thoughts?" I ask. "Why wouldn't they just ask me? And why wouldn't I just tell them the truth? Maybe even get some answers from them while I'm at it?"

"They won't ask because they don't trust human truth, and because they don't trust humans to tell the truth. You cannot let them into your head, do you understand? I took a huge risk letting you see me that first time, bringing you and Jackson here, talking with you. My team was against it. If you let the Committee find out about me, about this place—" She breaks off and shakes her head and the expression on her face gives me chills. "You can't let them find out. And you definitely cannot let them find out for certain that you've communicated with a Drau. If they do, you *will* be in danger."

She says that so matter-of-factly. Cold dread crawls along my spine. "Why—"

"They don't need a logical reason. They don't want humans and Drau connecting in any way except violent confrontation." She studies my face, her eyes impossibly green, pupils dilated and dark. She's afraid. For me.

Green. Even in the game. "Your eyes," I say. "Everyone's turn blue in the game. But not yours. They stay green.

Why? Is it because you aren't part of the game?" That's the most obvious answer.

"You've seen me there. In the *game*. So I must be part of it." She puts a weird inflection on the word *game*, but I'm doing the dog-at-a-bone thing, and I pursue my original question, refusing to be distracted.

"That's the logical conclusion, but is it the correct one?"

Her brows lift. "Good catch. And you're right. I can enter the game but I'm not part of the game. Not the way you are."

"So . . . no score for you. The Committee doesn't pull you"—the first time she saved me on the mission I led while Jackson was missing . . . and in the school basement the night the Drau crossed over into my real world . . . Every time I've seen her she's had a weapon that shot light, a *Drau* weapon, not a weapon like mine—"and they don't arm you."

"No, the Committee does not pull me or arm me. In fact, they don't know about me and I'd like to keep it that way. My life, and the lives of others, depends on it. And your life depends on you keeping the Committee from confirming their suspicions about your communication with the Drau." She studies my face. "Do you believe me, Miki? You need to believe me."

I think about that for a second, my gaze fixed on the brilliant white wall of the curved corridor. "I don't disbelieve you. I think the Committee is capable of doing pretty much anything for what they perceive is the greater good.

But . . . killing me because they think I communicated with a Drau? How would that be for the greater good? I can't see the angle."

Lizzie snorts. "The greater good? You mean their convenience. What's good for them and their entertainment."

"Entertainment? How is a war entertaining?"

"Isn't that the question?" She makes an impatient gesture in a way that definitely reminds me of Jackson, and asks, "What did she say to you?"

I open my mouth to answer, then stop. I run through everything Lizzie's said and everything I've said. Did I confirm that the Drau spoke with me? No. No, I didn't. Lizzie made the assumption. I asked some questions, but I didn't corroborate her assumption.

Now she's asking what the Drau said. She's telling me not to trust the Committee with this information, but she expects me to trust her, a girl I don't know, a girl wearing my boyfriend's dead sister's face. Not going to happen. Instead I ask, "Why am I at risk? Why harm me?"

"Because you could expose everything. The game. Their goals. Their cruelty." The words explode from her, too loud in the silent, sterile corridor.

"Expose it to who? Who'd believe me? We can't take weapons or harnesses out of the game, or even take pictures while we're there. Without evidence . . ." I shrug.

"You can see the other teams, the other lobbies."

Not a question, but I nod anyway.

"If you can see them, you can communicate with them.

With the team leader, anyway. You could tell all of them the truth. The Committee doesn't want that."

"Tell them what truth?" My skin prickles and stings. My fingers feel numb. I sway as the corridor starts to spin.

"Crap, we're losing you." She grabs both my hands. Her fingers are smooth and icy cold. My vision fractures into a trillion colors, then realigns.

I focus on what she said about the Committee not wanting us to connect with the Drau. "You're wrong about communicating with the Drau," I say, remembering when Jackson and I were in the caves, before we found the room with the rotting, brainless clones. We were alone—the Committee had activated Luka's con, sending him and Tyrone in the opposite direction. Jackson and I stumbled on a small patrol. He took out one Drau; I took out the other, and Jackson was anything but pleased because he wanted to question it. "Jackson's communicated with them before. He's questioned them, at least once or twice. And I'm pretty sure the Committee knows about it. They didn't kill him for it. Kind of blows your theory."

"Like I said"—Lizzie rolls her eyes—"violent confrontation. How do you think those sessions between Jackson and the Drau went? Sunshine and roses?"

Not so much.

"Miki, listen. It's fine if you don't trust me yet, if you don't want to confide in me," she says, tightening her hold on my hands. "But I need you to believe what I'm about to tell you. Your life depends on it.

"When the Committee tries to force their way into your head, and trust me, they *will* try to force their way in, you have to fill your thoughts with something they can't comprehend, something that will stop them in their tracks."

"Won't that piss them off?"

"Not if they can't blame you for it. They'll still be able to project the things they want to say into your mind, exactly the way they always do. But if you do what I tell you, they won't be able to root around for answers and steal your thoughts. And they won't be able to blame you for that because it'll be *their* failing, their inability to understand human emotion that stops them, not your lack of cooperation. It's important that they believe you're cooperating. You can't give them any excuse. Do you understand?"

I understand that either she's an incredible actress or she believes every word she's saying. "Fill my thoughts with something they can't comprehend? You mean like an image? Like the visualization techniques my grief counselor taught me?"

"Yes, yes. Like that, but different. Not an image. That won't do it. In fact, a single image gives them something to fixate on. It helps them get inside. It's like a beacon leading them."

When the Committee tried to steal Jackson's memories, he held fast to a mental picture of me. He thought that helped keep them out. Lizzie's saying it was exactly the opposite, that it made things worse. I remember the way he screamed in pain, the way his cries reached all the way into the game to find me.

"You have to pick an *emotion*. They aren't hardwired for feelings. Love. Hate. Terror. They can't understand any of it."

"Wait . . . are you sure?" I remember when I accused them of torturing Jackson, I thought I sensed surprise and amusement tingeing their replies.

"I'm sure," Lizzie says. "They can mimic human emotion to a tiny degree, to make them more relatable, to make players believe their lies. But feel it? Understand it? Never." Her tone takes on urgency. "Think of the strongest emotion you can come up with. The trick is to pick one and let it consume you, to let it overtake everything else. Let that emotion fill you."

"And that will keep them out."

She grimaces and dips her head to the side. "It's not foolproof. They might make it through the door, but they won't get past the entry hall. They'll still talk inside your head. They might even be able to pick up a few basic things, stuff that's weighing heavily on your thoughts, like your worry for your father and Carly. But that's as far as they'll get if you erect an emotional barrier. They won't be able to rummage through your thoughts and find anything you might want to keep hidden. Clear?"

"As mud." I pause. "They tried to steal Jackson's memories of me. They couldn't. He didn't let them. We thought it was because he called up a mental picture of me and pushed them out. But that wasn't it, was it? It was . . ." It was how he *feels* about me.

Lizzie smiles a little, her expression wistful. "I bet there's a story there. And I'm glad he found you." She squeezes my hand, her eyes on mine, her gaze clear and sincere, and for a second I believe completely and utterly that she really is Jackson's sister and not some kind of clone or shell or some other weird part of the game. I believe that she loves him and all this is about protecting him, and me.

"So, um, how does it work? And what emotion do I use?"

"Anything. Love, hate, fear, hope. Anything you can focus on completely. Emotion short circuits them. They just don't get it. They can't process it. And when they butt up against it in its purest form, they get tangled trying to figure it out. But it has to be a single one. The more emotions you allow in the mix, the more they're diluted, the . . . less . . . chance you . . . have for . . . success."

Again my vision fractures. Again my hands and feet go numb. I'm floating, weightless.

"Miki!"

I focus on Lizzie's face. She's like an overexposed photo, parts of her flaring bright. Like a lightbulb. Like a Drau . . .

Then I'm back, everything clear and in focus, and the certainty I felt about her seconds ago erodes and scatters like dust.

"We can't hold you much longer."

"Then it's my turn for questions. You said my friend's

name, more than once. Carly. How do you know that?"

"My team and I were there in your high school basement with you."

Of course. They were there at the Halloween dance, when Carly crossed into the game. When the Drau killed her.

"So you heard me call her name."

"She told me her name."

"Wait . . . when . . ."

"We saved her, Miki, then sent her back. How did you think she survived?"

"Jackson—"

She shakes her head. "The Committee would never allow that. It was us."

I stare at her, trying to process that information, remembering how Jackson and Luka and I rushed to Carly's house after the Drau attack at the dance, how we found her locked in her bathroom, terrified. She said, *My eyes were like theirs. Gray and scary. With slitted pupils instead of round ones. Not human. Like theirs.*

I didn't figure it out then. I was so grateful that she was alive, I didn't ask whose eyes she was talking about. But now, as I wonder how Carly knew the Drau have slitted pupils, an ugly suspicion uncoils like a snake.

"Where's the rest of your team?" I ask, glancing up and down the corridor. White floor. White walls. White like the walls of the underground Drau facility where we found row after row of rotting clones hooked to machines.

Clones that all looked like Lizzie.

Jackson told me that he's wiped out facilities like that, populations of clones wearing Lizzie's face, three times.

Hundreds of Lizzies. Maybe thousands.

"They're helping to hold you here," Lizzie says. "And doing other things."

"Things that keep me from seeing them. Gotta wonder why."

"I don't think you're wondering at all. I think you know the answer." She pauses, letting me digest that. "Miki, I'm not Drau. And I'm not a shell. We went through all that last time you were here."

"So exactly what are you then?"

"Ask me more important questions. We don't have much more time."

More important than whether or not she's teamed up with the enemy?

"Are you teamed up with the enemy?"

"Depends on your definition of enemy." She smiles a little, reminding me of Jackson, and one brow arches as she asks, "Are *you*?"

Her question makes me shiver, or maybe it's because she's losing me, her ability to hold me here fading. I can feel it in the way my limbs keep going numb and prickly. "I dreamed about you, about this place, before I ever came here. I woke up from that dream with burns on my shoulder."

"I know. I'm sorry. I was trying to contact you for so long and I almost managed that night, almost got you here.

The burns were accidental. I glitched and temporarily dropped you into the wrong place, wrong time. Definitely not in my plan. They healed?"

"Not even a scar." I frown. "So you can transport me from the game to here, and I guess from my real life to here . . . On the last mission, it felt like the game was lagging, like weird stuff was happening . . . was that you?"

"Yes."

"And when Jackson and I respawned at the hospital mid-mission. You again?"

"I thought I was doing something good, helping you. I thought if I snatched you back and let you know that your father made it through the surgery then dropped you back into the mission with no one the wiser . . ." She shrugs. "In the end, I think I just made things worse."

"Does the Committee know we got hauled out of the game?"

"I don't know. They might, but if they do, they'll just think there was some sort of glitch in the teleport. Which is another reason you need to keep them out of your head. They can't know about us, about what we're capable of."

"A glitch in the teleport. You say that like it's no big deal." I shake my head. "How does that work? How do they move me from one place to another? How do you?"

Something flickers in her eyes, her expression going closed and flat. Guess I stepped over the edge into the forbidden zone.

"Long-winded scientific explanation," she says. "Just know that the glitch is probably another thing the Committee will want an explanation for when they go digging around in your head. You need to make sure they don't . . . get . . . it . . ."

Her words drag. The white walls all around me glow blindingly bright. The sound of my pulse is like a freight train and the artificial smell of the air burns my nose, scraping my airway all the way to my lungs.

"Lizzie!" I can't go. Not yet. She has so many answers.

She lets go of my numb hands. "Remember what I told you. Be careful, Miki."

I want to thank her for trying to help when she pulled me out of the game, for being in the school basement and saving Carly, for saving my life on the mission before that, but she's spinning end over end, growing smaller and smaller as she revolves in darkness speckled with light.

So pretty. Like stars.

CHAPTER**FOURTEEN**

I STAND IN FRONT OF THE COMMITTEE, DIZZY, SWAYING.

The cloaked being on the far left lifts its hand and with a languid motion clears the amphitheater. All the shadowy figures in the tiers of seats disappear, leaving a massive empty arena, with me standing alone at its base, facing the three on the platform.

A buzz of fear chases through me as I wonder if they know about Lizzie, if they know she snatched me away from right under their noses. And if they do know, what they'll do to me now.

"You ask many questions, as always, Miki Jones." The Committee doesn't speak out loud. They send their thoughts directly into my brain, my nerves, every sense receptor in my body. Their voice crackles in my joints, flays the pain receptors in my skin, nearly bringing me to my knees. I cry out and cup my palms over my ears, as if that will help.

"Too much," I gasp, but they knew that already. They did that on purpose, a warning volley with specific intent.

They scale back the intensity and say, "Only your team was affected. A minor aberration."

I stare at them, trying to figure out what they're talking about. And then I remember what I was asking the second before Lizzie pulled me. I was asking them about the Drau and whether they crossed into the reality of all the other teams. I'm guessing that the fact that they're answering me as if there was no break in the conversation means they have no idea I was gone. One point for me. Yay, Miki.

"You're calling the Drau attack on my school a *minor aberration*?" Like all those kids at the dance don't matter, like Carly almost dying doesn't matter. Because to them, she doesn't. Anger flares and I bite the inside of my cheek to hold back all the ugly things I want to say to them. Instead, I say, "Send me back. My father, my friend, they need me and I need to be there to . . . to . . ." To what? Save them? Help them? There isn't anything I can do.

"They are safe enough, for now." Their words dance along my nerves. I hear them in my head, my lungs, my toes, not painful but uncomfortable. A reminder that they can amp it up and bring me to my knees any time they want.

"Safe enough for now? What does that mean?" As if

I don't know a clear threat when I hear one. I feel sick, shaken. All the times I imagined Dad pinned in the mangled wreck or Carly dying, I kept thinking it felt like those images were being forced on me . . . Maybe they were.

Maybe the Committee was threatening me even then.

Or am I only doubting them because of what Lizzie just told me? I don't know what to think, what to believe.

They don't answer my question, instead posing one of their own. "What transpired, Miki Jones?"

Are they asking about Lizzie, about how she hijacked me and what was said between us? Her warnings echo in my thoughts. I stare at the floor hoping they can't read the signs of my growing unease.

The question comes again, more insistent. "What transpired on the last mission?"

I sag in relief as understanding clicks. They aren't asking about Lizzie at all, which suggests they really have no idea that she detoured me to meet with her. And if I have any say about how this pans out, they aren't going to know. It isn't that I trust Lizzie—I don't know enough about her or her true motivations to make that leap. It's more that I don't trust the Committee. I have a feeling that at some point I'm going to need to pick a side, but right now, I'll just try to get some answers that might help me decide.

"Why are you asking about the mission? I mean, you were watching, right? You're always watching."

"We wish to hear your perceptions and conclusions."

"My perceptions and conclusions . . . You're asking for

my opinion?" And how unrealistic is that? I study the three figures on the floating platform, digging my fingertips into my thighs. Lizzie's paranoia is rubbing off on me.

Except, it isn't just Lizzie. The Committee didn't exactly endear themselves to me when they tunneled into Jackson's brain and tried to steal his memories of me, or when they tricked both of us into staying in the game. Or when they left me isolated and alone on the last mission instead of feeding me directions through my con. Then they fed directions to Lien and Kendra, who just happened to kill the Drau before I could get any important information from her. I could be making connections where none exist, making mountains out of molehills, but it just feels like there are a bunch of big and small things that don't quite add up.

"Miki Jones." Their words scrape my skin, explode on my taste buds. "Begin."

An order I don't dare disregard.

"We respawned in the factory. The Drau ambushed us from above with snipers on the catwalk," I say, and keep going from there, telling them everything about the last mission, from start to finish. Everything I can remember that my team said or did, everything I heard and saw, with a few key omissions. I don't tell them about Jackson's plan for Kendra to earn the thousand points and test the freedom rumor, or about feeling like the game was lagging, or about Lizzie pulling me back to the hospital mid-mission.

If they don't bring any of that up, I certainly won't.

I don't tell them about the white room and curved corridor and the moments I just spent with Jackson's dead sister.

And I don't tell them that the Drau communicated with me right before the Committee sent Lien and Kendra to kill her.

When I'm done, I stand facing them in silence so absolute I can hear the thud of my heart, the flow of my blood through my arteries.

"You asked us once before about the possibility of a player leaving the game upon earning a thousand points."

My breath catches in my throat. I did ask them that, the first time I met them. But why bring it up now unless they know about Jackson's plan . . . and if they know about that, what else do they know? About Lizzie, the Drau . . . ? Or is this a trick meant to throw me off balance, to make me think they know more than they do?

I scrape up whatever bravado I have left at the bottom of the pot. "I did. And you weren't exactly clear on your answer."

"We believe in being forthright. In the event we were not clear, no, a player does not leave upon achieving said score. They evolve to the next level."

"The next level," I repeat softly. As if this really is just a game. "What exactly does that evolution entail?"

"Change."

Why does that sound ominous? "Why do you let the players believe they can earn their way out?" I ask, angry, frustrated.

They don't answer my question, instead posing one of their own. "Miki Jones, you are familiar with our method of communication?"

Trick question? "You talk inside my head. Through all my senses." We just had a whole conversation that way.

"And how do you reply to us?"

"Out loud. I speak to you out loud."

"Why?"

I'm starting to think I know where this is going, and I'm a hundred percent certain I don't like it.

"Because you can't hear what I think. Not without my permission."

Or so they claimed when we had this discussion before. They choose not to enter without permission, not to force their way in and steal my thoughts and memories, but that doesn't mean they couldn't if they tried.

"We require that permission now."

So Lizzie was right. What else was she right about? My mouth goes dry. "Why? I answered your questions."

"There may be details that you feel are unimportant or that you have forgotten. We require those details. All of them. We require you to grant us access to see events through your eyes."

I tap my fingertips against my thigh, beating a rapid tattoo. "And if I don't want you to do that?"

"Your desires are irrelevant." I gasp and brace myself, expecting them to just shove their way inside. "But we would prefer your cooperation. What is it you fear?"

Other than the fact that they are aliens who will know my every thought, that nothing will be private? And the more disturbing possibility that what they find might make them decide to kill me? But I don't offer those arguments. Instead, I say, "Jackson was in agony when you forced your way inside his brain. I'm not exactly rushing to sign up for the same treatment."

"Understood. You fear the pain. There is no need. As we have explained before, you need only permit us access and there will be no pain."

What feels like icy needles poke at my brain, worming deep into my temples and the base of my skull.

"Wait!"

The needles withdraw. "Do you decline us entry?"

I can almost hear Lizzie whispering in my ear, warning me to be careful. "I—" Emotion. Pure emotion. Let it consume me. That's what Lizzie told me to do. Am I supposed to trust her, a girl who probably isn't even Lizzie at all, who may well be a Drau hidden under human skin? Or am I supposed to trust the Committee?

Maybe in the beginning I did, but every moment that passes in the game makes me wonder if they have an agenda I know nothing about, one that has little to do with the good of mankind or keeping the Drau from destroying Earth the way they did the Committee's home planet.

"I didn't say I'm declining you entry, but what you just did . . . that hurt. You said it wouldn't hurt."

"You must allow us entry and there will be no pain."

Again they prod at my thoughts. I panic, not knowing what emotion to choose, what will be strong enough, all consuming enough to confuse the Committee. I need to buy myself time to think. "Fine. Then give me a chance to prepare," I blurt.

They're silent for several seconds, each dragging like an hour, the elapsed time sending my pulse racing. They don't believe me. They don't trust me. They're going to push their way—

"Tell us when we may begin."

"Right. Okay. I will." I think of all the people I love. Those I hold dear, those I've lost, those who I may lose at any moment. But love isn't a single emotion; it's a million tiny nuances of laughter and joy and heartbreak, memories and trust . . . so many pieces of a complicated puzzle. And right now, the love I feel is tainted by sadness and worry, for Dad, for Carly.

Lizzie said to pick an emotion—*one*—and let it consume me.

Indecision sends me spinning. I've spent the last two years in the gray fog of depression, my emotions muted and choked. How am I supposed to connect with a single emotion? How—

Of course.

The fog. The misery.

That's what I'll focus on. That's what I'll let in. The all-consuming despair that was my full-time companion for so long. I've worked so hard to chase it away, and the idea of allowing it to regain even a tiny foothold is terrifying because I don't think the depression will ever be gone for good. I think it's an ongoing process of keeping it at bay, just like Dad said about drinking and how the craving will never leave him.

If I open the door even a little, if I let the misery take me down to the bottom of the dark well, will I be able to claw my way back out?

I'm afraid, but I'm more afraid of letting the Committee read my thoughts and find out secrets that could destroy not only me, but a whole bunch of other people I care about. Carly, if they found out Lizzie's team saved her, that she knows about the Drau even if she doesn't realize that she does. My team, if the Committee sees something in my thoughts they disapprove of. Lizzie, who's kind of growing on me. Jackson, who acts like he doesn't care because he cares so much.

Nothing in life is free. Nothing in the game is free. I don't get to just defy the Committee and not pay some sort of price.

But maybe they'll pay it right along with me. If I have to share anything with them, there's a certain vindictive satisfaction in imagining the Committee trying to navigate the bleak landscape of my darkest thoughts.

I *will* chase the gray fog out again because I'm not the

girl I was. I'm not the girl who will be afraid of the weight of my despondency ever again. I've learned so much about how to fight it, how to ride it when I can't make it go away, how to let people help me when I need them.

Depression is something I fight off. But in this moment, I intend to welcome it.

Happiness is something I fight for. I will fight for it again as I have for the past two years, and I will win.

They don't understand human emotion? Well, they're about to get a doozy of an introductory course.

The Committee grows impatient; I feel them poking at the edges of my thoughts. I'm out of time.

I visualize the events leading up to the very first time I got pulled, standing apart from my friends at the far end of the field, when I felt like the depression was a solid wall between me and them, between me and any healthy emotion. I remember wishing I could feel things the way they did, feel the same anticipation and excitement when they talked about the dance. I focus on that memory and the all-encompassing gray. I let it in. I sink into the depth of its icy embrace and I let every bit of that pain fill me to the brim, a miasma of hopelessness belching sulfurous fumes. I crash to the bottom of the endless, black pit.

And then I say, "Ready."

I hold my focus, hold the feeling, and I am sinking, drowning.

They didn't lie. It doesn't hurt. It's like my mind is made

of butter and they slide in like a warm knife.

Lizzie said not to focus on one image, so I don't. I let all the images, all the soul-sucking moments, run by like a slide show in my mind: Gram dying. Sofu in his casket, dressed in a suit, six coins in his hands for the River of Three Crossings.

Mom, skeletal and bleak, broken by the cancer, dragging in her last breath.

Mourners dressed in unrelieved black.

The sound of dirt hitting a coffin.

The moment when I imagine she's still alive, trapped in that box, the damp earth covering her, *thud, thud, thud,* trapping her, burying her alive.

The crippling sadness in that instant when I figure out Richelle didn't respawn with the rest of us, that dying in the game means dying for real.

The moment I respawned in the pizza place and realized Jackson hadn't made it back.

A thousand thoughts and memories twine foul, smoky tendrils together to weave a fog as thick as pea soup.

I feel them inside me, the Committee, fingers reaching, clawing, scrabbling at my thoughts and memories, the needles trying to grab hold of something, anything.

It all slips through their grasp. They can't connect with my emotions. They can't understand how I feel. It is impossible for them to move past the wall.

The sensation of their withdrawal is disgusting. Like

leeches pried from oozing skin.

My bones liquefy. I collapse, shivering, stomach heaving.

The fog holds me prisoner, sucking at my soul.

My teeth chatter. My body shakes.

Strong arms close around me, and it takes a Herculean effort to raise my head and find Jackson staring down at me.

CHAPTER FIFTEEN

I SPRAWL ON THE COLD HOSPITAL TILE BESIDE DAD'S BED, THE bottom of the privacy curtain brushing my shoes. On the far side of the bed is the massive sliding glass door between this room and the rest of the ICU. A nurse walks past. Someone moans—a patient, or maybe a family member who's just had tragic news. The sound punctures me, connecting with the unuttered moans and cries that batter my soul. I'm crumbling inside under the unbearable pressure of my sadness.

Expression grim, Jackson reaches back and yanks the privacy curtain over a couple of feet, just enough to shield me from prying eyes.

"Can you stand?" he asks, low.

I don't answer him; words are too hard. Standing takes

too much effort. Lying here takes too much effort. I just want to hide, sink into the choking fog inside me and hide.

Somehow, Jackson senses the change in me, the darkness. He hunkers down and cups my face, brushes his thumbs along my brows. "Miki? I need you to come back to me now."

I can't. I'm so far down at the bottom of the pit, I have no hope of clawing my way out.

I almost give in to it, almost let the sadness take me, but almost only counts in horseshoes and hand grenades. Mom always said that expression came from a movie. Dad said it was a quote about baseball. Every time they used that saying, they'd bicker back and forth, ending up laughing and bumping shoulders and, finally, hugging.

I can hear Mom's laugh somewhere, far, far away. It reminds me that I don't want to let her go, don't want to let the beautiful memories go, and that means fighting the gray fog, beating it.

The first step is getting up off the floor.

I focus on Jackson. "I can stand."

He cups my elbows and helps me to my feet, and I stand there swaying, my heart a shriveled, desiccated thing in my chest.

"You aren't alone, Miki," he says. "I'm here."

I stare at him, uncomprehending, ashamed that he is seeing me like this, the fog so thick I can barely breathe. I remind myself what Dr. Andrews told me, that there's nothing to be ashamed of, that I should be proud of my strength in battling this pain.

The Committee did this to me—maybe not directly, but by threatening to steal my thoughts, to climb inside my head without my permission, they forced me to choose to go back to this place of endless gray where I drown in the miasma of my despair. They forced me into a position where I gave up all the ground I had fought so hard to gain, just to bar them entry.

I shouldn't have had to make that choice.

Anger sparks along the borders of my despair. The wretched depths of my mood are familiar. I could stay here. I could float in the dark, cold sea. I could sink and drown, let the depression flow like a frigid ocean through my veins.

Or I can fight. Fight for my happiness.

"Fight. You can do this," Jackson murmurs, believing in me, always believing in me.

Reminding me that I believe in myself.

Reminding me that the sadness does not own me, that I chose to wield it as a weapon against the Committee, to keep them out of my head. I did that knowing how hard the path back would be, knowing, too, that I *could* travel that path.

I struggle to wrench control back into my hands. I open my heart and choose to let a million good memories flow through me. Mom, waiting for me every day after school. Dad, showing me how to put a worm on a hook. Sofu, believing in me, the only girl in a dojo full of boys.

Late nights at Nick Tahoo's with Carly and Kelley and Dee. Sitting in the tree behind Jackson's house, watching him through his mom's sewing room window, feeling the swell of joy to just know he was alive.

The feel of his lips on mine, his arms around me.

I think of my accomplishments. I think of hope. Of Dad coming home and Carly putting green streaks in her hair, or maybe blue or red. That's the thing about depression—it's the antithesis of hope.

I use the positive self-talk my therapist taught me, beating back the self-loathing I feel.

I think of all those things, pushing the fog back toward its cave. I don't manage to get it all the way there. To expect that would be unrealistic; it's going to take time to make up the ground I forfeited. But I make enough headway that I know I can function and I can continue the fight until the misery's back where it belongs, locked away.

So many things in my life are outside my control, but my thoughts belong to me and I beat the Committee to keep it that way. That victory buoys me.

"You with me?" Jackson asks, dipping his head to look at me over the rims of his glasses.

"Yeah." I pause. "You know what really pisses me off?"

"What?"

"How quickly I can pull the sad card, but how damn long it takes to get rid of it." I reach up to push my hair back off my face, then freeze.

"What?" Jackson asks.

"I was just on the floor, palms plastered against it. That floor is disgusting."

He strides to the wall and squirts some hand sanitizer into his palm, then stalks back to me and scrubs my hands between his until the sanitizer evaporates. The look on his face is enough to make the corners of my lips twitch. The way he's trying to make like hand sanitizer is macho makes them twitch a little more.

"You okay?" he asks.

Okay is a stretch. Functional is more like it. "Getting there. Just a little woozy." I take a step toward Dad's bed and have to grab hold of the metal side bar to catch my balance. "A lot woozy." I study Dad's face, pale and wan. "Why hasn't he woken up? How long was I gone?"

"You know the answer to that."

I do. I was gone for an eternity but I wasn't gone at all. The Committee dropped me back here at the exact second I left.

"You want to sit?" Jackson nudges the chair toward me with the toe of his boot.

"I'm okay."

"You're not. Have you eaten today?"

Have I? I shoot him a look. He holds his hands up in front of him, palms forward in a don't-shoot-the-messenger kind of gesture.

"So what did they want?" His tone vibrates tension. He doesn't like that I was pulled alone, without him. He doesn't like that he's out of the loop. But mostly, he doesn't like that he wasn't there, beside me, protecting me from whatever brought me back to him looking like this. He doesn't know the details, but he knows something's wrong.

Where to start? I have a heck of a lot to explain. But my tongue feels thick, my head full of cotton, and I don't trust the safety of saying anything out loud because I don't know if they're listening.

"You need to eat," Jackson says. "Something sugary will help."

I know that tone. It's the one he uses when his opinion is non-negotiable. "I can't leave Dad. What if he wakes up?"

Jackson circles me so we're face to face, his back to the door. He tips his glasses up to his forehead so I can see his eyes.

"If he wakes up and needs something, he'll ring for the nurse. You not being here for half an hour isn't going to make him backslide. We are going to go down to the cafeteria and get you some chocolate—"

"Really?"

"A salad," he continues without missing a beat. "A sandwich. Something healthy. With whole-grain bread and avocado and shit."

"Avocado and shit?" I give a little laugh. "Appetizing."

His smile is tight. "Thirty minutes, tops. We go down. We eat. We come back."

I shake my head and dig my heels in. "You go. Bring me back something if you want."

But I have nothing on Jackson when it comes to digging in my heels.

Seven minutes later, we're in the hospital cafeteria. Jackson isn't exactly the type to sway from his course once he has his mind set. Neither am I, but after a bit of back and forth, common sense told me to let him win this time.

"What do you want?" he asks.

I stare at the offerings. That's another thing about depression; making a decision is like scaling a sheer cliff with no handholds.

Jackson gives me another minute, then loads up a tray: a salad, three sandwiches, two apples, a banana, chocolate milk, water, and cookies.

"Are we expecting company?"

He pauses and studies the tray, then adds a bag of chips. "Did you want anything?" he asks, brows rising above the frame of his glasses.

I roll my eyes. When we get to the cashier, he won't let me pay. "Let me do this," he says. What he means is: *Let me do this small thing because there's so little else I can do to make any of this better, and that's killing me.*

And he thinks I'm the one with control issues.

We head to the far corner of the cafeteria, which isn't exactly crowded thanks to the fact that it's too late for the lunch rush and too early for dinner.

"We need to talk."

"If we talk, you won't eat." He unloads the salad, a

sandwich, and an apple and sets them in front of me. "You eat, then we talk." He holds an apple to my lips. "Bite."

My heart stutters. I remember the day we sat at the top of the bleachers behind the school and shared my lunch for the first time. He held my apple to my lips and I closed my hands around his wrist, his skin warm beneath my fingers as I held his hand steady and took a bite. Then he turned the apple and took a bite from the same spot, his eyes never leaving mine.

"Remember?" he asks, his expression turning wistful, telling me he's thinking about the same day, the same moments.

"Yeah." I take a bite.

He opens one of the chocolate milks and offers it to me. "Drink."

"I—"

"Drink it. The sugar will help the shakes."

Only when he says it do I realize my hands are shaking. I take the chocolate milk and drink about a third of the container.

"More," Jackson says, taking a bite from the apple, then holding it out to me again.

"You're exasperating." I bite.

"You love it. More chocolate milk."

I drink a bit more in slow sips, then set the container down. Of course he had to be right. My hands aren't shaking anymore.

I pry the plastic lid off the salad and stare at the

contents. It's a hospital cafeteria. I expected wilted lettuce and a couple of strips of shredded carrot. Instead, there's baby spinach, seeds, cranberries, feta.

Jackson hands me the packet of dressing he picked up. Low-fat raspberry vinaigrette. My favorite. I cut him a glance through my lashes.

"Eat," he says.

"I know you're a monosyllabic kind of guy, but at this point I'm half expecting you to haul out your club and start grunting."

He grunts and shoves my salad another few inches toward me.

I take a forkful just to make him happy. The plastic bowl's empty before I know it, half my sandwich has disappeared, and the apple's just a gnawed core. And of course Jackson was right; I do feel a little better—partly from the food, but mostly from knowing how much he cares.

CHAPTER **SIXTEEN**

THE CLEAR PLASTIC WRAPS FROM TWO SANDWICHES, COOKIE wrappers, an empty chip bag, a banana peel, and an apple core are piled on the otherwise empty tray in front of Jackson. He jerks his thumb at the remaining half of my sandwich. "You going to eat that?" He's already reaching for it before I answer.

I slap his hand. "I thought this was about you taking care of me. Feeding me."

His lips curl, baring white teeth. "You're fed."

I shove the rest of the sandwich in his direction. It disappears in two bites. I finish my bottle of water. He finishes his second carton of milk.

"So . . . ," I say.

He fishes out a pack of gum, offers me a piece and takes

one for himself. "Talk," he says.

I want to. I need to. He needs to know about the Drau who spoke to me and about the way Lizzie taught me to keep the Committee out. Right now, he's in the dark, and that could put him at risk. Plus, I want—need—his input on all of this. I feel like I'm flailing alone and I don't like it.

No more secrets. Secrets won't keep us safe.

But I'm scared to say it out loud. Since I first got pulled, I've been told that talking about the game is risky, that the Drau could somehow overhear. But what if they aren't the only ones who might listen in?

What if the Committee's listening to every word we say? I believe that they knew about Jackson's plan to have Kendra stockpile the thousand points. Oh, they never came right out and said they knew, but the implication was so blatant they might as well have hung out a pair of bright red boxers at the top of a flagpole.

I can't risk saying anything out loud. I can't risk writing anything down because the Committee might somehow be able to see it. Call me paranoid, but I'm convinced they watch us all the time. I just fought so hard to keep these secrets, let myself descend into the darkness to keep them safe. I'm not about to throw the information out there lightly.

So how am I supposed to communicate with Jackson?

I'm caught in an Ouroboros circle: Tell him. Don't tell him. I need a third choice, and I think I know how to make it work. But it's a risky and frightening move and I don't even know if it's possible.

I glance around. There's no one sitting anywhere near us. Still, I lower my voice until it's barely a whisper. "If you say something to me . . . inside my head . . . can"—I don't want to say *the Committee* out loud—"anyone else hear?"

"The only one who can hear it is you."

"Okay. Good. Get ready to do your thing, because we're going to have one of those Mind-Meld conversations."

"Security precaution?"

I nod.

"Just one problem," Jackson says. "It won't be a conversation. It'll be a one-way street because you don't have that particular skill set. So how would this work? I do my thing and you answer out loud? Kind of defeats the purpose."

I can't answer out loud, can't take the risk that I'll be overheard.

The risk I plan to take is a different kind.

"How did you question them?" I'm hoping I'm being vague enough to stay off the Committee's radar and specific enough for Jackson to know I'm talking about the Drau.

He leans back in his chair and crosses his arms over his chest, his posture closed, maybe even defensive. Sharing information, explaining himself, letting anyone in doesn't come naturally to Jackson.

"Full disclosure, Jackson. Tell me the whole truth," I say. "No more secrets, from here on out." I bump his knee with mine, then stretch out with my leg so my calf rests against his. "You aren't alone anymore. We're a team. We work together. It isn't every man for himself. It's all of us for each other. You have to trust me."

"I trust you." He pauses. "You're the only one I trust."

"With some of your secrets, yes." I press my palms flat on the table as I lean forward. "But you also have to trust that I can handle things. You have to stop trying to protect me, because you *can't*. No matter how much you want to wrap me in bubble wrap, you can't." That's the crazy part about all of this. Jackson originally intended to trade me into the game in order to gain his freedom. The thing is, once I was in, things didn't pan out quite as he planned. He realized that maybe he didn't want out after all. Instead of sacrificing me and getting out, he chose to stay in the game, to stand in front of me and keep me safe. Change of plans. "Give me the tools to protect myself. Give me information. Give me the truth, Jackson."

"Fine." He surges forward and captures my hands. We lean toward each other across the table. "You want to know how I questioned them?" The Drau. "I did to them what *they* tried to do to me," he says. I know he means the Committee and the way they pushed inside his mind. "I shoved my way in and foraged around until I found what I wanted. I'm fairly certain it was less than pleasant for them, and I don't give a shit. Ugly enough for you, Miki?"

He pulls his hands away and flops back again.

He thinks I'm going to reject him over this. He betrayed me into the game, turned my whole life upside down, and he thinks that his dark side, the fact that he doesn't feel guilty for pushing his way into the Drau's minds, is what's going to finally make me bail.

I don't let him retreat. I stand and walk around the table and come to sit beside him, scooting my chair over until our knees meet.

"You aren't telling me anything I didn't already suspect. And yeah, it's ugly, what you did to them." I look away because what I say next is hard. "Is the gray cloud that follows me everywhere ugly enough for *you*? You don't have a monopoly on dark and tortured, Jackson."

"And here I thought I was special." His fingers slide through my hair, his palms against my skull as he gently turns my head so I'm facing him once more.

"You don't need me to feed the fire of your conceit," I say.

He smiles a little. "Don't I?"

"No. It's already raging out of control." I sigh. "What you did to them . . . the way you questioned them . . . I think it's something we can use." I gesture back and forth between us, my implication—my invitation—clear. I'm giving him permission to do that to me. Trusting him.

He tenses, so still he isn't even breathing.

"No," he says, not leaving much room for negotiation.

"Yes."

When he just sits there staring straight ahead, jaw set, I take a deep breath. All or nothing. "Why didn't you ever give the new recruits better explanations when they showed up in the lobby? Why didn't you give me better explanations?" I ask.

He drums his fingers on the table in a staccato beat, then lifts his head. "I got tired of explaining it every time and dealing with the *this-is-bullshit* reaction. For some reason, most people have trouble believing they've been sucked into a game where they have to fight aliens."

"I can't think what that reason might be. But that isn't the whole truth. Come on, Jackson, you can do it. Tell me the rest." When he doesn't offer an explanation, I keep pushing. "Luka told me about your philosophy. About learning by trial and error to figure out how to progress to the next level. But you were never talking about video games, were you? You held back on explanations for new recruits so you could see the game through fresh eyes with every new player . . . so you could try to finally figure a way out."

"Not a way out, Miki." The smile he offers is feral. "I was kidding myself when I thought I wanted out. I already told you, there's a part of me that loves the game. The adrenaline high. The hunt. The challenge."

"You did tell me that. But it took almost finding a way out for you to realize that maybe you didn't want to leave. Originally, you *did* want a way out. At least, you thought you did. That's kind of how you and I ended up meeting, isn't it? Because I was your way out. Now answer my original question."

He blows out a breath. "Fine. You're right. Every time

I got a new recruit, I hoped they'd see something I hadn't, pick up on something I'd missed. Find the ever elusive answer."

"There you go. Was that so hard?"

"Harder than you know."

But I do know. He's been on his own for so long, standing on one side of the divide while the team he feels responsible for stands on the other, that sharing information with anyone isn't easy for him.

He takes my hand. His fingers are long and strong, his palm broad. His hand swallows mine.

I lay my other hand atop his. "We need to do this, Jackson . . . it's the only way. Not just because I need to be sure no one and nothing overhears, but because you need to see it all, experience it through my eyes. You might make connections I miss, see things from a different perspective. I need to be sure I don't leave anything out." I pause. "Plus, it might be something we can use the next time we get pulled. You barking orders in my head's saved me more than once. Maybe if we can get a two-way street going, I can even things up a little."

He shifts an empty milk carton to the right, taps it against the table a couple of times, and shifts it back to the left. "What you're talking about here, Miki . . . I'm not skilled at it. Think of it as someone doing surgery with a machete instead of a scalpel." He rubs his left arm, the one with the scars he got when he returned from the mission where Lizzie died, somehow bringing a Drau back with him. "I've only tried it twice. On two of *them*. Never on a person."

"Guess I'll be the first," I say. I sink my teeth into my lower lip, wondering what he's going to think when he finds out about the Drau begging for mercy, about how she didn't kill me when she had the chance, about my suspicion that Lizzie has Drau on her team and that those Drau helped save our lives the night of the Halloween dance. "It'll be okay."

"Will it? I can't go in and delicately pick out the bits you want to share," he says, his tone harsh. "When I did this before, I was pretty much like a backhoe shoveling out tons of information, then sifting through it to find what I wanted. Strategies. Attack plans. Locations. I'll see things you might not want me to see. Do you understand what you're asking me to do?"

I think of the Committee trying to force their way into my brain and huff an ugly little laugh. "Nothing that hasn't already been done to me."

"No." He surges to his feet, staring down at me through his mirrored shades.

"No, you won't do it? Or no, you're pissed that they tried?"

"Both. Miki—" He makes a visible effort to uncurl his fists, lower his shoulders, take a slow breath. He's back in control, but I figure it's by a thread. "Wait . . . you said they *tried*. They didn't succeed?"

I shake my head. "And you need to know why." I get to

my feet and methodically gather the garbage onto the tray. Then I carry it to the bin, dump it, and set the tray on top. "There's a bench out back. It's in this isolated little courtyard. I found it when Mom was here. I went there when I needed to cry and I didn't want anyone to see. We can do this there."

For once, Jackson lets me have the last word. He hooks his finger through my belt loop and follows me outside, but I can feel the tension radiating off him in waves.

CHAPTER**SEVENTEEN**

IN WARMER WEATHER, THE TREES IN THE COURTYARD ARE green, the flowers pink and yellow and red. But today, the world is a million shades of depressing gray—hospital walls, bare branches, and the patchy, frozen grass of early winter.

The times I've come here before, it was almost always deserted. True to pattern, there's no one but us here today, either.

I lead Jackson to the bench. We sit sideways, so we're facing each other.

"So how does this work? Do you ask me questions and then root around in my head for the answers?" I ask.

"Root around? Like a hog?" he asks dryly.

I smile a little, surprised that I can when I'm so wound

up. But that's the thing about Jackson. He always manages to reach through my mood, even when it's sad or angry or scared.

He takes my hand and slides his fingers through mine. The air's cold; his skin's warm. He lifts my hands to his lips to blow warm breaths against my fingertips, then tucks my hands in his coat pockets.

"Putting my thoughts in your head's pretty much second nature," he says. "I don't really think about it. I just do it. But the other half of the equation, hearing what you're thinking, that's foreign territory."

"It hurt them, right?" The Drau. "When you did this to them?" Just like it hurt him when the Committee tried to thrust themselves into his mind.

Jackson clenches his jaw. "Yeah."

I remember watching on the monitor while he dispatched the Drau with his knife on the last mission, his face expressionless, reflecting neither joy nor remorse. He isn't expressionless now. He's tense, wary.

"It didn't hurt me," I say. "When they tried to get in. They told me that if you had just let them in when they wanted inside your head, it wouldn't have hurt you, either. I'm guessing the—" I break off, reminding myself not to say the word *Drau* out loud, not to do anything that might flag the Committee's attention. "The *ones* you questioned weren't exactly thrilled to have you stomping around inside their brains. I'm guessing they put up a fight."

"You could say that."

"So we're going to work with the idea that if I just let you in, if I don't fight you, it won't hurt." I swallow and rush on. "But even if it does, even if it's agonizing, you have to keep going. You can't stop. I need you to know what I know. We need to make a plan."

Jackson shakes his head. "We don't have to do this, Miki. Think about it logically. If they were listening in on us right now, if they could hear us, then they'd know why we're sitting"—he gestures around us—"here. They'd know what we're planning to do and they'd have stopped us by now. Which means they can't hear us. So it's safe for you to just tell me."

"They can hear us. And they're smart enough to use our laissez-faire attitude to their advantage. You want it to be safe because you don't want to take the risk of doing this."

His brows rise. "Do you?"

"No, but I think we're out of choices. We can't assume they aren't listening in. They could have a million reasons for not stopping us right now. Maybe they don't listen in all the time, but they could just happen to tune in right when I divulge information we don't want them to know. Maybe they aren't listening at all. Maybe they can't.

"But maybe they *are* listening right now, amusing themselves at our expense, waiting to see if this experiment will work," I say. "Just waiting for us to slip up and say something by mistake. We don't know, and it isn't just my secrets I'm about to share. There are other people"—I pause over that word, thinking of Lizzie and her team, thinking that maybe that team isn't completely human—"involved. Other people at risk."

"When did they become the enemy?" he asks, meaning the Committee.

"I didn't say they are." Or maybe they always were. I'm just not sure anymore.

Silence hangs between us.

I pull my hands from his pockets and lift his glasses. He holds still and lets me, his eyes locked on mine. I will him to understand my turmoil. There's just a ton of stuff that doesn't add up: Lizzie, the Drau that Kendra killed, Lizzie's team that I never get to see, the Committee's harshness. Maybe if he knows what I know, he'll make different connections than the ones that are starting to haunt me.

Finally, he says, "We do it your way," his tone even. Sure. Confident. Now that we've made the decision, committed to a path, he'll stay the course, steady, strong. That's who he is.

"So how do we do this?" I ask.

"I bounce questions at you and I try to lock in on answers."

"But you might not just lock in on the answers. You might find out other things, too." Other things like my private thoughts and emotions, which won't confound him the way they did the Committee. That's an advantage that Jackson will have over them. No matter how much he pretends not to feel, I know he does. Deeply. So once he's in, I doubt I'll have much in the way of privacy, and I won't be able to use emotion to push him out the way I did them. I force a smile. "This is going to be interesting."

His lips draw taut. "Yeah."

Okay, then. "When you questioned . . . *them* . . . did you find out things about them? Private things?"

He frowns. "I never really thought about this before, but no. I just got answers to my questions." His expression tells me that something about that snares his interest. It snares mine, too.

"Because you were so intent on those questions that all you heard was the answers?"

"Could be. Or maybe they feel nothing, *think* of nothing except killing and hate."

"I don't—" I don't think so, but there's no sense arguing the point now. He'll be inside my head, seeing my thoughts, knowing what I know soon enough. I wonder if his opinion of the Drau will change once he experiences what I did: the Drau's pleas, her terror, the horror of her death.

"I'll try to stay on topic, Miki," he says softly. "Try not to see anything . . . private."

I wait for him to do something, to start the process, but he doesn't, and it hits me that he still isn't convinced. Or maybe he doesn't want to be the one to start. Maybe he's offering the first serve to me as a courtesy. But if that's the case, it's the wrong approach. The rules of this game aren't rules I know.

"It'll be okay," I say. If I'm honest, that's as much a

reassurance for myself as it is for him. When he still makes no move, I cup his cheeks and lift my lips to his, intending only a brief touch, a reaffirmation of trust.

But Jackson has something else in mind. His arms come around me like steel bands, drawing me tight against him as he lowers his mouth to mine, his lips firm and soft. His fingers tangle in my hair. He deepens the kiss, his lips parting and slanting on mine, tongues touching, heat coiling through me. He tastes like chocolate and mint.

Miki. His voice inside my head, followed by images and emotions, things he's seen that he wants me to see. He's done this before, melded his thoughts with mine so I could experience his memories, see myself through his eyes, the girl with the long dark hair standing in the crashing waves at Atlantic Beach. I see her now, see *me* now. The way he sees me.

But this time, it's more than that, deeper. I *feel* what he feels, every receptor in my body alive to sensation as he sends me his thoughts in words and images and emotions.

I see things he chooses to show me, the way he experiences the world. The exhilaration of the cold air on his skin. The way my hair feels to his touch. The way my lips feel beneath his. The way I look when I laugh, head thrown back, teeth flashing. The way I look when I sleep, curled up on my side, hands tucked under my chin. I see myself on missions, strong, fast, smart.

I see the girl he sees, and she is me.

Jackson touches the edges of my mind, looking for a

way in, not like when the Committee forced icy fingers into my temples and the base of my skull. Jackson's touch is gentle, testing the boundaries, slow, easy, like we have all the time in the world.

The air around us is cold, but I am warm from the heat of his body, his kiss like a fire inside me.

I open my heart, open my mind, an invitation. I don't feel him walk through the door, but I know he's there. I balk, backtrack, try to pull away. What made me think I could do this? What made me think I should?

He fires questions at me about the Committee and the Drau, about Lizzie and the conversation we had, too fast for me to follow. I panic, trying to scramble for answers.

I don't—

I can't—

He repeats them, slower, gentler, finding his pace as I find mine. And there are other questions, too—questions about me, the things I like, the things I don't like, questions about me as a little girl, birthday parties and balloons, Sofu, Gram, kendo, all the things I've never told him because there hasn't been time or he hasn't asked or I haven't thought about them in so, so long. But those more personal questions are faint, like echoes, like he's holding them on a leash.

Curiosity. I feel it. He wants to know everything about me, but he's holding back, keeping himself from digging deeper than I want to let him go.

"Where's the mystery then? A girl has to have some

secrets," I say, except I don't because his lips are on mine, my lips on his, the flames between us burning bright, licking at my limbs. Still, he hears me. His low laughter is effervescent in my blood, filling me until it runs over the brim.

In the way that thoughts do—popping up unexpectedly with no rhyme or reason—a memory surfaces of him shirtless in the tree behind his house, the planes and shadows of his abdomen, his arms, his chest.

Now his laughter has a tinge of swagger.

I focus on the things I need him to know, about the Drau who begged for mercy. About Lizzie and everything she said. About the Committee and what happened when I stood alone before them, the way I thwarted them, my fears of the next time I'm summoned to face them and what they might do to me then.

He knows what I know. He feels what I feel.

Carly. Dad. So much worry. So much pain. He takes it inside himself, shares in my burden.

I'm here. He is. He's here, holding me in his arms as I hold him in mine.

The gossamer thread connecting us wavers and Jackson begins to withdraw. I'm cold without him. I don't want him to go, not yet. So I follow him, one careful step at a time.

I'm not sure where I end and he begins.

He tugs on the thread, winding it into himself, towing me along. I am gliding, the path sparkling in the sun. I slide into a world I could never have imagined, a kaleidoscope of sensation. His world. His thoughts.

He isn't just talking to me inside my head anymore. He's invited me into his. He brought me in.

I'm a guest here. Jackson's guest. His thoughts and mine are one.

I see *him*, a dark silhouette against a gleaming gold background, hand reaching toward me, beckoning me closer, deeper. I feel the core of who he is. Loyalty. Love.

And the darkness inside him.

I see what he sees. I know what he knows, freeze-frame instances that play out, his knowledge through my eyes. Missions. Teammates. So many dead. I see the car accident that brought him into the game almost exactly as I saw it in my dream. I watch through his eyes as the Drau attack, shooting him, shooting Lizzie. I see him kill one. I see the pain and loss etched on another Drau's glowing, bright face. I see that Drau and Jackson locked in combat in this, the real world.

His hatred of the Drau is a vast, deep well. I drop a pebble and never hear a splash. Not just deep, then. Endless.

I inhabit that darkness, taste it, know it. Maybe it should frighten me more than it does, but there's something fascinating about it, something alluring. Something familiar. How many times did he tell me he isn't a good guy? He didn't lie. He isn't. He is what the game made him, a child soldier since he was twelve.

But he is so much more than that, and the light in him

is brighter than the darkness.

He is the boy who walks into a convenience store with a homeless woman who begged for money and buys her a sandwich.

He is the boy who shovels the neighbor's driveway in the predawn chill because her children and grandchildren live far away.

He is the boy who knows what candy bar is his mother's favorite, and leaves one for her on her pillow every once in a while.

He is the boy who would die for those he cares about.

And he is the boy whose hatred of the Drau is vicious and cold, a writhing, living thing.

My thoughts circle back to the Drau Kendra killed.

Jackson needs to know. He needs to understand. I live those moments again, live her fear, her panic, her pain.

He looks, but he refuses to see.

Please. He hears her.

He hears me as I beg him to listen. But will he? Will he listen?

His world, his mind—beautiful and treacherous. Living sunlight. The dying embers of a fire. The deepest reaches of a cave, cold and dark. That is the place he buries what he learns from me, the images of the Drau as she died.

He does not let me linger there. He brings me back to blink against the light, to inhabit only my own thoughts.

And then gently, so gently, he closes the door behind me.

"So now you know," he says, his tone flat.

"Now I know," I say. I look down at my hands, completely out of my depth. There are demons riding Jackson's soul, the bleakest of darkness in his heart. But light, too. The things I thought I knew about him—his fierce loyalty, protectiveness, intelligence—he's all those things and more. I look up at him. "You're damaged, just like me. No surprise there, Jackson. Did you think I didn't know it already?"

"Hard to miss."

"It is."

"And I did warn you."

"Again and again," I agree.

We're awkward with each other. What do you say to someone when you've been inside their head?

There's one thing I know I'm *not* going to say now, even though surely he must know it. I made up my mind that we would have our moment, one just for us, and I'm going to stick to that. "Did you know you could do that? Let me . . . in like that?"

"It didn't seem fair for that whole exchange to be just one way. Figured it was worth a try." He gets up from the cold bench and holds out his hand. I take it and we stand face to face. "I want you to try something," he says.

I nod.

Talk to me. Not out loud. Talk to me the way I'm talking to you.

"How?"

Just do it. Just think it. We forged a connection. Let's see if it's still open.

I close my eyes and try. I do. I focus all my concentration on making him hear me inside his head.

Click. My lids flip open at the familiar sound.

"I don't think scrunching your face like that guarantees success." He holds up his phone to show me the picture he just took. Not pretty. I slap his hand.

Doofus.

"Nicely done," he murmurs, one brow arching.

"You heard that? It worked?"

It worked. I guess the trick is to not try so hard.

Okay. I'm not trying now. I laugh. *Would have been nice if we'd been able to do this all along. Then the Committee—* I sober and say, "So now you know how to protect yourself, how to stop them if they try—"

Not out loud, Jackson says.

—if they try and steal your thoughts again. You can block them, thanks to Lizzie telling us how. Do you still suspect her? Still think she's the enemy?

Let's just say I have a suspicious nature.

I hesitate, not sure if I should keep going. Then I just dive in and say, *I saw something just now. Something through your eyes. The day you—* I reach out and stroke his upper arm, the one with the scars. He holds very still, waiting. *I know what you told me about that day. I know what you remember. But it was like I was there but not there, seeing it all*

184

through your eyes, watching it unfold without the emotions of the moment.

Eyewitnesses aren't always reliable, he says. *Especially when they have so much to lose.*

He lost so much that day. His sister. His last remnants of his childhood. His belief that the Drau were confined to the game.

I focus on what I saw in his thoughts, the minutia of the events as they unfolded. The Drau he killed just before one of them got Lizzie. The reaction of another Drau to the first one's death—pain, horror, grief. The way he brought that Drau back with him, the outpouring of his fury and rage, the way it struggled and fought to save its own life. Just as he struggled and fought to save his.

I will him to see it through my eyes. His nostrils flare and his grip on my hand tightens, but there's no other outward sign of what he's thinking. And when I'm done showing him all the things I saw, I stop, just stop.

All I feel for any of them is hate, he says. *But you don't. You feel regret that Kendra killed it—*

Her, I correct him. *Killed her. Don't you see? That's what the Committee wants. For you to depersonalize them. For you to not care about killing them. You don't feel regret or empathy for them. And the Committee likes it that way. We need to figure out why.*

Because the Drau are a threat to the world.

Are they? I ask. *Are they really?* I can't explain my doubts.

I've been in a bunch of battles now, fought the Drau, watched my teammate and kids on other teams die at their hands. They invaded my real world, almost killed Carly. Jackson bears the marks of their savagery on his skin. So why does one Drau begging for mercy make me question everything? Why does that one event make me wonder how many Drau bear the marks of *our* savagery?

Jackson flips his glasses down. *I'm not saying the Committee's without its flaws, but you're asking me to turn my entire world view upside down. To believe that the Drau are the good guys? Seriously?*

I shake my head. "I didn't say that. I'm not saying that. Not that they're the good guys. I just think we need a few more pieces of the puzzle to see the whole picture."

He's quiet for a moment, then says, "We should go back upstairs now." Last word.

I stand there for another second. "You don't get the last word this time, Jackson. You—"

He pulls me against him and kisses me, his lips firm, his tongue touching mine, then teasing, dancing away before touching mine once more. He bites gently on my lower lip. He licks the spot he nipped. My head spins. My fingers tangle in his hair. I kiss him back parting my lips beneath his. I love the taste of him, the feel of his thighs and abdomen and chest pressed against me, his fingers splayed across my lower back. I could spend hours just kissing him.

And when he pulls away, a satisfied smirk on his lips, I say, "Nice try, but you still don't get the last word."

The smirk disappears. "It's a lot to throw at me, Miki. I just need some time to process it all."

"Okay." I pause. "Thank you."

He kisses me again, gently, sweetly, like I'm made of spun sugar. "For what?" he asks against my lips.

For being so careful where you stepped, for not running through my mind like a train. For taking only what I tried to offer. I know you saw more than just the Drau and Lizzie and the Committee. And I know you tried not to.

"I kind of felt like I was sitting in your bedroom with my back to you while you stripped down and changed," he says, "and I was doing everything humanly possible not to look." He grins at me, that dark, sexy, sinful smile I know so well. "But man, the temptation . . ."

I blow out a breath and give a shaky laugh, wondering how long it's going to take me to get that too-tempting image out of my head.

CHAPTER**EIGHTEEN**

AS JACKSON AND I HEAD TO THE ELEVATORS, I CHECK MY phone. We've been gone for almost two hours. Hard to believe. It felt like we were in that courtyard for just a few minutes.

I reach for the elevator button and freeze; the back of my neck feels like a bucket of spiders has been dumped over my head. Jackson tenses at my side and I'm guessing he feels it, too.

"Someone's watching," I say softly.

"Don't turn," he murmurs, sliding his arm around my waist as he pivots so he's facing me, facing the open lobby behind me. He grins down at me like nothing's wrong, his fingers pressing a warning against my lower back. "Laugh."

I can't. I'm not that good an actress. Instead, I punch him in the shoulder.

He laughs, and the desired effect is achieved. We look like a couple oblivious to the rest of the world.

Behind him, the elevator doors open and people get out. It's going to look weird if we don't get on. Whoever's watching is going to know something's off.

Jackson takes care of the problem, nudging my jacket out of my hands so it hits the floor. I bend to retrieve it. He bends at the same time, purposely bumping heads with me, then making a big show of rubbing my forehead as if he just hit me with a sledgehammer. The elevator doors slide shut. The people dissipate. Jackson snags my jacket and we do an impromptu tug of war, and that's all the cover I need to look around.

At first I see nothing that stands out. The lobby isn't exactly crowded. There are a few people lined up in front of the coffee stand. A couple of people in the gift shop. A volunteer at the information desk. A girl sitting in one of the chairs by the floor-to-ceiling windows, playing with her phone. My gaze slides past all of them, then stalls and backtracks.

The girl in the chair is—

"Kathy Wynn," Jackson murmurs.

"Her mom works here. Maybe she's picking her up." I say it, but I don't believe it. The dream I had, the one where Lizzie was trying to get in touch with me, the one where Marcy grew and grew and Kathy shrank to the size of a thimble, plays through my thoughts at lightning speed. I focus and will Jackson to see what I see, know what I know.

But we must have lost the connection somewhere between the courtyard and here, because he doesn't give any indication that he's hearing what I'm broadcasting. I'm about to say something out loud when he surprises the heck out of me and goes on full-out frontal attack rather than opting for stealth mode. He snags my hand and stalks across the lobby, dragging me in his wake.

"Hey, Kathy," Jackson says. "Picking up your mom?"

She tips her head back and looks up at us, expression completely blank, like there's no one home. Her gaze locks with mine. Her eyes are brown, not Drau gray. Does that mean she isn't a shell? I have no idea. She stares at me, her features cardboard-smooth.

Icy talons claw their way up my spine.

"Picking up my mom," she says, her tone flat. She stares at me unblinking, and finally returns her attention to her phone.

"Hey," Luka says.

I spin to find him standing directly behind me. "Hey, yourself."

He and Jackson do the guy-nod thing.

"Visiting Carly?" I ask.

"Yeah." He looks uncomfortable, like he doesn't know what to say or do. "Sarah asked me to bring her and Kelley. They, uh, needed a ride."

I bump his shoulder with mine. "You don't need an

excuse to visit her," I say, then wish I hadn't because if anything, he looks even more ill at ease.

He nods, not meeting my eyes. "Looks like it's starting to snow," he says with a glance at the tall windows. "I should head out."

Kathy looks up as he looks down and they stare at each other for a second before she says, "See you."

And with a casual wave at all of us, he's gone.

"What the hell?" I whisper once Jackson and I are in the elevator.

He rests his index finger against my lips and shakes his head. "Later." As he drops his hand, he pauses for a split second, just long enough for me to get that he's pointing to the elevator surveillance. I remember the day Jackson and I first ran together, the day I found out Richelle wasn't coming back, the day he first told me the Drau could piggyback on human technology and watch us anywhere. And I remember the night we waited for news on Dad and Carly, the creepy feeling I had of being watched, my suspicion that maybe the TV in the waiting room was being used for surveillance.

But I have the feeling that maybe he isn't worrying about the Drau right now, that maybe he's thinking about all the suspicions of the Committee I shared with him in the courtyard.

The door to Dad's room is partially closed, the privacy curtain drawn, a woman's feet visible beneath.

"Can I come in, or should I wait outside?" I ask.

"I'll just be a second," the woman replies and a minute later jerks back the curtain. The nurse who sent me home that first night, Laila, stands in front of Dad's bed.

Over her shoulder, I catch a glimpse of Dad. He's lying on his back, hooked up to a bunch of stuff that definitely was not there when I went downstairs. He looks a lot like Carly looks: pale, soft, fragile. The ventilator's back. So are all the monitors. My stomach drops; my heart thuds uncomfortably against my breastbone as I clutch my folded jacket to my chest.

Jackson steps up beside me. "What's going on?"

Laila glances at him. "Are you family?"

"My brother."

She frowns, but before she can protest, I say, "He dyes his hair. What's wrong with my dad?"

"His temperature went up about an hour ago. He started having some trouble breathing. It escalated and the doctor had to intubate."

"Is it pneumonia?" They told me that people are at risk of that after a splenectomy. Double jeopardy for Dad, thanks to the broken ribs. The possibility terrifies me.

She gestures at the IV bags. "We have him on antibiotics."

Which doesn't exactly answer the question I asked. "So he's going to be okay?"

"He's in a coma, Miki."

My throat closes, locking the air from my lungs. It takes

me a second before I can manage, "Like Carly? A medically induced coma? To help minimize damage?"

"No, this isn't medically induced. Your father's slipped into an unexplained coma. We don't know exactly why—"

"You don't know?" I cut her off. "Who *does* know?" Even as I ask the question, an image of the Committee flashes through my thoughts.

"We're doing everything possible to figure things out. Dr. Lee's ordered some tests. Someone will be by soon to take your father down for X-rays." The intercom buzzes and a disembodied voice says a few words. Laila cocks her head and listens, then she touches my shoulder. "I'll ask the doctor to come speak with you. He's in surgery right now, but I'll ask him to come as soon as he can." And then she heads out of the room, leaving me standing there, bewildered and afraid.

"He was fine," I say. Then I say it again. Actually, I'm not sure how many times I say it. I just know that after a few minutes I'm sitting on the edge of Dad's bed and Jackson's sitting on the pleather chair. We don't talk. We just sit there holding hands, watching Dad's chest go up and down while the suction makes its ugly slurping sound and the monitors beep and the sounds of people in other rooms carry to us.

Voices. Sobs.

I feel their pain while at the same time feeling disconnected from it because I don't believe Dad's relapse is unexplained. The fine hairs on my arms prickle and rise and chills chase across my skin.

"They did this," I say. "To teach me a lesson."

When he doesn't say anything, I turn my head to look at Jackson. His head's cocked, frown lines between his brows, like he's listening for something. Or maybe feeling the same weird chill that I am.

Over his shoulder I see a shadow stretching across the doorway, as if someone's standing there, just out of sight, listening. I jump off Dad's bed and tear to the door, looking right then left and seeing nothing but the open doors of the other rooms.

Breathing too fast, I spin as Jackson comes up behind me.

"Someone was here," I whisper. "Right here. Watching us."

"Kathy?" he asks.

"I don't know. I didn't see. The shadow was long, but that doesn't mean it was someone tall . . . it could have just been the angle of the light." I mouth the words *Drau* then *shell*.

"Maybe."

"Maybe not," I finish for him. "I'll be back." I stalk from the room and out the doors of the ICU. I check the hall and the waiting room. No one's there. I spin to find Jackson right behind me.

"Bathrooms," he says and heads into the guys' while I check the girls'.

"Nothing," I say when I'm back in the hall and he

shakes his head, telling me he didn't have any better luck.

Back in Dad's room, I pull the privacy curtain around his bed, as if that really gives us any privacy. But there's something to be said for the power of illusion. I pause just before I pull it the last couple of inches, still feeling creeped out, still feeling like I'm being watched.

"This is payback. They know what we did, how we communicated. They know we're keeping things from them." When Jackson doesn't shoot down my words, I pace the length of the small room, then pace back to him and continue in a whisper. "This is too much of a coincidence. Dad was fine, he was getting better, then all of a sudden he isn't? It's a direct threat."

I pace three steps, turn, and pace three steps back.

Jackson grabs my arm. "You're making me dizzy, and you're just amping up your anxiety."

He's right. The room's too small and pacing like this is making me feel like a claustrophobic tiger in a cage.

"Maybe they didn't just make Dad fall into a coma now. Maybe they engineered all of this . . . the accident . . . the drunk driver . . . Dad . . . Carly . . . everything. They're capable of so much. What's to say they aren't capable of that?"

I think of the way I was pulled into the game, throwing myself in front of a truck to save Janice's little sister. Jackson was pulled in after a car accident. Richelle fell off a roof trying to coax her neighbor's son down. Did they set up every one of those events? Or did they only pull kids who would have died anyway?

"How did Tyrone end up in the game?"

If Jackson's thrown by my off-topic question, he doesn't show it. "Drowned after he got his kid brother out of the lake."

"The boy I replaced . . . what about him?"

"Don't know. Never asked," Jackson says. "Why?"

"All of us got pulled trying to help someone else. Except you."

"I got pulled because Lizzie didn't want me to die. So I guess you could say I got pulled because Lizzie was helping me."

"Right. Exactly. All of us were up against big stakes. Life-or-death choices. What if none of those events were actually accidents? What if they were orchestrated? Every single one of them?"

"You're crediting them with a huge amount of power. The ability to alter fate."

"Fate? Is that what this is?" I clench and unclench my fists. "They are powerful enough to bend time, to transport us in and out of missions . . . and you think it's too much of a stretch that they can cause a car accident?"

Jackson weighs my words. "There is no such thing as accident; it is fate misnamed."

"Did you make that up?"

He shakes his head. "Napoleon."

"Napoleon?" I stifle a laugh because I have a feeling that if I start, I won't be able to stop. I'll just cackle like a hyena, the way I did when I lost it that day with Luka in my driveway, the day I figured out Richelle wasn't coming back. "You're quoting a man who conquered most of Europe in a quest for personal power. Which is actually kind of appropriate, given what I'm thinking."

"Miki," he says, his tone carrying a warning, one I choose to ignore.

"I think everything that's happened was orchestrated. Not by fate. By the Committee," I whisper. "Everything. Not just what's going on now. Everything that happened before. The accident that pulled you in. The one that pulled me in. Your family vacation to Atlantic Beach. Your family's move here to Rochester."

I pause long enough to catch a breath, then continue in a rush. "Look what they've done to my dad. He was fine and now he isn't. This is a clear threat, directed at me." Because I managed to keep them out of my brain and figure out how to talk to Jackson in a way they couldn't hear.

"They aren't happy with me right now," I say. "They're reminding me what they can do to the people I love. They're telling me they can step in any time they want, do anything they want. This is like them pulling Carly into the game. Making a statement by nearly getting her killed there. They don't want me poking around, finding things out. They don't want us talking behind their backs."

I'm talking too fast, the words running together, my voice rising with each syllable. I get myself under control and say, "We're close to something important, Jackson.

Something they don't want us to find out."

I wait for him to tell me I'm talking crazy, but he doesn't.

Instead he says, "What makes you certain they were the ones who pulled Carly? There were other players involved at that point. Those players are adept at influencing the game. And they are capable of pulling us. Which makes them equally suspect."

He means Lizzie and her team, and I pause long enough to consider it. Lizzie moved me through time and space. She's part of the game but not, able to go in and out at will and not at the whim of the Committee. She admitted that her team saved Carly. Could they have been the ones who caused the damage in the first place? "What would they gain?"

"Your sympathy."

I stare at him. He's right. What better way to get me to believe them than to trick me into thinking the Committee's responsible when it was them all along.

I don't know who to trust. I can't tell the villains from the victims. I press the side of my fist against my forehead, feeling like my head's going to explode. "What if there are no good guys?" I whisper.

Jackson brushes my hair off my face and says, "You're the good guy, Miki."

Which makes me choke out a watery laugh.

"No more talk about this. Not now. Not here," he says. "We just went through that whole exercise in the courtyard to maintain a little privacy. Best we keep that in mind."

He's right, and now here I am blurting a bunch of stuff out loud. Nice one, Miki.

"Besides, from what I understand about comas"—he dips his chin toward Dad—"he can hear you."

I turn to Dad, horrified. What if my little rant has put him in even more danger by letting him overhear all of this, even if he *is* unconscious? What if the Committee can get access to his thoughts?

Jackson pulls me in for a one-armed hug and says against my ear, "Talk to him about normal stuff. Just let him hear your voice, like you did with Carly. It matters. Maybe it will help him find the way back. The rest of this will have to wait for later. Don't think about any of it. Just think about your dad."

I tip my head back and stare at him. "How? How am I supposed to do that?"

"Compartments. Right now, you only open the one where your dad matters. Lock the others up tight. Later we'll open those, okay?" When I don't answer, he leans back and studies my face. "Okay?"

I nod, edge my hip onto the side of Dad's bed, and take his hand. Jackson flops down on the familiar pleather chair. I'm hesitant at first, not really knowing what to say, my brain crowded with too many things. I talk about fishing and tying flies, and it gets easier the more I talk. I remind him of funny stories from Atlantic Beach, and about the year he thought it was December when it was actually

November and he stayed up all night getting the Christmas lights done because he thought he was late. I talk about how I think we should ask Aunt Gale to come home for the holidays this year.

I tell him how empty home feels without him. I tell him what I ate for breakfast and what I had for lunch.

When I falter, topics exhausted, Jackson asks me questions, drawing out stories of when I was a kid, keeping me going until my voice grows rough and hoarse, and when I can't talk anymore, I just sit there.

Every once in a while I look over at Jackson, kind of amazed that he's still here, that he still hasn't left.

The doctor doesn't come by, but eventually an orderly does. He tells me he's taking Dad for tests and I stand and watch him wheel the bed away down the hall, trying to hold in the anguish, my arms crossed tight over my belly, Jackson at my back, his arms around me, crossed over mine.

CHAPTER**NINETEEN**

VISITING HOURS END AT EIGHT. JACKSON AND I HEAD ACROSS the dark, snow-dusted parking lot toward the Jeep. We make it about halfway there when we're pulled. There's no warning, no tingling, no flares of light. One instant my foot's poised for touchdown on snow. The next, I foot-plant on grass, the sun high overhead, the trees bounding the open clearing.

The rest of the team isn't here yet. No weapons or scores. Just me and Jackson standing beside the familiar boulders.

From the corner of my eye, I catch movement in the mirror image lobbies. In one, there's just the team leader, waiting for her team to show up. In another, there's a bunch of people gearing up. In a third, I can see the black rectangle that reveals the scores, and the team gathered around it.

"Do you think they need us?" I watch the movement in the mirror image lobbies. "Specifically us, *this team*? Do you think they need *us*?" Because I don't think they do. I think the Committee's pulled us—*me*—to push me right to the edge, to make me crash. They aren't happy with the way I thwarted them, and everything they've done since is a clear message with clear intent.

"Does it matter? I think they do whatever the hell they want," Jackson says, then shifts his attention to a point over my shoulder. "Incoming."

"They're talking in your head, telling you that?"

Jaw clenched, he gives a taut nod. He doesn't like giving them even that much access. Then his gaze shifts to a point over my shoulder.

I turn to find Luka standing at the far end of the clearing, his posture rigid, hands fisted at his sides. He exhales and his whole body seems to deflate, sway, then buckle. With a low groan, he falls to his knees, head bowed.

"Luka!" I reach him a second before Jackson, skidding to my knees so my face is level with his.

"Have to stop," he mutters, his chest moving in shallow pants. "Miki, you have to stop."

He slams his palms over his ears and cries out in pain, then doubles over, his forehead resting on the grass.

"What's wrong?" I ask, touching his back, then his shoulder, then his arm. I don't know where it hurts. I don't know what to do to help him.

"Luka, talk to me," Jackson says.

But he can't talk.

He's shaking so hard his whole body jerks, his teeth clacking like castanets.

Desperate, I just throw myself on him, my front against his bowed back, my arms wrapped around him.

The contact seems to ease him. His breathing slows. His low moans stop.

"In my head," he manages, the words dragged from him. He starts to sit up, then with a hoarse cry doubles over again, sounds of agony torn from him as he curls up, his fingers clawing narrow grooves in the ground. "Can't keep them out."

I'm helpless. Again. I'm relegated to the sidelines watching someone I care about suffer, with no way to ease their pain.

I grab Jackson's leg. "Do something!" I yell.

With a snarl, Jackson grabs Luka and rolls him onto his back. He rips his sunglasses off and tosses them aside. "Put your knees on his shoulders," he tells me. "Hold him down."

I do what he says, scrambling around so my knees pin Luka's shoulders, his head cradled on my thighs. I'm terrified that I'm doing more harm than good.

Jackson straddles him and claps his palms against Luka's cheeks, holding him steady as he stares into his eyes.

He doesn't say anything, not out loud, but I can feel

the ripples of energy as he tries to talk to Luka inside his head the way he does with me. I don't think he's ever been able to do that with Luka before and I wonder if it's hurting him.

"He won't let me in. Damn it!"

"In my head. Can't keep them out." Luka's words slam me. Is he the one who won't let Jackson in now, or is it the Committee locking him out?

Their struggle pulses with power, Luka writhing beneath the weight of my knees on his shoulders and Jackson's palms flat on his chest.

"Come on, Luka," Jackson mutters, his whole body coiled with tension.

Luka screams, the sound shredding me.

For some reason, I remember what Jackson told me when we were trying to communicate without speaking in the hospital courtyard and I was failing miserably. "Don't try so hard," I say.

Jackson spares me a glance then looks back at Luka.

I take my own advice. I don't try. I just talk. *You're okay. It's okay. I'm here. Jackson's here. Talk to us. Tell us. What can we do?*

I feel Jackson's thoughts inside me and I know he feels mine, but Luka's a closed city, the wall around him so high and strong we have no hope of breaking through.

"He isn't that strong," Jackson says, and his eyes meet mine.

He isn't. Luka isn't. But we both know who is.

They're here. Right here. Inside Luka. They have been all along.

It wasn't Kathy watching me, watching us. It was Luka.

The Committee's been watching us through Luka's eyes.

The first time I ever tried skateboarding, the board went forward, while I went back and landed hard. It was the worst winding I've ever experienced. Except for now. I feel like my lungs have collapsed and will never inflate again.

A bunch of memories slap me, running past like a slide show, and I see them all from a whole new perspective.

Bam. After the very first mission, the one where Richelle died, when I was back in my real world, getting into the Explorer for Dad to drive me home . . . I had this creepy feeling like I was being watched and when I turned, there was Luka, staring at me from way down the street.

Bam. The times Luka acted odd, like he was interested in me, then interested in Carly, then interested in pretty much anyone, then not interested in anyone at all.

Bam. Luka not firing on the Drau, holding back, as if he were watching, waiting to see what everyone else would do.

Bam. The moment at my house when we were eating takeout and I thought he was going to say something . . . something important.

Bam. Luka at the hospital, acting awkward and strange. Because he wasn't really there to see Carly.

He was there to see me. No . . . not *see* me. *Spy* on me.

A ton of tiny moments when Luka acted like Luka, and others when he didn't.

The moments he didn't were the ones when the Committee was staring out through his eyes.

Oh God. What do they know? What have they found out through him? Lizzie. Her Drau team. Has everything been betrayed?

I can't remember all the things I've said in front of him, all the things he's seen.

But even as I struggle to cope with this horrific revelation, my heart breaks for Luka, my friend, whose body is rigid with pain. Pain because he's fighting them, trying to keep them out.

What he said when he first showed up in the lobby were words of warning for me. He told me I have to stop. He was trying to tell me to back off, to warn me that the Committee is watching.

He had to have known they wouldn't be happy with him. But he risked that, for me.

His back bows, his whole torso lurching off the ground, throwing me off. Jackson tries to press him down. I scramble over and pull on Jackson's arm.

"Let him go," I say, heartbroken, wary, not sure who Luka is. *What* Luka is. Not sure what to do to help him.

"Stop. Stop fighting," I whisper. "It isn't worth the agony. Just let them do it. Let them do what they want."

"Betray—" The word comes out on a gasp as Luka

arches and claws at the ground.

"I don't care. It doesn't matter. They already know what they know. Stop fighting." I glance at Jackson, desperate.

He grabs Luka's shoulder. "She's right. Stop fighting."

"Don't . . . want . . . to . . . let . . . them . . ."

"What makes you think you get a choice?" Jackson says.

I don't think Luka ever had a choice. I know what Jackson suffered when he tried to keep the Committee out of his thoughts. I remember the feel of icy needles poking at me when they tried to force their way inside my head. I had inside information on how to keep them out. Jackson had the strength and knowledge he's built through his interactions with them over so many years.

What did Luka have? What chance does he have against them?

Luka gasps and deflates, then he lies there, not moving, every breath shuddering through his torso.

Eventually, his eyes open. He stares at Jackson. At Jackson's eyes. Without his glasses.

"Surprise," Jackson says.

"Not really," Luka rasps. "Had to be a reason you wear those stupid shades all the time. So you're a Drau?"

"No."

"A shell?"

"This matters now?" Jackson asks. When Luka says nothing, Jackson says, "No, not a shell. I'm just a guy with a few alien genes thrown in here and there."

"So you're a spy?" I ask Luka.

He turns his head to look at me, his expression pained. "I didn't—"

"Don't say it," I cut him off, holding up my hand. "You had a choice. We always have a choice." I push to my feet and hold out a hand to help him up. "You chose to stay alive by giving in to them. I'm not going to fault you for that. You think I don't know"—I gesture back and forth between me and Jackson—"*we* don't know what they're like?"

He takes my hand and I put my toes over his for counterbalance and haul him up.

"Let me explain," Luka says.

"Are they listening now?" I turn a full circle and yell, "Are you listening now?"

"No," Luka says. "They left." He shakes his head. "But I don't know why."

"How are you feeling?" I ask.

He cuts me a look and runs his hands through his hair. "Guilty. Effing guilty. That's pretty much it."

Then that's why they left. Emotion overload.

Jackson touches my arm, making sure I'm not about to trust Luka with any inside information. I give him the death stare. Does he really think I'd be that foolish?

"So what the hell was that, Luka?" Jackson asks. "How long have you been spying on us?"

Luka stares off in the distance for a second and then says, "It didn't seem bad at first. They asked if they could just take a look at my memories of that first mission after Richelle died, see it through my eyes so they could help protect us better. It made sense, you know? And they asked. They didn't make me. I didn't see the harm." He pauses. "Not then."

When Jackson didn't respawn with us after the mission in Detroit, and Luka and I were trying to figure out a way to find him, Luka acted like the existence of the Committee was news to him, all surprised. But that was a lie. If he had known about them since Richelle died, then he knew about them long before the day Jackson went missing.

Which means Luka's a better actor than I would have given him credit for. So how can I trust him now?

Easy answer: I can't. And even if I wanted to, I don't dare, because while he may be telling the truth about the Committee not being here right now, the second they come back, they'll have access to his thoughts and memories and they'll know everything he knows.

He nudges the ground with the toe of his shoe.

"How do I know they aren't listening right now?" I ask. "How do I know they aren't inside you, looking out at me through your eyes?"

"You don't." He scrapes his fingers back through his hair, then does it again.

"That's how we know," Jackson says, low.

I look at him, then back at Luka. He's right. The Committee have no concept of emotion. If Luka was hosting them right now, he wouldn't be nervous, edgy, because they aren't capable of that. I think back on a ton of moments since I first got pulled into the game and I see it, clear as can be, all the moments that Luka was . . . Luka. And all the ones he wasn't. The ones when he seemed off, weird, sort of flat, not really acting like he ought to. Almost as if he was trying to be what someone thought a human teenager should be. The mixed signals, the times he did things that made no sense . . . now they make sense.

Hands linked behind his head, elbows angled out, Jackson takes a step closer to Luka. Classic intimidation posture. I doubt he's even aware he's doing it.

With a sigh, I step between them.

"You said it didn't seem bad at first. When did things change?" he asks.

"It wasn't a single moment or day. At first it was just them coming into my head more and more. Each time, it felt creepier. That first time, all they did was replay my memories of that mission, but every time after that, they just wandered wherever they wanted, flipping through my thoughts like they were flipping through a filing cabinet. If I try to fight, it hurts. I can't—" He shakes his head and rubs the heel of his palm on the center of his forehead, like it's hurting him right now.

"Been there," Jackson says.

Luka swallows and nods. "So"—he shrugs—"they'd be there in the game, out of the game, whenever. It creeped me out. Pissed me off."

"And Kathy?" I ask. "Where does she fit in?"

"Kathy?"

I have to remind myself that he made me believe he didn't even know the Committee existed, because looking at him right now, the confusion on his face, it seems like Kathy's not part of this at all.

Jackson snags his glasses off the ground and settles them in place. "Incoming."

Luka inhales sharply and looks at me. "Are you going to tell them? About me?"

Am I? To what end? I don't know how much of what Luka is saying is the truth and how much is lies being fed to him by the Committee. One thing I do know is that the Committee can't be pleased that Jackson and I figured out we're being spied on. Until I know if and how the Committee plans to retaliate, why put the rest of the team at risk? Especially when I can't really see the benefit of them knowing.

"Not right now," I say.

He looks at Jackson.

"No," Jackson says. He taps the side of his sunglasses. "You going to tell them about me?" About his Drau eyes. I can just imagine how that would go over, especially with Lien. I have a feeling she'd shoot first, ask questions later—or not ask questions at all.

Luka shakes his head as Tyrone strides over and says, "Hey."

CHAPTER **TWENTY**

WE STAY IN THE LOBBY JUST LONG ENOUGH TO GET OUR WEAP-
ons and our scores, then we respawn on a massive
flat-topped rock, trees rising around us, mountains ser-
rating the horizon. The air's warm, but there's a wind
that rustles the leaves all around us. On instinct, we form
a circle, backs toward one another, weapon cylinders
ready.

Nothing moves. Nothing shoots.

There's no one else here.

"So, what's the mission?" Lien asks.

"Don't know yet," Jackson says and leaps down to the
long grass, prowling forward, weapon cylinder and knife
in hand.

"I don't like it." Tyrone jumps down after Jackson and

walks a few feet in the opposite direction, wary, tense. "Feels wrong."

"Does it ever feel right?" I ask, hopping down and choosing a third direction, watching the shadows, the swaying branches, the dancing grass.

"Not so much," Tyrone concedes.

Lien snorts a laugh.

Jackson checks his con, then turns to Luka. "They feeding you a map?"

"No."

"Anyone?" Jackson asks.

We all check our cons. Mine swirls with varying shades of green. No map. I shake my head and look around to see everyone else answering in the negative.

"Then we have a problem," Jackson says and holds up his wrist. The flat rectangle of his con shimmers with color, but no triangles, no map.

"What now?" Lien asks after a long second of silence.

"We wait," Jackson says, then tenses and looks up. "Or not."

"What is it?" Kendra asks.

"Drau." He turns a half circle, scanning the trees. "I can't see them, but I can feel them. Not close."

"I don't feel anything," Lien says.

"Been doing this a while. Trust me. They're here."

As if on cue, Drau fire rains down on us from somewhere to the right. We dart behind the boulder, taking cover. Not that we need it. Their shots fall short.

I search for the cell-deep terror, the genetic memory that always warns me when the Drau are near. It isn't there, which scares me because if I can't rely on my instincts, then what's left?

"Where are they?" Tyrone asks, looking to the tree-tops.

"Wherever they are, they know we're here," Luka says.

More fire comes our way, again falling short.

"All the shots are coming from that direction," Jackson says, pointing. "High up. They might be on that ridge." He shifts his finger to the right. "Or that one."

"Why are they wasting their time shooting at us?" Kendra asks. "If they're on those ridges, they have to know how far away we are. Can't they see they aren't getting anywhere near us? All they're accomplishing is to give us a heads-up as to their location."

"That's exactly what they're accomplishing," Jackson says, his tone contemplative.

"And that's why it isn't a waste of their time," I say, turning to look at the forest in the opposite direction. "Bait and switch. Make us think they're coming at us from one direction when they actually have a second team circling from the opposite side."

"Maybe a third or fourth team," Jackson says.

"We need to move," Luka says, scanning the trees.

"Move where?" Lien asks. "Which direction do we go? Which way leads away from the Drau? If Miki's right and we take off from here, we could be running right to them."

"Process of elimination," Jackson says. "The Drau are shooting from that direction, so we can rule that out." He turns his head to the other side and studies the forest. "They probably have a team coming from the opposite direction, because they'd assume we'd run from enemy fire. So we can rule out going that way."

"But you said there's more than one team coming for us." Kendra's eyes are wide, her voice high.

"I said maybe. That's what I'd do if I had the manpower. Cover all my bases." He holds a finger to his lips and we all fall silent.

I don't know what he's listening to. All I can hear are the sounds of the forest and the faint roar of a distant river. Jackson lifts his brows at me.

"We go that way," I say, pointing toward the direction the sound is coming from.

"Why?" Lien asks.

"Sounds like water," Jackson says. "Loud enough that it's moving fast and there's probably a lot of it. Close enough that we can hear it. The river will give us at least one angle they can't come at us without being seen."

"That's the best you've got?" Lien asks.

"Best I've got."

She shrugs. "Good enough for me. I haven't got anything better."

"Tyrone, take point," Jackson says. "Luka, you're with me. We'll cover the others in case the Drau are closer than we think."

What he really means is that he doesn't plan to let Luka out of his sight. And I can't say I blame him. How much of what Luka admitted is the truth and how much is a version of the truth the Committee wants us to know? At this point, I doubt Luka even knows which thoughts are his and which are planted.

I stare at him as another possibility strikes me. What if he isn't Luka at all? What if he's a shell? I shake my head; that wouldn't make sense. The shells are Drau creations, and Luka's a pawn of the Committee. I'm losing it, my thoughts jumbling.

Drau fire splatters across a massive branch directly above us, igniting it. Sparks and burning twigs and leaves rain down on us. Lien gets the worst of it, and Kendra and I slap at her shoulder, smothering the fire before it can catch.

"I didn't know their weapons could light things on fire," Kendra says, sounding scared.

"Live and learn," Jackson says, then, "Tyrone, go." He pops up, stabilizing his weapon cylinder along the top of the boulder, covering Tyrone as he makes a break for a narrow gap in the foliage. I keep my focus on that spot, weapon ready, pulse pounding as I wait for Tyrone to come back and signal the all clear. Minutes crawl past. Then he's back, thumbs up, and we run to join him.

We move fast, keeping to a jog, leaping over fallen branches and large rocks, the terrain anything but friendly.

"What's the rush?" Lien asks. "We don't even know what the mission is."

"Right now, the mission is to stay alive. Priority one," Jackson says, then pauses. "The Drau are getting closer."

Lien doesn't argue further, and I suspect it's because, like me, she can feel the uneasiness in her gut growing, the certainty that the Drau are tracking us.

We keep up the pace until we're forced to slow as the ground slopes down, the way peppered by holes and ruts and jagged chunks of rocks. We might have extreme stamina while we're in the game, but we're still at risk of a twisted ankle or broken bone if we go down hard. Tyrone stays ahead of us, scouting the terrain, then doubling back every once in a while so he can flash the thumbs-up and let us know the way is clear.

I know the Drau are following us. Each time I look back, I see nothing. But that doesn't mean they aren't there. Watching us. Stalking us. Maybe herding us exactly where they want us to go.

"Let's slow it down," Jackson says as the terrain grows even rougher.

"We can keep the pace," Kendra says, her eyes darting to the trees that surround us. "They're out there. All around. I can feel them." She spins and stares back the way we came, walking backward as she does.

"Kendra!" Jackson surges forward, hand outstretched, a millisecond too late.

Her foot sinks into a hole and she goes down hard. She cries out, then presses the back of her wrist against her mouth to hold back the sounds.

"Keep watch," Jackson says as he and Lien hunker down beside Kendra.

Luka and I move back to back, giving us a three hundred and sixty degree perspective.

A low moan escapes Kendra. "My ankle."

"Let me see," Lien says. She eases off Kendra's shoe and then her sock. The outside of her ankle's already swelling. It looks like there's a golf ball under her skin.

With a hiss, Jackson pulls his knife and uses it to slice off the bottom of his T-shirt, then slices that in half and wraps her ankle like an expert.

"Sprained your ankle once or twice?" Lien asks.

"Took first aid," Jackson answers. "Kendra, we need to get this shoe back on and it's going to hurt like hell. Don't scream."

"Are you ever not bossy?" Kendra asks, aiming for light, but the words come out tinged with pain.

"Nope. Hold still."

"Wait," Lien says, and pulls her belt from the loops of her jeans. She doubles it over and hands it to Kendra. "Bite."

With a little whimper, Kendra bites down on the leather.

Jackson takes her shoe and with surprisingly gentle hands wriggles it back and forth until it's on and then ties her laces. To Kendra's credit, she doesn't make a sound. He helps her to her feet and she takes a couple of tentative steps. Barely.

Lien looks at Jackson, panic all over her face. "She isn't going to be able to keep up."

"No, she isn't."

"I'm sorry," Kendra says. "That was so stupid, so—"

"Stop," Jackson orders, his voice hard. "It is what it is."

She swallows and nods.

I shake my head. "Your bedside manner needs work."

He turns his head my way and despite the circumstances, a tiny smile tugs at his lips. "Hey, I don't need a bedside manner. I just want to be a runway model."

"Seriously?" Luka asks at the same time Lien and Kendra say, "What?"

I laugh. I can't help it. "Never mind. Inside joke."

There's a beat of weird silence and then Jackson says, "We should move."

Lien tries to angle her shoulder under Kendra's to bolster her. Problem is, Lien's at least a head taller. It makes for an awkward support system.

Jackson snags a thick branch off the ground and uses his knife to strip away the stray leaves. He hands it to Kendra. She clings to the branch as if it were a cane and takes a few shuffling steps forward.

"I'm going to slow everyone down, put everyone at risk," she says.

"You guys go ahead," Lien says. "I'll stay with Kendra."

"No. You go. I'll keep up as best I can—"

I stride over, cross my arms, and grab Lien's hands.

"Lien and I can make a sort of chair if we cross arms like this. I used to do this when I was a kid."

"This'll work," Lien says, nodding. "We can—"

There's a rustling sound and we all fall silent, weapons aimed and ready. Except Jackson. He doesn't even glance up.

Tyrone stalks through the foliage, expression pained. "I've been standing here listening and none of you had a clue—" His gaze lands on Jackson and he amends, "Almost none of you. Enough with the chatty chat. Miki, the handchair thing isn't a practical solution. If your hands are locked together, how do you defend yourselves? And how long do you think you'll last, moving through this terrain like that? With our luck, it'll be fifteen minutes before someone else sprains an ankle."

Lien deflates. "He's right." She looks at him. "Got a better solution?"

He lifts his chin at Jackson, then Luka. "Rock, paper, scissors?"

"Might as well," Luka says.

They go through the motions. Jackson wins. "Luka, you got my back?"

Luka stares at him for a long moment. "You know it." Except Jackson can't know it because there's no way to know when the Committee will jump back inside Luka's head or what their agenda is.

Jackson pulls his knife and goes into a crouch, his free arm positioned in front of his chest, hand protecting his face. "This is basic stance. Cover your vital organs, like this. Hold the knife like this. Stab like this." He goes through the motions twice, then offers the knife to Luka, hilt first. "Show me."

Luka takes it and goes through the routine. Jackson makes him do it a second time and a third, then turns to Tyrone. "Take point. Miki, back him up."

"Hey," Luka says. Jackson turns to him. "Thanks. For . . . you know . . . trusting me."

"You run faster with a knife," Jackson says.

Gamer joke. First-person shooters carry a ton of weapons. If they pull out a massive bazooka, they run slower. If they pull out something small, like a knife, they run faster. But technically, they ought to be running at the same speed because either way, they're carrying the same amount of weapons all the time.

Luka makes a sound somewhere between a grunt and a laugh. "Yeah, but you don't want me running. You want me right here, watching your butt."

"You don't need to watch it, just protect it." Jackson turns to Kendra. "Piggyback time."

Kendra just stares at him.

He offers a cocky grin. "You're about to enjoy a first-class ride." He crouches a little to accommodate her much shorter frame. "Get on."

CHAPTER TWENTY-ONE

THE SUN MOVES ACROSS THE SKY. STARS SPECKLE THE HEAV-
ens. I welcome the night. The Drau are slower in the dark,
and the glow of their bodies will be all the more apparent
if they aim for a sneak attack. Every so often Lien and I fall
back and scout for Drau following us. I don't see them, but
I feel them, drawing ever closer.

"How long can he carry her?" Lien asks, worried.

"Till he can't carry her anymore, and then Luka and
Tyrone will space him." I hold up my hand for silence and
scan the leaves, looking for any sign of movement, any
flash of light that might give the Drau away. Nothing.
"We were in these underground caves once for days, and
Jackson was like a machine. Didn't need to rest or sleep or
anything."

"We're all stronger in the game," Lien says. "Faster. More resilient."

"Until we aren't."

She meets my gaze and nods. We're not so resilient that we can't get hurt. Sprain an ankle. Get shot by Drau weapons. Die.

"I can't lose her," she whispers. "I can't. She's—" She blinks in quick succession and looks away.

"You won't. We're all going to be okay," I whisper back, and silently will it to be true. And how weird is it that the girl with the cloud over her head is suddenly playing the role of Suzie Sunshine? I guess my optimist panties are holding up well. I need them to be superstrong because it isn't just the game I'm worrying about. It's Dad and Carly and what's going to happen to them.

I close my eyes for a second and pinch the bridge of my nose, forcing myself to clear my thoughts. Worrying about them isn't going to accomplish anything other than distracting me from the task at hand.

"You okay?" Lien asks.

I drop my hand and nod. "Yeah. Peachy. You?"

She laughs softly. "Peachy keen. My mom always says that. I thought she was the only one."

I shake my head. "My mom used to say it, too. That, and groovy."

"Groovy. Nice." She looks away. "Sun's coming up."

"Welcome to another day in paradise."

We do another check of the perimeter, then quicken

our pace to catch up to the others.

"Can I ask you something?" Lien says. "You never said anything to me about me and Kendra. Like . . . about us being together . . . Our last team leader was kind of freaked out . . ."

My brows knit. "Is that a question?"

"Observation."

"You never said anything to me about me and Jackson."

"Good point," she says. "Not my business. Plus, I'm kind of happy for you."

"Kind of?"

She laughs. "Hey, it's Jackson we're talking about."

"Well, I'm kind of happy for you, too. It's about finding a connection, someone who helps make you the best version of you."

"Yeah." She pauses. "If what we see is the best version of Jackson, the one you've helped him become, I'm glad I didn't see the version before you came along." I bump her shoulder and she holds up her hands in surrender. "Kidding. Seriously, just kidding. He's okay. Asshole with a heart of gold."

"Look who's talking."

She laughs and ruffles my hair like I'm her kid sister or something. "You're okay, Miki."

We catch up with the others and keep pace as we press on, the sun rising higher in the sky.

"So . . . where are we going?" Luka asks. "I mean, I get that we need to walk in the opposite direction of the Drau.

For now. But at some point, we need a goal, don't we? A mission?"

"At some point," Jackson says, hitching Kendra higher on his back.

"Your con still not telling you anything?"

"Nada. Zip." Jackson turns his head and even with his eyes hidden behind his shades, I know he's giving Luka a hard stare. "Unless you have an inside track and therefore a suggestion."

Luka shakes his head. "Got nothing."

And I believe him because when I think back on all the missions and even all the times we've been together in the real world, I can almost line up the times I think the Committee was in Luka's head and the times it wasn't. There are subtle differences in his behavior that give it away.

Right now he looks worried and edgy and that makes me think he isn't Luka-the-spy, he's Luka-the-guy-trying-to-stay-alive. Just like the rest of us.

"How long do you think we've been here?" I ask Luka.

He shrugs. "Hours. Days."

"You tired? Hungry?" I'm asking him because I'm not either of those things, and that's nagging at me.

"No. Why would I be? We never are on a mission."

Jackson holds up a hand to call a halt and crouches down so Kendra can clamber off. "And that's the point, isn't it?" he asks me.

"What point?" Luka looks back and forth between us.

"The cons are working to alter our physiology just like

they always do," I say. "We don't need to eat or rest or pee. But they aren't working to feed us a direction."

"So what gives?" Tyrone asks. "That's the question, isn't it?"

"Isn't it?" Jackson agrees.

Given the state of our cons and the lack of directive, I wonder if the Committee dropped us all here to die. Not a pretty thought, so I try not to dwell on it or let it swell out of control.

"Anyone have a preference on where we go from here?" Jackson asks.

"You're asking? Miracle of miracles," Lien says, one brow arched, hip cocked to the side. She's all attitude. Gotta love her for her consistency, if nothing else.

Her question echoes what I'm thinking, what I suspect we're all thinking, but I keep it to myself. Because on every other mission, Jackson hasn't had to ask. He's had the Committee feeding him inside info. But now the connection's down and Jackson's too smart to act the dictator when someone else might actually have something valuable to add.

Thanks for the vote of confidence, he says in my head.

I shoot him a startled glance and catch the whisper of a smile. Guess I was projecting my thoughts to him. I have to remember that I can do that if I don't try. And can't do it when I do. Figures.

He ignores Lien's sarcasm. "We could head into the trees, there"—he points at a break in the thick undergrowth—"or stick to the edge of the cliff and see where it takes us."

I take stock of our options. Forest and undergrowth to one side. To the other, the earth drops away in a steep cliff that ends in a roaring river at the bottom of the gorge. Behind us are the Drau. Ahead of us, low scrub that's easier to navigate than the forest.

"Cliff's risky," Tyrone says. "We could get stuck in the open with no way out but down."

"I think we should go back," Lien says. "We don't know why we respawned in that spot or what the mission is. Maybe we've gone in the completely wrong direction. Maybe if we go back to where we started, we'll get some information through your con."

As if in answer to her suggestion, the tops of the trees behind us light up and burst into flames. Just a little reminder of how close the Drau are.

"Sooo . . . nix that suggestion," Lien says.

"You think they're setting the fire on purpose?" I watch the smoke rise. "So we can't backtrack?"

"Kind of herding us in the direction they want?" Kendra asks.

"Okay, that's just horrifying," Lien says.

I walk over to the edge of the cliff and look down. It's a long way to the bottom of the gorge.

Lien comes up behind me. "A roaring river in front of us. Fire behind. No map. No idea what the mission is. Just bad choices in any direction."

"Love your optimism," I say, and she laughs.

"It's a gift."

"We know they're behind us for sure. But if you were right about what you said earlier and there is another group in there?" Tyrone jerks his head toward the trees. "They could burn us out."

"If the choice is between drowning and burning, I vote for the cliff," Kendra says with an apologetic look at Lien.

"Cliff," Luka agrees.

Jackson looks at me.

"What's your gut telling you?" I ask.

"Cliff," he says.

"Your gut's saved me enough times that I trust it. My vote's for cliff."

"Guess we have our answer," Jackson says.

He scoots down so Kendra can hop up, but Luka walks over, holding Jackson's knife out hilt first. "My turn."

"Fair enough." Jackson takes the knife and shoves it in its holster.

Kendra climbs on Luka's back, and he walks toward the others, leaving Jackson and me behind.

"What?" Jackson asks when he catches me staring.

"I was just thinking that we have weapons. The Committee gave us those, at least. So it doesn't seem likely they just sent us here to die, does it? I mean, there could be a bunch of reasons your con isn't working properly."

"There could."

I chew my lower lip, wondering if the Committee's listening somehow. Then I decide to take the risk and whisper, "What if it has something to do with Lizzie and her team? What if they're jamming the signal?"

"For what reason?"

And that's a question I can't answer.

We press on, the terrain growing rockier, the forest to our right dense and dark. To our left, the ground drops away to the deep gorge. At the bottom, white water slams against rock, undulating and coiling like a living thing. Mountains rise on either side of us, blocking the sun. But the Drau and the fire follow us, the scents of smoke and burning wood stinging my nose.

"Wait," I say and scramble up some boulders, using them as a staircase to get to a ledge above us. Below me, Luka sets Kendra down, giving her a chance to hobble around a bit.

From this height, I have a better view of the forest. "Looks like there's smoke rising from three different spots, and they aren't on a linear path." Which suggests more than one group of Drau hunting us.

If Lizzie were to pick a time to intervene, now would be it. Because the Drau on her team might be all about cooperation between the species, but I'm betting the ones behind us don't share those feelings.

"We need to keep moving," Jackson says as I climb down.

"Why? Moving to where?" Lien's mutinous expression is one I recognize.

"Away from the fire," I say.

"Which is probably exactly what the Drau want. Kendra's right. They're herding us, and we're going along with it like dumb cattle."

"Miki just told you there's a shitload of Drau back there," Tyrone says. "So by process of elimination, we go forward."

"This has been a clusterfrack from the get-go," Luka mutters, and as he does, Drau shot rains down on us from a vantage point I can't track. From above us, somewhere on the forested ridge to our left. Which means that it's coming from a new Drau team, not one of those behind us. Which means that Lien might well be right.

"Move," Jackson barks, reaching for Kendra.

Tyrone gets there first, not even waiting for Kendra to climb up on his back. He just scoops her up in his arms and takes off at a jog. She loops one arm around his neck and twists her fist in his shirt for balance, her weapon cylinder in her free hand.

Lien and Jackson and I stay to the rear, watching for Drau until the ridge curves, cutting off the view of whatever's behind us.

"If we can't see them, they can't see us," Lien says. "Maybe I should hang back." She shades her eyes and looks up, then points. "Take a vantage point up there. Pick them off as they come along the ridge."

"We stay together," Jackson says.

"I—"

"We stay together," he repeats in his argue-at-your-peril voice. "I'm not going to be the one to tell Kendra we left you behind."

Lien closes her mouth and we take off after the others. We keep the pace at a steady jog and round the bend to see that the path narrows, ending in a rickety hanging rope bridge that sways in the wind. Below us, the river widens, rocks jutting from the swirling, frothing waters.

"No," Kendra says as Tyrone sets her on her feet. She crosses her arms over her abdomen and stares at the bridge. "No. Not happening. No."

"Can't say I'm in disagreement." Tyrone eyes the bridge askance. "That thing has to be over a hundred and fifty feet long."

"And a hundred feet up," Kendra says with a shudder.

"Try double that," Lien says, but at Kendra's distressed look amends her estimate. "No, you're right. A hundred feet up. Definitely not more than that."

"Either way, I'm not crossing that," Kendra says.

I study the bridge. Two massive footropes hang suspended from stone pylons, providing the main support system for the bridge and creating part of the rope-and-wood floor. The boards are cracked and rotted, and some are missing. The horizontal handrail ropes are intact, but probably half of the vertical side ropes meant to provide extra stability have frayed apart and hang off the bottom of the bridge like tassels. Getting across isn't guaranteed.

I'm wondering if it's even *possible*.

My vote's with Kendra and Tyrone. There is no way I want to cross that thing.

"Maybe we should go back," I say.

As if in answer, Drau shot arcs across the sky, falling short of us, but still a threat. I pause and study the trajectory. "That didn't come from behind us," I say, and look up until I pick a spot on a distant ridge that appears to be the point of origin. "I think there's another group of them stalking us. Unless the ones behind us moved hella fast." I look at Jackson. "It's only a matter of time before they're close enough to pick us off this ledge one at a time."

"We cross here, then," Jackson says.

"We are not going across that bridge," Kendra says, her voice high, the words running together.

Lien walks to her and loops her arm around Kendra's shoulder, lowering her head so their foreheads touch. "I don't think we have a choice."

"We could go up," Kendra says, turning to the rock wall that ascends beside us, the sheer face hundreds of feet high.

Hands on hips, Jackson assesses it. "Anyone ever been rock climbing?"

"Once," Lien says. "School trip to the Rock and Chalk. You?"

"Climbed when I lived in Arizona for six months. Kept it up in Texas. But haven't gone in a while. And never anything this high." He looks up at the rocks. "We don't have ropes. No carabiners. And there aren't many handholds. I'm guessing the highest we could go is maybe fifteen, twenty feet. Thirty, tops. Which doesn't gain us much." He turns his head toward Kendra. "And with your ankle, you wouldn't make it even that far. We take the bridge."

"They'll pick us off one by one," Kendra argues.

"That outcropping's blocking them, giving us some protection, for now," Jackson says. "If we move quickly, we should all be able to get across before they're close enough to do real damage. And I'll go last, watch your backs till you're across."

Kendra wraps her arms around herself, eyes wide, her whole body shaking. "I'll do it. If I have to, I'll do it. But I can't go first. Someone else needs to go first."

"I'll go," Tyrone says, then, "Let's hope our luck holds."

"Get ready to test it," Jackson says.

They clasp hands for a second, and then Tyrone's gone. I don't recall them ever doing anything like that before. I stare at the spot where their hands were joined, that small gesture terrifying to me.

CHAPTER **TWENTY-TWO**

THE BRIDGE SWAYS AND CREAKS AS TYRONE STARTS OUT, HIS hands sliding along the rope handrails. He takes it slow at first, testing each wooden slat with his toes before settling his weight full on his forward foot. Ten steps in and he turns with a grin and offers a mock salute.

"This won't be as bad as it looks," Lien says to Kendra.

"I don't know if my ankle will hold."

Lien tugs one of Kendra's blond curls. "Don't walk across. Crawl. That'll make it easier anyway. Your center of gravity will be lower."

"Right. Okay. Crawl."

"Clear," Jackson's voice carries from around the bend where he went to stand watch for Drau coming up from behind. I scan the ridges, looking for movement or flashes of light, but see nothing. "Clear," I call back.

I argued that we should whistle some sort of birdcall so that our voices wouldn't invite Drau attention, but after a couple of tries, Jackson and I both conceded defeat. Birdcalls are not among his repertoire of awesome skills, or mine. Besides, as he pointed out, the Drau know where we are. It's more a question of watching out for their inevitable arrival.

Tyrone's about a third of the way along when he stops dead and glances back. At first I can't see what the problem is, but then one of the vertical support ropes unravels, the top end falling away from the handrail, the bottom end still anchored to the bridge. For a second, he just stands there, still as stone. Then the bridge lists to the left, taking Tyrone with it.

"Oh, no." Kendra gasps. Lien stands, hands fisted at her sides, jaw set.

Tyrone flails and grabs tight to both rope handrails, spreading his feet to try to regain his equilibrium. He lurches left, then right, then left again, the bridge twisting under him. I take three steps before Luka grabs my arm, jerking me up short.

"Any more weight on that bridge before he's farther along just might make things worse," he says.

Stomach knotting, I watch as Tyrone rights himself, clinging to the rope handrails. After a minute, he offers a backhanded wave and takes a careful step forward. I watch, heart in my throat, as the bridge sways and bucks.

"Will it hold?" Kendra whispers.

"Isn't that the question," Luka answers.

Lien gives him the finger. "Way to be encouraging."

"He'll be okay," Luka says. "It's the bottom ropes that carry the load. The vertical ones on the sides are just for extra support and the top ones are for holding on to. So unless the bottom ropes snap, he's fine."

Kendra exhales. "Okay," she says at the same time as Lien asks, "And you know this how?"

Luka shrugs. "Eighth grade science project. We had a choice between building a trebuchet or a suspension bridge."

"I'd have gone with the trebuchet," Lien says.

"That, or a battering ram, right?"

Lien sends him an arch look.

"We're all going to make it across just fine," I say, managing to sound like I believe it. "Look at Tyrone. He's almost there."

Almost there is pushing it, but Tyrone's closer now to the far side than he is to us.

Leaning on Lien, Kendra hobbles to the bridge. Lien stares at her for a long moment, then leans in and presses a quick kiss on her mouth. "See you on the other side."

Kendra nods, her whole body shaking. She's terrified, but she doesn't say a word about it. She's different ever since she stepped up on the last mission to save Lien—not any less afraid, but better able to cope with that fear. It's something I recognize and admire. My fears are never far from the surface; the trick is to ride them out rather than letting them rule.

After taking a couple of slow, deep breaths, Kendra drops down on all fours, crawls forward, and starts out, dragging herself along. I wonder if that approach might be the one for all of us to take. Her progress isn't as fast as Tyrone's, but the bridge sways and dips a lot less.

Minutes crawl like sloths. Tyrone hits the far end. Kendra's halfway along now.

Jackson jogs up behind us. "The wind's picking up," he says. "Better get out there, Lien."

As she walks to the bridge, bright flares of light—Drau fire—arc across the sky, still falling short, but closer. Ever closer.

"Go," Jackson calls to Lien, then he scrambles up the boulders at the base of the cliff, climbs to a higher vantage point, and settles his weapon cylinder against his forearm. He doesn't return fire. Not yet. They're too far away to hit, but he's ready just in case they come within range.

"Why are they even firing?" Luka asks. "They have to know the range of their weapons. That they won't even come close to hitting us."

"Maybe they're trying to stoke our fear," Lien answers. "Or maybe it's some sort of signal to other Drau teams out there."

Other Drau teams. How many of them will we have to face when they get here?

"Go," I say.

Lien squares her shoulders and steps out, posture rigid, her head held high, telling me she's looking straight ahead at the far side. Not down. Never down at the raging water and rocks below.

"Miki, you're next," Jackson calls down to me once Lien has her rhythm, moving at a slow, steady pace, body shifting to accommodate the sway of the ropes.

I glance at Luka, thinking maybe I ought to send him.

"Non-negotiable," Jackson says.

I look up at him for a second, hating the thought of leaving him behind, of knowing that he'll be the last one to cross the bridge to the comparative safety of the other side. Words hang on the tip of my tongue. Words I refuse to say. Not here. Not now. I remind myself of my promise that when I say them again it will be in a moment just for us, a moment of joy, not a moment where death breathes on the backs of our necks and the game rules our choices.

So I just memorize the way the sun hits his hair, the tilt of his head, the arrogant curve of his lips, and then I head for the bridge.

Kendra's almost across. Lien's just past a third of the way, and Tyrone's safe on the far side. I test the slats with a couple of careful steps. Jackson was right. The wind is picking up, sending the bridge swaying to and fro. I cling to the hand ropes, focusing on each step, borrowing a page out of Lien's book and staring straight ahead. From the corner of my eye, I catch the bright spray of more Drau fire, closer than before. I don't turn my head and I definitely don't look down at the raging river crashing over the rocks below.

Lien stumbles, catches herself, her wrist winding through a loose rope that dangles down the side of the bridge. It snaps, whipping out like a tail. She falls to her knees, the whole bridge bucking beneath us.

I step sharply, scrabbling for balance, the rotting board beneath my foot crumbling. I cry out as my foot slams through, the broken edges of the wood scraping through my jeans, tearing my skin. Clinging to the ropes, my leg dangling through the jagged hole, I hang there, panting, fighting for control. I look straight ahead and drag myself upright, forcing myself to ignore the damp warmth along the front of my shin and the sharp pain that tells me my leg's in less-than-perfect shape.

Pausing to catch my breath, I hold tight as the wind sends my hair whipping in my face.

Ahead of me, Lien tips precariously to one side, her legs sliding all the way over the edge. I bite my lip to keep from calling her name, not wanting to distract her.

Inch by agonizing inch, she drags herself upright. Again the wind catches the bridge, making it rock like a tiny boat on a big wave. She drops to her knees and crawls forward.

Maybe she has the way of it. I glance down, thinking of following her lead, and see that the front of my leg from the knee down is stained with blood. I can't worry about that now. The only thing I can allow myself to focus on is getting to the other side.

I clutch the rope handrails, the rough length biting into my palms, and drag myself forward, avoiding the rotting boards, trying not to limp and unbalance myself. It's slow going. Ahead of me, Lien's at the two-thirds mark. I'm nearing the middle, gaining on her, and I glance back to see Luka start out after me.

Lien pulls herself to her feet and takes a dozen steps, covering ground. With a cry, she stumbles again, a rotted slat giving way beneath her. The bridge sags and twists. She flails for balance, one hand waving wildly, the other clawing at the rope.

"Run," I yell. "Just go. You're almost there. Go!"

She flings herself forward and makes an awkward run for the far side. The bridge in front of me lurches and rocks as she moves, the undulation carrying back to me in waves. I tighten my hold on the handrails and widen my stance, struggling for balance. She's almost at the end. I watch, not daring to move, holding my breath. Tyrone reaches out and grabs her sleeve, using it to yank her against his chest. She's shaking so hard her legs won't hold her. He wraps her in his arms and cradles her against him, his eyes meeting mine over her head.

Three safe. Three to go.

I start forward again, barely daring to breathe. Five steps. Ten. Each one brings me closer to the other side.

"Stop!" Tyrone yells, letting go of Lien as he gestures at something in front of me. "Hold on! Miki, hold on!"

On instinct, I do this thing I once saw when Mom and Dad took me to see Cirque du Soleil. I weave my wrist through a side support rope, once, twice, a third time so the rope snakes up my forearm. I barely have time to finish the move before the section of bridge directly in front of me sags and drops and I tumble forward, my shoulder yanked hard as my wrist stays secured.

I hang there, my body twisted, my torso stretched along the boards. Several of them fall away, and I watch as they shatter on the rocks below, pieces bouncing up then scattering across the surface of the rushing water, swept away the second they touch down. Panting, I tell myself to look away, look up, stay focused on my goal.

As I raise my head, the slats beneath me shift. A glance back shows Luka closer to me along the bridge and Jackson just starting out. He yells something to me, but I can't hear from this distance, with the wind snatching his words and the roar of the water drowning him out. I just shrug and shake my head.

He yells again and points. Flashes of light flicker on the ridge where we spotted the Drau, closer than they were before. My gut churns. My skin crawls. *Enemy.* The thought whispers through me, forced to the forefront of my mind. Like it was shoved into my brain, just like those horrible images of Dad and Carly that I saw on the last mission and again at the hospital. There's no time for me to ponder the similarities.

I glance back at Jackson and Luka to see Drau surging

along the path that brought us to the bridge, glowing and bright and deadly.

"Go, Miki! Get to the other side," Jackson yells. The wind shifts, carrying his words to me instead of away.

Luka scrambles toward me, Jackson behind him. I start to unravel my arm from the rope. The Drau fire on us, pinpricks of light arcing across the chasm, falling short. Except one spark of light that surfs the wind and lands on the rope handrail ahead of me. One spark of light that catches and flares. It flickers and flames, burning the rope, cutting it in two.

The severed ends fall away.

"Run," Kendra screams.

I yank my hand free and leap forward, landing flat on my belly, my fingers clawing at the side suspension ropes, the whole bridge lurching and swaying. I scuttle forward as Tyrone jumps out onto the sagging slats, one step, two, until he grabs me and hauls me to my feet. Wrapping his arms around me, he throws us both to the solid ground.

I surge to my feet, weapon cylinder in hand, and spin back to face Jackson and Luka and the Drau on the ledge behind them.

One of the handrails is on fire, flames licking along the rope, sending a shower of sparks that ignites the vertical side ropes. Boards break loose to spin away to the rocks below.

Luka clings to the intact handrail, double-fisted.

"Go," Jackson yells to him. "I'll hold them off."

With a snarl, Luka yanks his weapon free and fires on the Drau, still clinging to the rope with one hand.

"Go," Jackson yells again.

Luka hesitates, torn between obeying the order and having Jackson's back.

Endless seconds tick past, and then he finally backs up a step and then another, still shooting as he moves. His effort is wasted; his shots don't hit their targets, and the ropes along the sides of the bridge flame and then turn to gray ash one after another, falling like dominoes.

CHAPTER TWENTY-THREE

LEGS SPREAD FOR BALANCE ON THE SWAYING BRIDGE, JACKson fires a volley of shots at the Drau, most of which fall short. The only good thing is that theirs don't find their mark, either. It's a long way from one end of the bridge to the other.

Kendra hunkers down at the edge of the cliff, weapon at the ready. Frustration skewers me. If Jackson's shots aren't doing any good, what can she possibly hope to accomplish? She's even farther away from the oncoming Drau. Lien runs to a second vantage point, firing at the Drau on the opposite side of the gorge. More wasted effort.

Luka backs up along the bridge toward us, covering Jackson as best he can, which means he's pretty much accomplishing nothing. I want to dive in and save them both. I can't. All I can do is watch, helpless.

The ropes dip and creak. Jackson winds his calf and ankle into one of the side ropes for stability, the way I did earlier with my wrist. Two more vertical support ropes snap away as Luka passes them, his weight the final nail in their coffin. The bridge tips far to one side. Luka stumbles, then rights himself, spinning toward me.

"Come on," I yell, panic punching through me. "Run! Just run. You can do it. You can make it." I yell at them again, "Run!" as I hold my weapon up double-fisted and fire on the Drau.

Another rope frays, this one at the bottom of the bridge, a main support rope. Icy terror races through my veins as the footrope snaps, the edges recoiling, the whole bridge listing to the side. With a shout, Luka scrabbles for balance. Jackson lurches and almost falls.

Slats tumble into the gorge, tearing free on either side of the severed section.

With a cry I start for the bridge only to haul up short. I can't risk my weight on there. It could send all of us tumbling.

Helpless, terrified, all I can do is watch as Jackson and Luka remain trapped on the failing bridge, Drau fire raining down, sparking on their clothes and the remaining ropes. I fire, again and again. But I hit nothing, the black ooze disgorging from my weapon spinning, useless, to the frothing water below.

Luka lurches three steps closer as another side rope

snaps and the bridge bucks and drops another foot. His head comes up and he stares straight at me as the wood beneath his feet works free and fails, one slat at a time. The whites of his eyes are visible all around his irises, terror enveloping him.

Luka lurches to the side, stumbles, catches himself.

With a snarl, Tyrone takes a step forward, then freezes, helpless to do more than watch the scene unfold.

The rotting boards drop off, one at a time, until there's nothing but air beneath Luka's feet.

My heart stops. My breath stops. The whole world stops as the bridge falls away.

With a cry, he falls, arms windmilling, his weapon lost.

I scream and hold out my arms, throwing myself toward the bridge. But Luka's far beyond my reach.

Jackson shoves his weapon in its holster and dives forward like he's bungee jumping, his leg wrapped in the rope, hands reaching as he yells Luka's name. They both race toward the rocks, freefall.

Jackson catches Luka by the wrist.

The rope hits its limit and snaps them both to a stop, Luka's weight jerking Jackson's shoulder, Jackson's fingers digging tight around Luka's wrist and Luka's locked around his. They hang, just past the midway point, over the gorge and the rocks below, their lives dependent on the fraying, rotting rope that coils around Jackson's ankle and calf.

"Don't let me fall," Luka cries, his free arm flailing as he reaches for Jackson. "Don't let me fall."

Jackson answers him, but I can't hear what he says.

The two halves of the bridge are connected by only the single remaining footrope and a few vertical supports that suspend the opposite side of the floor from the handrail. Broken slats jut in all directions like brownish gray teeth.

The wind sends Jackson and Luka twisting. Terror gnaws at me.

I don't know how long the rope around Jackson's foot will hold. I don't know how long Jackson and Luka can hang on to each other. Jackson must be thinking along the same lines because with one hand stretched out, holding Luka, he contorts until he can get his other wrist wrapped in one of the vertical support ropes, his hand closing tight around it, reinforcing the connection.

The Drau come to the very edge of the far side of the gorge and fire. The spray of light doesn't come close to reaching Jackson and Luka, but a shift in the wind could change that, could carry a spark to them and set the last of the ropes ablaze. They can't hang there forever. Either the Drau will get them, or gravity will.

"Swing up, Luka," Tyrone yells from beside me. I catch his meaning and gesture at the one remaining footrope that spans the gorge.

"Come on!" Lien screams. "You can do it!"

Luka nods and starts climbing Jackson's arm like a

ladder, reaching for the rope. They're in this crazy-awkward position and I don't know how Jackson's managing to hang on. Even from this distance, I can see the rope growing red with blood where it's chafed his hand raw.

The wind picks up, twisting them like a weather vane and with a cry, Luka slides back, saved from falling only by Jackson's steely grip.

This isn't going to work. We need another option, fast.

Panting, heart slamming against my ribs, I squat by the edge of the cliff and start hauling up the remains of the severed footrope.

"Help me," I yell.

Together, Tyrone and I get the rope gathered.

"We need to get the boards off." I stand and slam my foot down on a board, snapping it off. Tyrone does the same and we work as quickly as we can. With her sprained ankle, Kendra can't be much help, but Lien comes to stand next to Tyrone and smashes her foot down on a board.

It feels like eternity before the rope is stripped. One end is still anchored to the stone pylon, and Tyrone winds the free end into a coil.

"I'm going to throw this to you," he yells to Jackson.

Jackson nods and Tyrone throws the rope.

It misses Jackson by at least a dozen feet, the end snaking into the gorge.

A lone Drau ventures onto the bridge. Jackson's whole body jerks as Drau fire hits him full on the back. Kendra shoots from her vantage point at the edge of the cliff, but she has no hope of hitting it. Luka tips his head back and looks at Jackson, then lets go with one hand, his whole weight suspended from the point where he and Jackson clasp wrists. He grabs Jackson's weapon from its holster and fires at the Drau.

Misses.

Fires again.

The Drau is swallowed by the black surge.

Deterred for the moment, none of its teammates venture out. They wait on the ledge, probably coming up with a new plan.

"I'll swing Luka up," Jackson yells.

I don't get what he means until he shifts his body back and forth a few inches, the arc growing bigger and bigger until the two of them move like a pendulum, toward us then away again. Jackson says something to Luka. I can't hear it, but from the way they both look in our direction, I think he's telling him he'll need to let go of Jackson at the last second and grab for the rope when we throw it.

Tyrone frantically re-coils the rope.

"On three," Jackson yells.

Luka looks over at where Tyrone and I stand side by side. His face is twisted with fear.

The Drau surge forward again, two of them stepping onto the swaying bridge in tandem, targeting Jackson and Luka. Jackson takes the worst of it, his body jerking and contorting like a marionette as they shoot him again and again. Luka fires back. They retreat. For now.

Luka shoves the weapon into his holster, then closes his fingers around Jackson's wrist, doubling his grip.

"One," Jackson yells as he and Luka swing away from us. "Two." They start back toward us. "Three," he yells when they're at the closest point.

Tyrone throws the rope. Luka throws himself forward, making a motion like he's going to clap.

The free end of the rope starts to drop.

I think he won't make it. I think he'll miss.

Horror congeals, glutinous and thick.

Luka's hands slam together and the rope's between them, and then he drops, his weight like a wrecking ball swinging toward the sheer cliff face.

More Drau venture out onto the bridge. They fire and keep firing, light falling like hail, not quite reaching Luka or our side of the gorge.

I glance at them, my eyes off Luka for only a second.

When I look back, the rope is on fire, flames licking up and down the length.

"Luka," I scream as the rope snaps.

"Luka," Jackson yells, swinging toward him, hand outstretched.

Still clinging to the severed edge of the rope, Luka falls back, eyes locked on mine.

The world freezes. The moment freezes.

Luka pulls out the weapon and fires on the Drau,

getting the two in the lead as he plummets down, down, down, his final action selfless.

I leap for the edge, falling on all fours, loose earth and stones breaking away beneath my hands.

It takes Luka forever to fall, his cry of terror echoing off the sides of the gorge, carrying up to the sky. The sound digs talons into my heart and rakes bloody runnels. I fall to my knees as he crashes to the rocks, arms and legs splayed.

He lies there, unmoving, face to the sky, eyes wide and staring. Blood stains the rocks beneath his head, running in rivulets into the foaming water, turning the water pink before the current washes it away.

"Luka!" I scream, crawling closer to the edge of the cliff, searching for a way down. "Luka!"

The rock beneath his head is crimson. The water swirling at his limbs, foaming white. He slides forward, his feet, his legs, his hips. Slowly, the water takes him, sucking his body into the churning spray.

And then he's gone. Gone.

Gone.

Shaking, sobbing, I lift my eyes and yell, "Jackson." I scuttle to the edge of the cliff, desperate, searching. There's a way. There has to be a way. To get to Jackson. To get to Luka. To save them.

He tips his head back, and I realize that somewhere in the craziness, his glasses were torn off. His eyes meet mine.

I effing love you, Miki Jones. Don't ever forget it.

With a roar I surge to my feet, blindly firing on the Drau, my gaze locked on Jackson. And I watch in sick despair as the flaming remains of the bridge carry him down, down into the gorge toward the jagged rocks that reach for him.

CHAPTER**TWENTY-FOUR**

I RESPAWN ON MY KNEES, HUNCHED FORWARD, SCREAMING. The pain inside me mushrooms like a nuclear cloud.

"Miki!" Strong arms close around me.

My head jerks up and I stare at Jackson, not daring to believe he's real, that he isn't some cruel trick conjured by my imagination. He looks calm and unflappable, shades in place. Then he shoves his sunglasses up on his forehead, his eyes molten silver, and I know he's anything but calm. He doesn't speak as he traces his fingertips along my brows, my lashes, my nose, my lips, like he's memorizing me. Or proving to himself that I'm real.

"I thought—" I shake my head. It doesn't matter what I thought. It just matters what *is*.

Laughing, I throw my arms around him and hold on

tight. He isn't dead. He's here, right here. I pull back to look at him, to follow his lead and trace my fingers along his jaw and the seam of his lips. I touch his hair, the scar that bisects his eyebrow, the curve of his ear. Then I lean in and press my mouth to his, ebullient, my joy bubbling and bright. We bump noses, shift, bump chins, shift again, and I laugh against his lips at the awkward perfection of this moment.

"You came back to me."

"I will always come back to you, Miki Jones. As long as I'm breathing, I'll find the way back."

"Don't say that," I whisper. "It's too much like tempting fate. Just tell me again that you love me, for now, right now, and that's enough. Not just enough . . . perfect. Don't say it in my head. Out loud, say it out loud so I can hear it."

"I love you," he says, his voice gravel rough.

He could have died on that bridge and I would have missed the chance to tell him, would have missed the chance for all the wrong reasons. Not because I don't love him, but because I'm afraid. Afraid to love. Afraid to lose. Afraid to mourn again. The thing is, not saying *I love you* wouldn't have changed the outcome, but saying it would have. Because he'd have heard me say it. They're worth something, the words. He deserves them.

I swore the next time I said it would be in a moment of pure joy, a moment just for us. This is that moment. I won't squander it. "I love you, Jackson Tate."

His lips curl just a little. "I know," he whispers and

drags me against him to kiss me, his mouth fitting to mine like they are two parts of a whole, once separated, now joined.

I fist my hands in his hair, my body pressed tight to his, desperate to get him even closer than this, to feel his breath as my own, his heartbeat in time with mine. His hands splay across my lower back, pulling me to him, then he tumbles me onto the grass, his weight coming over me, heavy and welcome. Thigh to thigh. Chest to chest.

He kisses me like I am the moon and stars, the sun and blue sky, the whole universe. His universe.

All I know is his kiss. It consumes me, endless and deep and so beautiful it makes me shake. My arms loop tight around him, my hands press against the solid, smooth planes of his back, drawing him closer and closer still, running up and down the ridges of muscle that flank his spine. I want to kiss him forever, live here forever, in the warmth of his embrace.

But I can't, and he can't, and my heart breaks a little when he drags his lips from mine. Slowly, he pushes up, away from me, and already I feel cold without him.

Or maybe I feel cold because of the expression on his face. Pain. Regret. Loss.

He takes my hand and pulls me up so we sit facing each other on the grass. The cut on my leg's gone—no blood; no pain. Despite being hit repeatedly by Drau shots on the bridge, Jackson's unhurt, his clothes exactly the way they were before we went on the mission, his weapon back in its holster. The trees rise around us, the familiar boulders off to my right. Suddenly, this strikes me as odd. We've respawned in the lobby, which makes no sense. After a mission, we don't come back here—we go back to our lives, our real lives.

Jackson cups my cheeks and stares down at me, and my heart clutches as I read his expression, so serious and sad. The effervescent euphoria of finding each other alive and safe leaches away, replaced by cold truth and numbing despair.

"Luka," I whisper, refusing to believe.

Jackson's lips thin and he shakes his head.

"You're wrong," I say, surging to my feet, pacing away then back. "*You're* here. He will be, too."

"Miki . . ."

I blink against my tears and look away, at the grass, the trees, the familiar boulders. We're alone here, just Jackson and me. No one else from our team.

"No one else has respawned, either," I point out as he gets to his feet. "Not yet. But when they do, Luka will be with them." I want to believe he survived. If there was even the faintest hint of orange edging his con, then he survived.

Again Jackson shakes his head. I clench my fists and slam them against my thighs.

"You can't know," I say. "You can't know for sure. Look! Tyrone's not here, either, or Lien or Kendra. Just because Luka didn't respawn yet doesn't mean he isn't okay. They'll all be incoming any minute. You'll see." But even as I blurt my assertions, I know I'm lying to myself, because in my mind's eye, I can see Luka as he was pulled under the water, and the bloodstained rocks that broke him.

The loss sledgehammers me, leaving me breathless. Jackson catches me as I weave, closing his hands around my wrists, and we just stare at each other, the horror of what's happened tunneling through us.

I drop my chin to the side, lids lowered. The image of Luka staring sightless at the sky, the river raging all around him, fills every corner of my mind. I try to think of his grin, the way he laughed the day he chased Carly at the bleachers, the awkward look on his face that day we both reached for the groceries at the same time, our hands bumping, our renewed friendship too fresh for easy comfort with such physical closeness. The way he poked at Carly's dead fish. The way he raked his fingers through his hair when he was nervous or worried. But every image I call up melts away until all I see is Luka's slack features, animation and life stolen from them, and the rocks stained crimson with his blood.

"We couldn't figure out what the point of the mission was," I say, anger lacing every word. "The Committee dumped us there with no maps. No instructions. They weren't talking in your head. Why the hell did they send us there if there was no task for us to complete?" Jackson opens his mouth to answer, but I don't give him the chance. I barrel on, my voice rising. "Because *Luka* was the mission. That's why we respawned as soon as he died. I can see their whole plan now." I swallow. "They killed him."

Jackson doesn't answer, but I can feel the tension radiating from him in waves, and it hits me that he probably thinks I'm talking about the Drau.

"The Committee," I say. "Not the Drau. Don't you see? The Drau were just the weapon, but it was the Committee that pulled the trigger."

"They might be listening," Jackson says, low, leashed rage and pain in his tone.

"Let them." I tip my head to the sky and yell, "Are you listening? Can you hear me? I know what you did. You sent us there to get Luka killed." *That* was the point of the mission. To murder him. Because he'd served his purpose to the Committee, and once we figured out they were using him as a spy, they decided he had no purpose at all anymore.

"He was a danger to them," Jackson says. "He knew too much. They didn't want to risk him telling us all about it."

I press my palm against my lips, the horror of it all overwhelming me. "We figured out he was a spy. *We* killed him," I whisper.

"No." Jackson slides his hands to the base of my skull, tipping my head back so he can look into my eyes. "No, Miki. We didn't. They did." He looks away, a muscle twitching in his jaw. "You're right. The Drau were the weapon but the Committee had their finger on the trigger.

There was no other way that mission was going to end. They meant for Luka to die, and if that meant the rest of us went with him . . ."

"No." I shake my head. "The Committee isn't that arbitrary. They meant for Luka to die and us to live. They still have a use for us." I pause, then continue bitterly, "Team leaders aren't that easy to replace."

I lean forward and rest my head against Jackson's chest, focusing on each breath, only each breath, in, out, blocking out the pain, the rage, the hate that threatens to swamp me.

"None of this makes sense," I say. "None of it. I'm not just talking about Luka dying. I'm talking about the whole thing. The Drau. The Committee. If this is all about fighting off the Drau invasion, all about saving mankind, why send us on that useless mission just to kill a valuable soldier because they're pissed we found out what they were doing? Why use Luka to spy on us in the first place?" I exhale, trembling. "What if we're making a mistake? What if—"

"Go on," Jackson says. "What if . . ."

"What if . . ." Do I dare say it out loud? The Committee is no doubt listening to every word we've said. They know what I think of them. So does it matter if they hear me confirm it? I wet my lips and whisper, "What if the Drau aren't the enemy?"

Lightning doesn't strike me down. I don't get whisked to the amphitheater. It's still just me and Jackson standing in the lobby. So maybe the Committee doesn't care what I think. Or maybe they're just sitting back and seeing where this goes.

"Were you not just on that bridge?" Jackson asks. "Did you not feel the sting of the Drau's weapons?" His jaw clenches. "They saw Luka hanging there. They shot the rope knowing exactly what the end result would be. I think that spells out pretty clearly that they aren't exactly friends or allies, and if it doesn't—" He curls his fingers in the neck of his shirt and yanks it down to bare the top of his shoulder and the scars there, testament to his life-or-death fight with the Drau that followed him back from the game.

"It isn't that clear-cut." I shake my head, my thoughts spinning too fast. "You killed someone that Drau cared about right after they killed Lizzie. The Drau followed you back into our world and attacked you out of grief. It was life or death for both of you."

"If we weren't in a war with them, a war *they* started, the life-or-death situation wouldn't have existed."

Again I shake my head and demand, "But how do we know? How do we know any of it is true? The binary star system the Drau supposedly come from . . . their attack on the Committee's home planet . . . the motives behind the Drau's actions . . . Everything we know comes from the Committee. They told us the version they want us to believe. Who started it? Who really started the war? The Committee says the Drau. Is that the truth? What if the Drau believe it was us?"

Jackson just stares at me, brow furrowed, and I can see

he isn't discounting my questions. He's considering them, trying to come up with answers. It must be impossible to reconcile everything he's believed for five years with the evidence pointing to the possibility that it's all lies.

"It sure as hell wasn't the human race that started it," Jackson says. "Most people don't even have a clue the Drau exist." He pauses. "What are you looking for here, Miki? Some sort of reason in the chaos? There isn't any." He looks away and swallows, then looks back at me. "Five years. *Five years*, I've balanced never knowing where I'll be when I open my eyes, never knowing who'll die, who'll live, who'll lose it. Dealing with the Committee. Dealing with kids who have no clue, who wouldn't believe me even if I told them, who are probably going to die before their next birthdays. I survived it because I thought I was serving a cause bigger than me." He pauses again, then finishes softly, "I have to believe that."

I wrap my arms around his waist, my cheek against his shoulder. "The only knowledge I have of the Drau, other than what I've seen in the game, is what you told me or the Committee showed me in my head the first time I encountered them. The same information they gave you." I lean back, holding his forearms. "What if they lied? The Drau want to conquer us, want to use us as a food source. That's what the Committee says." I swallow and stare up at him. "You don't think that's cliché, like some sort of creepy sci-fi movie? Like something too out there to be true?"

"Luka's dead because of the Drau."

"But he isn't. He's dead because of the Committee, and that's the most terrifying thing of all." I'm so sick of this, so sick of having no control, of just reacting to whatever gets thrown my way. My life is running like a train off the rails, careening to one side, a millimeter away from tipping over. My father and my best friend are lying in the hospital, maybe dying, all because the Committee is trying to rein me in, threaten me, control me.

I'm done with being reactive. It's time for me to be the one to choose, to determine time and place, to determine my own outcomes.

I stare at the trees that bound the clearing, letting my peripheral vision catch the movements in the other lobbies that are reflections of ours. There are other teams there, some big, some small. I wonder if the Drau have pushed through the boundary into their real lives. I wonder how many of them have faced down the Committee.

"We need to talk to them," I say.

"You think I haven't tried?" Jackson asks. "There's a barrier in place, like the ones on missions that don't let you walk away until you're done."

I encountered the barrier he's describing the first time I was team leader, on the mission to Detroit. I told Luka and the rest of my team to get out of the building, get to safety, but they couldn't. They were trapped by invisible boundaries, with no choice but to fight and see the mission through to the bitter end. The only way the Committee lets you out is if you finish the mission.

Finish the level.

Finish the game.

But they never really let you out. They just allow a temporary reprieve.

As I stand there, one of the team leaders in another lobby turns. She stares somewhere off to my right and it hits me that she's looking at me. If we turn and try to see each other straight on, we fail. But if we don't look, if we just let the corner of our eye catch the movement, then we see each other just fine.

It's that instant of awareness that decides my course. Jackson might have tested the barricade, but I haven't. And maybe he didn't have Lizzie on his side when he tried. But I do. I know I do. She told me that's what the Committee is afraid of . . . that I'll tell the other team leaders what I know. I think she was telling me to do exactly that.

I've had enough—enough of letting the Committee move me around like a chess piece, enough of leaving my life in their hands, enough of their non-answers and the possibility that everything they've told me is a lie.

Enough of them letting my friends die.

I take a couple of steps toward the trees.

"Don't," Jackson says.

"You're worried they'll do to me what they did to Luka."

"I am."

I curve my palm along the base of his skull and go up on my toes, pressing my mouth to his in a brief, hard kiss.

"I have to," I say. "I refuse to be a pawn anymore."

I wait for him to ask, *What makes you think you get a choice?* I ready my arguments. I do have a choice. I can do more than be a dandelion blown by the wind.

"Then we do it together," he says, showing me just how far we've both come.

I walk toward the trees. He walks beside me, each step bringing us closer to the team leader who stands looking at me, fists clenching and unclenching at her sides, expression anxious. She doesn't walk toward us, but she doesn't walk away, either. Maybe Jackson and I aren't the only ones who've said enough is enough. Maybe we aren't the only ones having major doubts.

I've never tested the boundaries of the lobby. So maybe I'm going to hit the outer limit and bounce back and land on my ass just the way I did when the Committee was holding Jackson prisoner and I slammed against the invisible wall. I know there's a possibility of failure. But there's a one hundred percent guarantee of failure if I don't at least try.

Jackson takes my hand. We're at the tree line now. Three more steps and we'll be in the forest.

Two more . . .

One . . .

CHAPTER **TWENTY-FIVE**

THIS TIME, THE JUMP'S EASY. THERE'S NO DIZZINESS, NO burst of color, no painfully loud sounds. There's just the fraction of a second where I blink, my lids lowering, and when they come up again, Jackson and I stand side by side in a hallway so white it burns. He pulls his weapon cylinder and his knife, his body coiled and ready.

I leave my weapons sheathed.

"Jax," Lizzie says, walking toward us, her lips curved in a welcoming smile. "You don't need those."

He doesn't say anything. And he doesn't lower the weapons.

"The cylinder won't work here," she says.

"The knife will."

"Will you stab me? Will that make you feel better?"

She spreads her arms. "Go ahead."

Jaw tense, he stands there for a long moment, then finally rams the cylinder in its holster and the knife in its sheath. I don't need to climb inside his head to know what he's thinking, what he's feeling. Jackson's just watched his best friend die. The game he believed he'd mastered is suddenly unpredictable and foreign. The sister he believed dead is standing in front of him. I understand the urge to fight, to lash out, to let rage rule. Without saying a word, I slide my hand into his. His fingers close on mine and he holds on tight enough that I know he needs me, just like I need him.

Lizzie steps closer, head tipped back as she studies his face. "When I left, you were this high." She lifts her hand level with her chin. "You used to have to look up at me."

"I was twelve," he says. "And you didn't leave. My sister died."

"Your sister. Lizzie. But that's the conundrum, because I'm Lizzie."

His fingers clench on mine.

"Fine. Call me Liz. Is that better?"

"No."

"I'm her, Jax. I'm me."

"You're not," Jackson says. "Even if you are my sister, which I'm not ready to concede, you're not *her*. Not the girl I knew. Five years have passed. Five years where you've been places I know nothing about. Where you haven't aged, which makes no sense. Five years where I grew up fighting a war you—" He breaks off and takes a deep breath, and when he speaks again, his tone is cold and flat. "A war my sister introduced me to. In those five years, I changed. I'm not Jax anymore and you're not Lizzie."

My heart breaks for him because I've seen the beating heart beneath the frozen exterior. I've seen what he's willing to sacrifice for his team, his friends. I've been inside his head, felt what he feels. His love for his sister is vast and strong. This has to be killing him, not knowing for certain, not daring to believe.

I can't imagine how I'd feel, what I'd think, what I'd do, if it were Mom standing here in Lizzie's place.

"You're right. I'm not her and you're not him. But at the same time, I am. And you are. You need to figure out a way to reconcile that."

"Do I, now?" he asks softly, the words edged with menace.

I squeeze his hand, willing him to remember we're guests here—or, given the fact that we have no idea how to leave, prisoners. So maybe antagonizing our host isn't the ideal plan.

Lizzie sighs and turns to me, reaching out to rub her hand up and down my upper arm—the greeting of a friend. And she *has* been a friend to me, saving me when I almost died on a mission, saving Carly the night of the Halloween dance. Why us and not Luka?

I can still hear his scream, feel his terror. She could have stopped it.

"Where were you?" I ask. "Why didn't you come?"

She tilts her head, frowning. "Come where?"

"On the last mission. Why didn't you save him the way you saved me?"

Lizzie's eyes grow wide. "Save who? Miki? What's going on?" She grabs my free hand and lifts it between us and I look down to see tears splashing on my skin. I didn't even realize I was crying. I yank my hand from hers and swipe at the tears, angry to be this girl who weeps and chokes back sobs.

"Luka," I say. "He's dead. They killed him."

"What—" She looks at Jackson, then back at me. "I didn't know. I didn't even know you were on a mission. I thought you'd just arrived in the lobby."

"We did," I say. "They respawned us there after the mission. Lobby, mission, lobby. Everything's out of order. Did you know Luka was working with the Committee?" I pause. That question makes no sense. Everyone in the game is working with the Committee. "I mean, did you know they were using him to get inside information, to spy on us? They pushed into his head, stole his memories. They even . . . I don't know . . . somehow inhabited him in the real world, to watch us every day during our real lives . . . Did you know about that?"

As I say it, a chill chases up my spine. Lizzie's made it clear to me that the Committee can't find out about her. But Luka saw her on at least one mission, heard me talk about her on another. She could have viewed him as a threat, a way that the Committee could find out about her and her team. To what ends would she go to keep her team safe? Would she see letting Luka die as a valid sacrifice?

I don't know what to think, what to believe.

"Inhabited him? Like a shell?" Lizzie stares beyond me down the corridor, then looks back at me. "You said they were using him to spy on you. What did he know, Miki? What did he give them that they could use against us? Do they know about me?"

"There they are," Jackson says softly. "The questions that paint you guilty."

"Or paint me logical," Lizzie replies.

"Is that why you didn't save him?" I ask. "Because he was a threat to you? Did you let him die on purpose? To keep any knowledge of your existence from the Committee? Would you let me die, too? Or Jackson?"

"Oh, Miki," she says on a sigh, her tone both sad and consoling. She rubs my arm again, like she forgives me for saying these horrible things to her. "I didn't save him because I wasn't there. Didn't know I should be."

It dawns on me that my questions don't make sense, not even to me. Lizzie saved me, protected me, protected my team the night of the dance. She's done nothing but have my back since the first time I saw her. I take a shuddering breath. "Could you have saved him? If you had known? If you had been there?"

"Maybe. I don't know." Again, she stares beyond me for a few seconds, brow furrowed. "What we do . . . It isn't foolproof. I don't always know when you're pulled. I'm not always here to know."

"Because you track other teams," I say. "And follow them into missions."

"Sometimes."

"How does it work? How does any of it work? The game? The Committee?" I gesture at the white walls, white floor. "All of it."

She looks at Jackson and holds out her hand, pleading. "I can explain, if you'll let me."

"Let you?" He huffs a dark laugh. "Hell, I'll beg you."

"It's easiest if I show you. Okay?"

He gives a brief nod.

Lizzie turns to me. "Miki?"

I don't know what she's asking me until I get the hint of an image in my thoughts, an image of me, not the way Jackson sees me, but the way Lizzie does. She's asking if it's okay to convey images inside my head, the way that Jackson did when he showed me the first time he saw me at Atlantic Beach. The way the Committee did the day they showed me the Drau destroying their planet.

"Sure," I say. "Why not? Everyone else does."

It's like my permission was the key she needed to open the door. Images, knowledge, certainty flood my mind and I understand things so far beyond my reach it makes me dizzy, makes me grab for Jackson's arm and hold on to keep myself from spinning away.

The fabric of the universe unfolds and I *see* it, *understand* it. Everything in the universe is made of molecules, which are made of atoms, which are made of protons, neutrons, electrons. Protons and neutrons are made of quarks. Quarks are made of strings—tiny, tiny particles that vibrate and move.

Everything is made of strings. The universe and every other universe that exists and will exist. The Big Bang happening again and again. Infinite connections. Infinite reactions.

If the strings oscillate one way, we see one thing. If they oscillate a different way, we see a different thing. How many dimensions, how many realities overlie one another?

The basis of the universe, the basis of everything, explained by tiny loops of vibrating energy.

Lizzie takes me by the hand and leads me into space. Endless, beautiful. Stars. Galaxies. The universe expanding at an exponential rate. A vast expanse. Somehow, she folds space, and two distant points align one atop the other, connected by a wormhole. Points separated by distances that are beyond my comprehension suddenly become neighbors. One step, and you can be somewhere you were never meant to be. Time and distance don't mean anything anymore.

Her hand in mine, Lizzie steps forward and back, then side to side, drawing me with her. She jumps and lands.

"Three dimensions," she says. Or maybe she just thinks it and I think it with her. Up, down. Right, left. Forward, back. Three dimensions. That's what we know. What humans know. But there are more, so many more.

Jackson steps between us, disengaging her hand from mine. Protective, always protective. He doesn't trust her, doesn't want to let her lead me on a dangerous path.

She grabs my hand again, and his. "Think of a TV show. It's only two dimensions but we perceive it as three. Imagine an actor could step right out of the screen and into our dimension. That's the explanation for it all."

"It doesn't explain anything," Jackson says.

She laughs and lets go of our hands and pulls out a deck of cards, shuffling them then tapping the end so all the cards align in a neat block. "Imagine that the universe is contained on a single card. Just one. A flat, two-dimensional card. But look how many more cards there are next to us. Right next to us. We can almost reach out and touch the cards beside us. Almost but not quite. Other realities. Other dimensions. The universe is infinite space within a dimension and there are other universes and other dimensions. Do you see?"

"The Committee inhabits one of those dimensions," Jackson says. "And moves us around between others."

"In a simplified sense, yes." She takes a single card and bends it into a C shape, so the ends are just millimeters from each other. "The Committee bends time and space. They create wormholes here"—she taps the edges of the C—"and make use of others that already exist. They can move themselves, you, the Drau, wherever they want, whenever they want."

"How do you know all this?" Jackson asks.

"I only know what the Drau know, what they've been able to teach me," Lizzie says. "They're advanced in so many ways." She grins. "Less advanced in others."

"So Miki was right. They're part of your team."

She laughs again, the sounds like crystal goblets clinking together, filling me to the brim. "Really? Jackson, you're so much smarter than that."

I don't know what makes me turn. Some sort of sixth sense or maybe something in Lizzie's posture, her tone. Two Drau stand less than three feet away, glowing and bright, weapons protruding from thigh harnesses but still holstered, not drawn.

When Lizzie looked beyond me up the hallway, she was looking at them. And I didn't even sense they were there. Neither did Jackson. No warning sensation; no cell-deep certainty that the enemy was near.

But they've been there the whole time, watching.

CHAPTER **TWENTY-SIX**

JACKSON TURNS AS I DO AND STEPS SOLIDLY BETWEEN THE Drau and me, his weight distributed so he's hunched a bit to the right in a boxer's stance, left foot forward, arms on guard, right elbow close to his body. Ready for a fight. Always ready.

Don't look in their eyes. The rule's been pounded home since the beginning.

But I do, because I know the Drau can choose not to hurt me. They can choose not to kill me. Just like the Drau that Kendra killed, who begged for mercy, who showed me mercy, sparing my life when she could have drained me. I looked in her eyes, her mercury eyes. And all she did was hold my gaze.

Now, I look at the Drau and for the first time, I have a

chance to really study them, close enough to touch, without the blinders of fear to limit my view. I get my first real lengthy look at them and what I see is more confusing than edifying.

"Their skin . . . ," Jackson says.

"Is not skin," Lizzie clarifies. "It's an artificial covering, sort of like a cross between clothing, a vehicle, and a wet suit you'd wear to go diving. They can't survive in our atmosphere. The barometric pressure would kill them. We wouldn't be able to survive in theirs."

An artificial covering. How could I not see that before? Maybe because when I encountered the Drau in battle, they glowed brighter, stronger, their light nearly blinding.

"Why do they glow?"

"Natural bioluminescence. Light energy released by chemical reaction."

"Like fireflies," I murmur.

"Same concept, but the Drau are more like jellyfish. And they glow all the brighter in our atmosphere because of the oxygen content. Oxygen reacts with a pigment in their bodies to create light."

Without thinking about it, I start to step toward them. Jackson shifts, barring my way, the move bringing him even closer to them. If he lifted his hand, he could touch them. I wonder if he's ever been this close to a Drau he wasn't trying to kill or question.

"Why a vehicle?" he asks, voice tight, muscles coiled.

"They don't move like we move. They don't actually

look like what you see. They're more gelatinous, comfortable in the viscous environment they're originally from. But when they began exploring other realms, they created these . . . I guess you can think of them as space suits . . . to adapt and make them faster, more resilient, more able to navigate varied environments."

"But when I—" Killed them . . . hacked off their heads . . . I saw their blood. I saw the bones of their spines. I can't say that. I can barely stand to even think it. "They have bones," I say instead.

"The suit has a skeleton-like support system similar to bones and a viscous environment they need in order to survive," Lizzie says.

Bones, and blood, of sorts. "But this suit or covering or whatever it is," I say. "It moves like skin over muscle. It reveals their emotions, their expressions, just like our faces do."

"It does," Lizzie agrees. "The suit sort of becomes part of them."

"So they can't take it off?"

"They can, but it's a long and complicated process."

I think of everything Lizzie's said so far about what she's learned from the Drau, about them exploring other realms. I look at the white corridor and picture the control room with the creepy nanoagents, the control panel Lizzie sank her hands into, everything foreign and different than any human technology I know of or could imagine. The

Drau are so advanced that their space suits are practically alive.

"They're not part of your team," Jackson says, picking up on the same things that suddenly coalesce for me. *"You're* part of *theirs.* This place"—he gestures at the stark, brilliant walls of the corridor—"they created it. The nano-agents, the control room, your ability to pull us out of the Committee's grasp . . . It's all Drau technology."

"There you go," Lizzie says. "I knew you would figure it out. Yes. They created this place specifically for me, because I could not survive in an environment designed for them. They saved me after my con went red. Revived me. Gave me a life."

"Why?" Jackson asks.

"Because of you. Because of what your eyes allowed you to do. They saw our energy exchange and they interpreted events to mean that I was part Drau. That we were all part Drau."

"The word *exchange* implies a two-way street," Jackson says. "The way I remember it, things were pretty one way that day. I was dying. You told me to make like a Drau and borrow some of your energy. But I couldn't stop at *some.*" His chest expands on a deep breath. "So I took it all and I killed you."

I make a sound of denial, but Lizzie voices her objection before I can. "By mistake," she says.

"I killed you. And they saved you." The emphasis

Jackson puts on the word *they* speaks pretty clearly to how he feels about that.

"Jax," Lizzie says softly.

"They saved you because they thought you might be part Drau. But they must have figured out pretty quickly that they were wrong," Jackson says, not giving her the opening to say anything kind. "So why do all this"—he gestures at our surroundings—"to keep you alive? Once they realized you weren't Drau, why not let you die?"

"That isn't their way."

"Isn't their way? They kill us in the game all the time."

"In the game, they have little choice. Kill or be killed." She shrugs. "With one lone, dying girl, they had a choice."

"What did they do with you while they were creating this place?" I ask. "It must have taken a while. How did they keep you alive in the interim?"

"They kept me in the game, on endless cycles of missions."

"Fighting for which side?" Jackson asks.

"Neither. I was in spectator mode. And let me tell you, it was an eye-opening experience."

Jackson shakes his head. "Why keep you here? Why didn't they just send you home?"

She takes a sharp breath and her chin comes up. "Because the second they did, the Committee would have terminated me."

"Believable words, but that's not the answer," Jackson says. "Or maybe not the whole answer. Try again."

"You always did know when I was hedging. The truth?" She holds his gaze. "No one leaves. No one escapes. Once you're in the game, there's no going back."

"That can't be true," I say. "There were no adults on any of the teams we've encountered. And the Committee told me that adult brains don't do well with the jump. So at some point, kids get old enough that the Committee lets them go, right?"

"No one ages out," Lizzie says, gentle. "Your friend Tyrone doesn't have much longer. They'll kill him soon. He's too old."

My pulse kicks up a notch and I shoot a look at Jackson. "Why not just let him go?"

"No one ever goes."

"You did," Jackson says.

Lizzie touches his cheek, her heart in her eyes, so loving, so sad.

"I died five years ago, Jackson. In the dimension you inhabit, I died. I can't ever go back. No one who dies in the game can. My life, your life, Miki's . . . all the lives of all the players who have been or still are part of the game. They were stolen by the Committee. None of you will ever go home completely. And if you die in the game, you can't go home at all."

I knew that. On some level, I'd known it all along.

Still, I can't help but protest. "The Committee said that if a player earns a thousand points, they evolve to the next level," I say.

"The next level," Lizzie echoes. "Death's a form of evolution, isn't it? The truth is, everyone dies in the game at some point. Like your friend Luka."

I cringe, the pain of Luka's death too fresh.

"He didn't just die," I whisper.

"He was murdered," Jackson says. "To keep him quiet."

"Or because they thought he'd outgrown his usefulness," Lizzie says.

I wrap my arms around myself. "In the lobby, before the last mission, he warned me, warned us. Told us what the Committee had been doing, the way they'd been spying."

"One more reason they wanted him gone. Payback for leaking their secrets," Lizzie says.

"Or maybe they wanted to make certain he didn't leak any more." My voice breaks. I glance at the Drau, standing there like silent sentinels, then I look back at Lizzie. "I never imagined he could die. Stupid of me, huh?"

Lizzie's half smile is sad. "Not stupid. Optimistic."

"Yeah, that's me. The consummate glass-half-full kind of girl." I try for a smile, but I can feel it fall flat.

"So . . . your con went red in the game, but you're here. Is everyone else here, too? Richelle? Luka? All the kids who died in the game?" I ask, even though I suspect deep down that it's a futile hope.

Lizzie shakes her head. "Only me. And only because of what happened with Jackson right before my con went red. It was a fluke. They can't save every human who dies in the game. The Drau can't even save themselves."

I study Lizzie's face, trying to read her, trying to figure out what exactly her agenda is.

And while I'm studying her, the Drau are studying me; I can feel their interest, their curiosity. What I can't feel is the cell-deep genetic memory that labels them as my enemy. In the game, every alarm would be clanging right now. But not here. Because that wariness *isn't* cell deep, I realize. It's a construct of the Committee, a trick they feed into our thoughts. It isn't real. Still, I can't help the wariness, the distrust that lurks in my thoughts.

"There's still a war going on, still a threat against the human race," I say, parroting the Committee's assertions. "The Drau want to invade, conquer, cut us up and make people stew."

Lizzie throws back her head and laughs, the sound dancing along the corridor. "Actually, they're what humans would describe as vegan."

Jackson's head whips toward her. "What?"

No harm. We mean no harm. Peace. Pacifism. Fight only if our lives are threatened. Raw thought pours through me, lighting every neuron in my brain. I gasp and stumble and it takes a few seconds before I realize Jackson's holding me, his arms the only things keeping me from hitting the floor.

"Scale it back," he snarls.

RegretRegretRegretRegretRegret—their version of an apology.

The thoughts dampen to a whisper, butterfly wings dancing through my mind.

Panting, I look up at Jackson. "You heard them."

He offers a spare nod.

"But it didn't affect you the way it did me." The intensity didn't seem to bother him.

"I've had more practice," he says with a tight smile.

He has. He's had the Committee talking in his head for years. He's questioned the Drau, had their thoughts in his mind. "But—" I think it's more because of his Drau genetics. I shake my head. The reasons he's less susceptible to the intensity of their communication aren't important now. "I think they're telling the truth. That they mean no harm." I straighten but don't pull away, and stare at Jackson's face until I know he's focused on nothing but me. "I believe them."

It's easy to read the anger that darkens his expression. So I'm surprised when he grinds out, "So do I."

He rounds on Lizzie. "Straight answers. Now. What is this place? Where exactly are we? What are we doing here? If the Drau aren't a threat, then what the hell is going on?"

Despite everything, I can't help the hint of a smile that tugs at me now that the tables are turned. Jackson's been the sullen, uncommunicative, uncooperative source of almost every non-answer I've had since being dragged into the game. It's almost funny to see him on the receiving end of evasions and non-answers.

Almost funny, but not quite, because I want answers to those same questions.

"Is there a particular question you'd like me to answer first?" Lizzie asks.

"You can start with an explanation of which side you're on," Jackson says. "What are you? A rebel faction against the invasion? You're fighting the Drau leaders that want to take over the world? Allying with the Committee?"

Reasonable questions, but somehow they feel wrong, like Jackson and I are standing at a fork in the road and he's choosing the wrong path.

"No." Lizzie's gaze locks with mine, green and bright.

My heart stutters. "Allying with who, then?"

"Knowledge is power?"

"Pretty much."

"What you think you know about the Committee are half-truths and stories," Lizzie says.

"According to you," Jackson shoots back.

She inclines her head, conceding the point. "You don't have a reason to trust me. I get that. In fact"—she grins— "I might feel the same way if our positions were reversed." The grin fades. "Think about that for a second, Jackson. If you were the one who'd gone missing. If you were the one who returned. What would you want me to do? To say?"

He looks away, and again my heart twists at the sight of his pain. There has to be a part of him that wants to drag Lizzie in for a bear hug, lift her off her toes and spin her round and round. The part that believes she is who she says she is.

I think Lizzie sees how hard this is for him because she says, "Let's go somewhere we can sit down and discuss this more comfortably."

"And have milk and cookies? Maybe join hands and sing?" Jackson fires back, keeping his hard-ass shield in place as a defense. "I'm not interested in comfort. I'm interested in answers. Right now. Right here."

Lizzie sighs. "I can tell you what I know, and you can choose to believe or not. How's that?"

At Jackson's terse nod, she continues. "The Committee lies. Trust nothing they tell you."

"Specifics," Jackson orders.

"The first lie they told me was that they're the collective consciousness of a long-dead alien race. They aren't dead. They are immortal and powerful. They can transform energy and matter. Manipulate time. Teleport. According to the Drau—"

"Right there, that's a problem," Jackson says. "Why would I trust anything you preface with *according to the Drau*?"

"We agreed you'd listen and then decide what to believe."

Jackson clenches his jaw but gives another nod.

"According to the Drau, the Committee have always existed and will always exist. They are almost omniscient. Almost omnipotent. And eternity has made them bored."

"Bored?" I echo as a seedling of memory unfurls inside me. Gram, taking me to the hairdresser with her when I was little. The smell of dye. The heat of the dryers—the kind that look like helmets and settle over your whole head.

Gram, I'm bored.

Play a game, Miki.

But there's no one to play with. It's boring here. They have no toys.

Make up a game. I remember Gram's smile, patient, loving. She riffled through her purse and took out a little plastic tub of Play-Doh. She always carried toys and games in her purse. I loved that purse; it was like a treasure chest. *Here,* she said, *make little dolls. Create a whole army of Play-Doh dolls.*

Delighted, I did. I created a whole tiny army with round balls for legs and round balls for heads and arms and torsos. The only things that weren't round were their tiny kendo swords. Those I rolled into cylinders, then squished them flat with my thumb.

Why am I thinking about that right now?

Creeping unease makes me shiver, leaves me feeling sick and I don't know why. I look over at the Drau, standing there in their suits . . .

Their suits are creations.

Just like every human in the game is the genetic creation of the Committee. They tinkered with our DNA, added some of their genetic material to ours way back in our family trees. Did they do the same to the Drau? Do they have genes from the Committee, or human genes, or maybe some other alien spliced into their genome?

It's important. I just don't know why. Not yet.

I'm collecting puzzle pieces, so close to the solution.

Again, I glance at the two Drau. They haven't moved, haven't spoken again, but I feel like they're anxious, hanging on my every word, waiting for me to see the big picture.

I look at Jackson, harness crisscrossing his torso and hips, posture rigid and alert. Always alert. Always the soldier the game made him.

He turns to the Drau, frowning. "You said those suits allow them to tolerate this environment."

"That's right," Lizzie says.

"Those suits make them faster than us. Stronger." He steps closer until he's eye to eye with one of the Drau. "So why create human shells if you already have life-sustaining supersuits?"

I take a sharp breath as a piece of the puzzle clicks into place: The perfect genetic mix creates the perfect soldier.

Creates . . . We are all the creations of the Committee, like a bunch of GMO fruits and vegetables, like soybeans or corn, genetically modified to possess qualities not found in nature.

Click. Another piece locks in place.

"Who makes the shells?" I demand. And when Lizzie doesn't answer fast enough, I ask again, louder, "Who makes the shells?"

"You know," she says.

I feel like I've been staring at a book, trying to read the words, and they've been dancing and blurring, hovering just beyond my ability to see. But as I stare at the answers, the letters sharpen and grow clear, every one bold and readable, and I see, really see, what's there.

I just solved the puzzle box.

Sofu would catch me up under my arms and toss me in the air, so proud. Problem is, the solution—the conclusion I've reached—is horrific.

"Oh my God," I whisper, feeling sick, the answer to my own question glaringly bright. "The Committee. The Committee makes the shells, just like they made us. But they didn't want to stop at modifying what already exists. They want to create from scratch. The clones are part of their experiments to create the perfect supersoldier. And they send us in to clean up their messes when their experiments fail."

"Is anything they told us true?" Jackson asks.

"Half-true," Lizzie says. "Twisted for their purposes."

"You aren't some rebel faction rising up against the Drau leaders who want to destroy mankind," Jackson says without inflection, his expression closed. "There are no Drau leaders bent on destroying mankind."

"There never were," Lizzie says.

"There's just the Committee." Jackson clenches and unclenches his fist. "They engineered us through generations purely to play this sick game. *Generations.*"

"They have eternity." Lizzie shrugs. "What are a couple of centuries to them?"

"So the Drau . . . they're just like us." My stomach churns, bile crawling up my throat. I keep talking, very fast. "Pulled against their will, with no clue what the hell is going on? Thrown out there to fight kids . . . Are they kids, too? Drau kids?"

Lizzie nods, lips compressed, brow furrowed.

"It really is a game to the Committee," Jackson says softly.

"A game," I echo, horror a congealed ball in my chest. I back away, shaking my head, not wanting to believe. Memories slap me, of Luka and Tyrone when we were on the elevator mission, of them talking about how the place seemed familiar, like a level from *Resident Evil* or *Half Life*. The Committee must have lifted those images out of Luka's head and created a game environment based on what they took from his thoughts.

"This is all the Committee's version of some twisted RPG," Jackson says, then with a quick look at the Drau, he explains for their benefit. "Role-playing game."

"They're the Dungeon Masters, the game masters," I say.

"And we're the pawns they've been moving around for years," Jackson finishes my thought.

An RPG. *Dungeons and Dragons.* Was Luka trying to tell me something the night he brought dinner over to my place? Was he trying to warn me?

"Tell him he's wrong," I whisper, hunching my

shoulders and wrapping my arms around my waist as I look at Lizzie.

She lifts her hand like she means to touch me, then clenches her fist and drops it back to her side. "I can't. He isn't. But you already know that."

"So we're like gladiators fighting for the entertainment of the masses," Jackson says, his tone flat. "*Fight Club.* Or cock fighting. Or dog fighting. We're the dogs. We fight and die while the Committee watches and cheers."

"Humans aren't the first game pieces they've drafted. They've been doing this for a very long time," Lizzie says. "All across the universe. Across the universes. Plural. They find planets with sentient beings. They seed the population with specific genetic material, specific traits that they want to pit against each other."

"Hold up." Jackson lifts his hand. "How is our DNA, *human* DNA, compatible with theirs? How is my DNA compatible with a Drau's? How the hell did they splice all this together?"

"All DNA has the same basic building blocks," Lizzie says. Her lips curve in a faint smile. "Humans share fifty percent DNA with a banana."

"Okay. I feel special," I mutter.

Lizzie arches a brow. "The genes the Committee seeded confer specific skills . . . the ability to tolerate tele-portation being key. They breed soldiers. Then they play their games, pitting species against species in a war neither can win." She pins Jackson with a clear-eyed stare. "You, me, Miki, Luka, everyone who's ever been recruited . . . we are their Master Chief, their Marcus Fenix, their Captain Price. This is their *Halo*, their *Call of Duty*, their *Bioshock* or *Gears of War*. This is their entertainment."

"You died for their entertainment!" Jackson roars as he jerks a step toward her. "It nearly killed Mom and Dad—" He shakes his head, panting, trying to get himself under some semblance of control. "Luka. Richelle. Amelia. Jerry. Ryan. Dozens of kids I can name just from my team alone in the past five years. What about all the other teams? All the other kids?"

"All the other kids from species across the galaxies. The Committee has been repeating this pattern for eternity."

"I stayed sane by telling myself I was saving the world," Jackson says. And I hear what he doesn't say: How does he reconcile all those dead kids now? I think he hasn't even gotten to the point of thinking about all the Drau he's killed.

I reach for him, but he backs away.

"Miki," he says, my name ripped from him. "I lived with what I did to you by telling myself we could stop the annihilation of mankind." The pain in his eyes is almost more than I can bear. "What do I tell myself now?"

My lips part, but there are no words to offer. I forgive him—he knows that—but he has to find a way to forgive himself.

Lizzie lays her hand on his forearm. He twitches but doesn't pull away.

"There is no war. There is no threat." The words come low, dragged from his soul.

"Oh, there is a very real threat," Lizzie says. "Just not the one you expected." She looks over at her Drau companions and nods. I figure they're talking to her telepathically. "Time to go back," she says to us.

"Back? To get pulled? To go on missions? To fight? I can't," I say in a rush.

"No," Jackson says, expression contemplative, attention focused on Lizzie. "We go back to the lobby, to do exactly what we were planning to do before my sister brought us here. We find a way to get to the other teams. We tell them what we know."

It doesn't escape my notice that he refers to Lizzie as *my sister*. From the shift in her expression, it doesn't escape hers, either. But I suspect that any mention of that will only make him shut down, so I let it go, for now.

"So let's say we're successful, that we share the knowledge," I say. "Tell everyone we can. Team members. Team leaders. Spread the information. Tell them how to use emotion to keep the Committee out. What does that gain us?"

"Numbers," Lizzie says. "We're going to create a revolution, effect change."

"One team at a time? What's stopping the Committee from killing us before we can bring the teams over to our way of thinking?" Jackson asks.

"We don't bring them over one at a time. We convince them as quickly as we can. One after another. The

Committee will be scrambling to catch up, to react. If we can get everyone on both sides to lay down weapons and refuse to fight, the game system will overload. The Committee won't stand a chance."

I think about that for a second. "Start dropping water into a bucket a teaspoon at a time, and you won't see much. But if everyone drops in a teaspoon at the same time, everyone does their little part, then next thing you know, the bucket's full. I get that. What I don't get is how that helps us. The Committee keeps themselves segregated from the players. It's like they're behind a protective wall. Even if we overload the game system, how do we get at the Committee?"

"They rely on technology and keep themselves at a distance. They're used to acting as puppet masters, not getting their hands dirty," Lizzie says. "And getting at them has posed a challenge. One we believe we've overcome. We're going to upload alterations to their GUI."

I glance at Jackson to see if he knows what she's talking about.

"Graphical user interface," he says. "It allows the gamer to interact with the game."

"So . . . mess with it and they can't play?"

"That's the idea."

"Will it work?" I ask.

"There's only one way to find out," Lizzie says.

"You're planning to use the teams' refusals to play as

a distraction," Jackson says. "Keep the Committee busy while you hack the system and take down the wall they hide behind, the one separating them from us."

Lizzie grins at him. "It's going to happen fast and hard. You need to convert as many players as fast as you can. We'll work on it from our end."

"Converting the Drau teams."

"Of course. This won't work if only one side's on board. Plus, we'll be working at masking you from the Committee. It won't be foolproof. They'll know what you're up to. But we can protect you to some extent."

"If the Drau technology is so advanced," I say, "why don't they just use it to take out the Committee? Why did they ever participate in the game in the first place?"

"Compared to us, they're advanced. Think of it like this: compared to the Drau, humans are pretty much amoebas on the technology scale. And compared to the Committee? The Drau are snails." She tips her head, and again I have the impression her Drau companions are speaking with her.

"It's time." She hugs me tight, then draws back, her hands resting on my shoulders. "Work fast," she says. "There will be only so much I can do to keep you safe, and the Committee will be working to take you down. I don't know exactly what will happen once I'm in, how fast the walls they've created will come down or what will happen inside the game when they do. Be ready for anything."

She turns to Jackson. The air around them crackles with tension. Slowly, she lifts her arms, takes a step toward him.

He doesn't move, doesn't even blink.

"Jax," she says and closes the last of the distance.

He stands rigid as she embraces him, his expression set. Only as the floor spins away and the burning white glare of the walls grows unbearably bright does he take the leap of trust, and I hear him whisper, "Lizzie."

CHAPTER **TWENTY-SEVEN**

WE RESPAWN BACK IN THE LOBBY; OTHER KIDS MOVE THROUGH their mirror lobbies in the periphery of my vision. The team leader I was watching just before Lizzie pulled us stands with hands on hips, her face turned toward us.

"She's first," Jackson says. "She's alone. We'd only have to sway one person's opinion rather than a whole group. And from the way she's been watching you watching her, I'd say she's interested in talking."

"They'll kill us," I whisper. "You know that, right? If the Committee hasn't figured out that something's going on, they will soon. And they'll kill us, like they killed Luka."

Just saying his name brings a crushing wave of sadness and loss. I don't fight it; I let the icy sensation crash through me, over me. Then I float to the surface, riding the wave until I can breathe again. Jackson pulls me against him, and I loop my arms around his waist, letting myself hold tight, letting the solid strength of him anchor me.

He tugs lightly on my ponytail. "They'll *try* to kill us. That doesn't mean they'll succeed. Lizzie's keeping an eye on us," he says, his voice rough, telling me he, too, is reeling from losing Luka. "She hasn't let them kill us yet."

"True, but she can't watch us every second. Which is why I should do this alone. They won't go after you if you aren't part of it—" I say at the same time he says, "And that's why you are going to stay right here while I cross into the other lobbies. I take the risk. The Committee won't go after you if you don't participate."

With typical Jackson arrogance, he flashes a grin. "Great minds think alike . . ."

"And fools seldom differ," I finish for him.

His brows shoot up. "Is that the other half of that quote?"

"That's the way Gram always said it." I take a breath and step back, his hands sliding along my waist, reluctant to let me go. "I'm afraid to do this," I say, and when he opens his mouth to tell me again that he'll do it alone, I rest my fingers against his lips. "But I'm more afraid not to."

He laces his fingers with mine and together we start for the edge of the clearing and the team leader I saw standing alone in the mirror lobby. She sees us moving toward her and she walks closer to the edge of her lobby, watching us, waiting, her expression tense.

I drop Jackson's hand and run full tilt at the trees. For a second, it's just me, the slap of my feet on the ground, the rhythm of my stride, familiar, comforting. Then he's there beside me, long legs eating the distance as we sprint, side by side.

I don't know what to expect. Mostly, I think I'm going to slam up against an invisible wall and bounce back on my ass. But I don't. I pass through the barrier, stumbling out the other side. Maybe it's the force of our will that carries us through, or maybe this is the first sign of the success of Lizzie's überhacking skills. Either way, it hurts like hell, my skin burning like I've been stung by a thousand hornets, my stomach heaving.

Doubled over, hands on my thighs, head down, I take a couple of breaths, trying to master the nausea and pain. From the corner of my eye, I catch sight of Jackson. He's still upright, but his lips are pulled taut and his face is pale.

"Well, that was fun," he says as I straighten up, his voice like gravel.

The team leader walks over, staying well outside our reach. Her lobby is larger than ours, and lacks boulders. It's just a flat, grassy oval surrounded by trees.

"Incoming?" she asks, studying us like we're a couple of alien specimens, hand hovering above her weapon cylinder. Can't say I blame her. If she'd just popped into our lobby, I'd probably feel pretty wary, too.

"Not exactly. More like party crashing," I say. "I'm Miki. This is Jackson. We're team leaders, like you."

She shakes her head. "Not possible. I've seen you on the same team. Both of you in that lobby." She juts her chin to the left. "There's only one leader to a team."

"Our team's a little different," I say. "It's complicated."

Her eyes narrow. "Why are you here?"

"We, uh . . ." I look at Jackson for help.

"We come in peace," he says, lips curving in his trademark cocky smile. Way to win friends and influence people.

"That was eloquent." I roll my eyes and he laughs and somehow that's enough to make the team leader drop her guard a little. "I'm Tara," she says. "How did you get here? What are you doing here?"

"We're here to talk. There are things you need to know. Things about the game."

"Okaaaaaay." Her gaze jumps between the two of us, her hand still uncomfortably close to the hilt of her weapon.

"How long have you been in?" Jackson asks.

"Eighteen months." There's a hint of pride in her tone. It hurts to know we're the ones who will strip that pride away, divest her of the comfort of believing everything she's been forced to do is for the good of mankind.

"Guess you've seen a lot of things you never thought possible in those eighteen months," Jackson says.

She laughs, the sound rusty and dry. "You could say that. What about you? How long have you been in?"

"Five years."

She gasps. "But, that means you would have been—"

"Twelve, first time I got pulled. I've been killing Drau

for five years and that's important for you to know because what we're about to tell you is going to be hard to swallow, and I need you to understand that it was hard for me, too."

He tips his head at me and I start to talk, telling her everything Lizzie told us in concise terms. Tara doesn't believe us. Not at first. But I ask her questions and use her answers to guide me to new questions. I push her, make her think, make her draw her own conclusions. I stumble a few times, then finally get the groove, trying to judge from her expression how hard to hit, how deep to go, trying to copy the technique Lizzie used to help us reach the conclusions we did.

I get it now, why Lizzie made Jackson and I figure everything out for ourselves, nudging us in the right direction rather than just saying it plain and simple. Tell someone a truth that seems impossible, and she probably won't believe it. She's more likely to shut you down than climb on the bandwagon. But give her the tools to reach the conclusions on her own, to make decisions based on experience, let logic win the argument, and the truth speaks for itself.

That's what Lizzie did.

That's what Jackson and I do, and as Tara answers my questions, dragging out memories that don't quite paint the Committee in a rosy light, her posture changes, her expression alters, flitting from worried to afraid to angry.

"Have you ever met with the Committee?" Jackson asks, his voice low.

I glance around, wondering if they're listening to us right now. Wondering when they're going to intervene.

"Once," Tara says with a shudder. "Mostly they just talk to me on missions. Inside my head, you know?" I nod, and she keeps going. "But this once, something happened and they brought me there, to that place . . ."

"The amphitheater?" I ask.

She nods. "With all the silent, faceless things watching."

"Why did they want to see you in person?" Jackson asks.

"To reassure me, they said. But I felt more like I was on trial, like something bad would happen if I didn't give the right answers."

"What did they need to reassure you about?"

"There was this girl on my team. She got cut off from the rest of us. When we found her she was hysterical. Sobbing. She kept saying the Drau saved her and she wasn't going to shoot them anymore. That they weren't all bad and that maybe we should try to negotiate with them."

"You think she encountered Lizzie's team?" I ask Jackson.

"Could be. Or maybe just a group of Drau who couldn't bring themselves to kill a lone kid. What happened to that girl?"

Tara stares off at the trees. "She died on the next mission. My first loss as team leader. She was fifteen." She sighs. "It didn't make sense. We were done. We were supposed to jump in thirty. I could swear her con was yellow. Then she goes all sweaty and starts to moan and I check her con. Suddenly it's red. And she died, right there in my arms." She pauses and then whispers, "I hated them for that."

I wonder if the *them* she's referring to are the Drau or the Committee.

She jerks and lifts her head like she's just remembered we're there, or just remembered that we're strangers to her. Her expression closes. "I don't know why I told you that."

"Because your own evidence supports what we're telling you. And because we get it," Jackson says. "Like no one else ever can. I held my sister while her con went red."

Tara's lips part and she stares at him in horror. At first, I think it's because of what he's just said, but there's something in her expression, something . . . distant. Like her attention's split between us and—

The Committee's talking to her. Right now. Probably telling her to take us out. Jackson's voice, inside my head.

Her hand slides to her weapon cylinder.

I reach back between my shoulder blades and grasp the hilt of my sword. I won't kill her. But I'm skilled enough to know how to temporarily disable an attacker, nullify the threat.

Her weapon cylinder's half out of the sheath now, her hand shaking, sweat beading on her upper lip, her eyes wide with fear. "What do I do?" Tara chokes out, the words forced from between her lips. They're pushing her and she's pushing back.

"Fight them," Jackson says. "Pick an emotion. One emotion. Focus on it. Let it fill you. Think of that girl, the one who died. Think how it made you feel. Focus on that. Only that. The sight of her con. The sight of her blood. The way her eyes closed on her final breath. Think of her. Only her."

Tara cries out, covering her face with her hands as she sinks to her knees. Jackson grabs her elbow and guides her down.

Her head snaps up. She jerks away, her hand closing on her weapon cylinder, drawing it halfway from its holster.

I slide my sword up, almost free of the sheath.

Jackson holds out his hand to me, palm forward, telling me to wait . . . wait . . .

Tara's whole body shakes, shoulders hunched, as she drags her hand from the hilt of her weapon. Her breathing's ragged. Her fingers curl like talons, as if one part of her is trying to make a fist while another part is trying to straighten her fingers.

I wait, poised to disarm her, when she slumps forward all the way, then tips over to one side, her eyes rolling up in her head.

"Tara!" I drop to my knees beside her, one hand on her back, the other pulling her cylinder. I toss it to Jackson, out of harm's way. Just because she defied the Committee for a moment doesn't mean she'll be able to do it long term.

After a few seconds, she lifts her head and then lifts

her brows as she sees Jackson holding her cylinder, muzzle toward the ground.

"Thanks for the concern." There's no missing the sarcasm.

"I'm concerned," I say. "I'm also careful."

She gives a shaky laugh. "I did what you said. I thought about the girl who died. I felt . . . so sad." She shakes her head. "But I didn't think it would work. They're so . . ." She closes her eyes tight, her lips compressed. "I almost shot you both. It was just that close. They were so strong. I didn't think I had a choice."

"You always have a choice," Jackson says, sounding like he means it.

"This is a nightmare," Tara says.

"Steer the nightmare," I say, my eyes on Jackson. "Grab hold and steer it where you want it to go. You can't escape it, but you can push it in a different direction."

She coils up to a sitting position, pressing the back of her wrist to her temple. "Good advice."

"Isn't it?" I ask with another glance at Jackson. "Someone smart told me that."

Jackson lifts a brow and offers me his hand, hauling me to my feet. Then he helps Tara up.

From the corner of my eye, I can see other teams moving around in neighboring clearings.

"Incoming," Tara says.

"We need to go," Jackson says.

"I know."

"So what am I supposed to do with all this information?" she asks, her words short and clipped. "Is knowing what they really are"—she waves a hand at the trees—"what all this really is going to stop us from getting pulled? Is it going to change whether or not we go on missions? Is it going to stop the Drau from killing us?"

"We have an alliance with a group who can tell the Drau teams the same things we're telling you," I say.

"Share the information. There's power in unity, all of us working together. We all lay down our weapons at the same time, resist the Committee together, and we have the power of our numbers to combat their strength," Jackson says. Funny how far he's come from being an every-man-for-himself kind of guy. "And be ready. I don't know exactly when the walls will come down, but when they do, it's going to be hard and fast. And unpredictable."

Tara snorts. "Thanks for the reassurance."

"That's Jackson. A real people person and font of comfort."

She laughs, the sound shaky and forced. Then she asks, "What are the walls you're talking about? What happens when they come down?"

Those are questions I can't answer, but I figure telling her that won't help our cause, so I say, "The Committee protects themselves behind a wall of anonymity and technology. Our—" I pause, not sure what to call Lizzie and her Drau team.

"Our allies," Jackson says, picking up where I left off, "have the technology to combat the Committee. The walls are artificial constructs that define the game. We need to destroy them. Force the Committee out of hiding."

"Look. Tara, if we all band together, if we make sure everyone knows the truth, once enough people know, we can organize, unite, fight the Committee. We just have to get the information out there," I say. "We have to start somewhere."

She looks green, like she's going to throw up. "Really? And once the information's out there, what changes? What really changes?"

"We figure out ways to start saying no to them," I say.

"But in the meantime, we still get pulled, we still go in to fight and kill. Be killed. How long until it all ends?" Her shoulders sag. "It was hard enough to do this when I thought I was saving the world. How am I supposed to do it now that it means nothing?"

"What you're doing does mean something," I say. "You're still fighting for a reason. A good reason. It's just the enemy that's changed."

"All those kids who've died . . ."

"Can't be brought back. But we can save the ones who've yet to be pulled. And we can put a stop to the Committee. It's just a matter of time," Jackson says, calm and sure, like there's no question about the outcome.

Jackson is the soldier the game's trained him to be, his thoughts working with military precision. He's committed to the new mission, to Lizzie's plan. He believes it will succeed. He allows himself no doubts.

I want to be that sure. But according to Lizzie, the Committee has been doing this for millennia, pitting species against species across galaxies and universes, all for their entertainment.

The best I can manage is guardedly hopeful.

CHAPTER TWENTY-EIGHT

WITH LIZZIE AND HER DRAU TEAM WORKING FROM THEIR END
to hold the Committee off, Jackson and I run through the
barriers between lobbies dozens of times, speak with dozens of teams. In real-world time, we must have been at this
for days. Every time my mind wanders to Dad and Carly,
or Luka, I wrench my thoughts back to the moment, this
moment. Because this is the moment I'm living in, the only
one that matters. All my worrying won't change a thing.
And every time I let myself start thinking about them, let
my focus shift, I can feel my control slipping away.

Some lobbies have whole teams standing in front of
score screens. Others have just a few players. Some have
only a lone team leader, like Tara. They all turn and stare
at us as we suddenly materialize on their turf, breaking

through a boundary they've either never tested or never succeeded in passing.

It isn't easy to convince them all. Some groups take more effort than others, and some listen but don't buy what we're selling. We ask that they keep an open mind, consider the possibilities, and then we move on. Once we've exhausted our arguments, there's no point in wasting our breath.

One guy's such a total asshole that no matter what we say, he won't listen. He challenges Jackson, getting in his space, in his face. He puts both hands on Jackson's chest and shoves.

Jackson holds his arms wide, refusing to fight, and keeps talking, talking, calm and steady, trying to get the guy to just listen.

I'm about to step in when the guy disappears, just vanishes mid-sentence. Jackson gets this amused look on his face, teeth flashing in a dark grin.

"What?" I ask.

"Guess Lizzie figured that he might believe her team over us. I suspect it'll be the Drau that greet him." His brows rise above the frames of his glasses. "Wish I could be there to see it."

The leap to the next lobby is worse than any of the others have been. The hornet-sting sensation on my skin makes me feel like I'm on one of those beds made of nails, the kind you're supposed to lie on and the nails don't break skin. But I feel like they're doing more than breaking my skin—they're digging deep, gouging clear through to my bones. We fall into a clearing that flickers and sparks with static electricity. I stare at the treetops and breathe, just breathe, trying to master the pain. And as I stare, my vision wavers and distorts and I realize it isn't me, it's what I'm looking at. The trees, the grass . . . they swell, then shrink, undulating like flames. Then the lobby disappears, just flickers out, a match snuffed.

I stand in darkness so complete that it has texture and substance. No light. No sound except the harsh rasp of my own breathing. Tiny knives carve strips from me, and I scream, running my palms over my arms, my legs.

Snap. The lobby's back, the team turning to face us, my palms damp as I rub them against my jeans.

"Okay?" Jackson asks softly.

"Not so much. That was bad."

"Worst yet," he agrees.

But we don't get to dissect what it means because the team leader's striding toward us. Jackson starts talking, telling the kids who stand watching us with wary interest who we are, why we're here. We've perfected the routine now, and when he falls silent I jump in. Tag team.

This group's easy. It's a fairly new team and they lost three members on the last mission alone. They're scared, their confidence worn, and they're definitely open to what we have to say.

We keep moving, keep meeting new teams, keep talking. Running through the barrier is easy sometimes; others it's a repeat of the less-than-pleasant experience that left my heart racing and my palms wet. And sometimes it's something in between, the edges of the lobby we land in flickering and fraying, like the very texture of this world is coming apart at the seams.

"Is it Lizzie?" I ask when we stumble into an empty lobby. Nothing here but grass, trees and sky that pixelate and pop. "Is it starting?"

"That'd be my guess," Jackson says.

I stare up at the sky. Big sky, blue and cloudless. "Why hasn't the Committee stopped us? Why are they letting us get away with this?"

"They aren't. I figure they're trying to intervene and that's what's causing some of the jumps to be so brutal. Lizzie keeping them busy or somehow blocking them from getting to us might be all that's protecting us."

"Or they find our pathetic attempt at rebellion amusing and they'll step in when we bore them—"

Jackson hooks a finger in my belt loop and pulls me close. "What happened to the optimist panties?" He turns me to face him and slides his fingers into my back pockets. "Should I check if they're intact?"

"Seriously?" I ask, throwing up my hands. "Seriously? The Committee could obliterate us at any second and you want to canoodle?"

"Canoodle?" He laughs. "I'm in."

I can't help but smile. "You are such a guy."

"That I am." He shrugs. "Red-blooded male. Gorgeous, brilliant, brave girl. It's a combustible combination. Besides, no one's going to hand us precious moments just for us. We have to seize them."

"Like spoils?"

A flash of white teeth. "Just like."

He dips his head and kisses me, his lips smooth and firm. I come up on my toes, molding my body to his. I love the way he feels against me, solid and strong. I love the way he holds me, like he isn't afraid I'll break. I love the way he smiles a little when we kiss, the way we bump noses, the way his fingers push deeper into my back pockets.

"I love you," he whispers.

"Why?" I whisper back.

He shakes his head and laughs. "Because you're the girl who asks me why instead of just saying *I love you* back." He tips his glasses up, his voice lowering, growing soft as he continues, "Because you win and lose every day while you battle the pain and panic inside you, and you never say die. You come back stronger every time." He kisses the tip of my nose. "Because you told Carly the truth about her belly-up fish instead of taking the easy way out and buying her a new one." He kisses my right cheek. "Because you climbed the tree in my backyard when I didn't answer the door." He kisses my left cheek. "Because you force me to be my best version of me. You won't accept anything less." He leans in until our lips are a breath apart. "You make me want to be the person I want to be."

My heart does a trippy little dance. "Does that last sentence make sense?"

"It does to me."

And then he lowers his mouth to mine and kisses me again, lips and tongue and teeth, his hands splayed across my lower back, my fingers twining in his hair, my pulse racing in the best possible way.

He's right. We deserve this moment, and the only way we get to have it is if we take it.

We step through into another empty lobby and alarm bells start clanging at the base of my skull. There was a team here. I saw them. But they aren't here now, and there's no way they had enough time to make the jump. I would have seen them disappear.

"This is wrong," I say, spinning to face Jackson. The grass beneath our feet is patchy and brown, so dry it crunches and breaks under my soles. The trees that bound us are stark gray, bare branched. Not winter gray with the promise of rebirth in the spring. Dark gray, almost black. Brittle, like the slightest touch will make them turn to ash.

Dead.

"We need to go. Now." Jackson grabs my hand and pulls me back toward the trees.

We both skid to a stop, just inches away from hitting

the forest as the weave of this reality unravels, revealing patches of endless dark. Cold. Infinite. The darkness a physical entity, thick and choking.

I shudder, backing up a step, and then another.

"This way," Jackson says with a tug on my hand.

We run in the opposite direction, my heart pounding, fear driving me. Whatever time Lizzie's managed to buy for us, the sand's run out. Maybe she's hacked the system and everything's coming apart. Maybe the Committee's found us, or they've just gotten tired of humoring our little rebellion. The why doesn't matter. What matters are the stakes.

We cross the clearing and are about to fling ourselves at the forest when the two sides of the boundary pull apart, like tearing a piece of cloth in two, revealing the limitless darkness behind.

Darkness—the word doesn't capture the reality of it. It's . . . nothingness. Just . . . nothing.

Jackson skids to a stop and jerks me back just in time, his reflexes a shade faster than mine.

Panting, I turn a full circle, watching the forest all around us unravel.

I pull my kendo sword and weapon cylinder as Jackson pulls his own cylinder and his knife. We move to stand back to back in a well-practiced dance, though I can't think what value these weapons will bear against the unraveling of the universe.

Terror grips me, not just because I don't want to end

here in this place, my death marking no extra meaning to my life. It's because we have so much to do. It can't end this way. We can't fail like this. The Committee can't be left to destroy lives for millennia. For infinity, if everything Lizzie said is true.

Back to back, weapons at the ready, Jackson and I turn and turn, watching the world around us come completely apart.

The edges of the lobby inch toward us, the darkness creeping ever closer. The desolation of the void touches my skin, like spiderwebs on my arms, my neck, my lips.

"To your right," Jackson says. "See it?"

I do. From the corner of my eye, I catch movement. People. Branches heavy with leaves. Green grass. Blue sky. I jerk my head to the side, trying to get a better look, and see only the darkness. Inky darkness, like the oily sludge that shoots from our weapon cylinders to swallow the Drau whole.

"Don't look. Just run," Jackson says, grabbing hold of my hand. "Now!"

I duck my head and stare at my feet as I run full tilt for where I thought I saw a lobby, all the while hoping that Lizzie's watching and if Jackson and I are about to leap to our deaths, she'll grab us somewhere before the point of no return.

I glance back. Once. Behind me, the lobby we inhabit disappears, trees and ground and sky caving in on itself, imploding, the spot where we stood swallowed by a surge of darkness.

Jackson shoves the middle of my back. I go flying forward, arms outstretched, and I feel myself breach the barrier, feel it tear away. The sensation of being stung by a thousand scorpions eats my hands, my arms, my face, my torso. I scream and fall face-first, slamming hard on the ground.

I lie there, facedown, panting, waiting for the sensation that my skin's on fire to subside. It hits me that my cheek is pressed to grass. I curl my fingers, grabbing two hefty clumps, and lift my head to see a half dozen kids staring down at me. It takes me a second to realize they're faces I've seen before, a group we already approached. One of the boys walks over and hunkers down beside me.

"You okay?" he asks.

"She's peachy keen. Come on, Miki. Up you go."

"Lien!" I roll onto my back to see her standing over me, hand outstretched. I grab it and she pulls me to my feet.

I'm so happy to see her I throw my arms around her and hug her tight. She pats me awkwardly on the shoulder, then finally caves and hugs me back. When I let her go, I turn, looking for Jackson, panicking when I don't see him. I spin back, mouth dry, pulse slamming like a piston, and find him standing behind Lien.

"Hey," he says.

"Way to scare the crap out of me."

"What fun is it if I don't keep you on your toes?"

I turn back to Lien. "What are you doing here? Where's Kendra? Tyrone?"

Lien's not the most demonstrative girl I've ever met, but there's no mistaking the worry that hardens her expression. "I got pulled and arrived here about a minute ago. I haven't seen Kendra or Tyrone or Luka."

My chest locks down like someone suctioned the breath out of me.

She stares at me and her eyes slowly widen. "No," she whispers, shaking her head. Her hands come up like she's warding off a blow. "No." The word explodes out of her. Her fingers curl into fists, and she looks around, frantic, searching for something to hit. Jackson grabs her and pulls her against his chest, his arms coming around her as she says Luka's name, a pitiful wail. It reaches inside me and twists around like a knife shredding my guts. I swallow convulsively, choking back the urge to puke on the grass at my feet.

Her grief scrapes away the too-thin scab over my own.

Jackson speaks softly against her ear. I can't hear what he says, but I imagine words of comfort. At least, as comforting as he can manage. He isn't exactly the fuzzy, warm type, but then neither is Lien. So maybe they get each other. Whatever he says, she nods and uses the hem of her hoodie to rub the tears from her eyes, and when she steps away from him, her jaw's set, expression hard, even if her eyes and nose are red.

The team leader we spoke with last time we were in this lobby stares at us, eyes narrowed. It hits me that he isn't staring *at* us, but rather, *behind* us.

"What's that?" he asks as I turn to see what it is that's grabbed his attention.

The edges of the trees waver and fade, then pop back into clear relief. The darkness that swallowed the lobby we escaped has followed us here.

"Run for the trees, there," Jackson orders, pointing to the opposite end of the lobby. "Don't think. Don't stop. Close your eyes if you have to. You'll feel a stinging sensation. Push through and you'll be fine."

There are murmurs from the group, and all I can think is that I'm glad they aren't kids we've never seen before, kids we have to convince from scratch. At least Jackson and I have already been through here. These kids accepted us after a bit of persuasion. I'm hoping and praying they'll listen now.

"What's happening?" a boy asks.

"The game's unraveling," Jackson says. "Now move!"

"Listen to him," Lien says over the rising murmurs, then louder, "Do what he says." When no one moves, she throws up her hands, mutters, "Whatever," and runs for the spot Jackson indicated. There's complete silence after she disappears into the trees.

"Go," Jackson barks.

They go, following Lien's lead.

In moments, we're all in a neighboring lobby, the team

that's already there startled by our arrival. Again, it's a group we already met.

"We're being herded," I say to Jackson as we hang back, waiting as the others run through into the next lobby, following Jackson's instructions.

"The question is, by Lizzie or the Committee?"

I look back at the far end of the clearing, the trees turning charcoal gray as they fold in on themselves, the sky falling, the ground curling like charred paper. "Right now, I'm not sure it matters."

We follow the last of the teams into the next lobby, and the next. I lose count of how many times we run for the trees, collecting people as we go. Right now we're in a lobby with at least a dozen teams standing in small clumps, eyeing one another warily. The edges are already fraying, coming apart to reveal not grass and trees, but the all-consuming darkness. It's as if the lobbies are illusions projected on an obsidian screen.

The next jump is worse, leaving me feeling sick, bones aching, stomach churning, my skin prickling like I'm covered in a layer of fire ants. At the edges of my vision, the lobby breaks down even more.

Beside me, Jackson tenses, his head tipped to the side. "Don't look head on," he says.

I stare at a spot in the distance, letting my vision grow unfocused, concentrating not on what's before me, but what's off to the sides. I see them, tiers of seats and the shadowy forms that fill them.

The Committee.

"We're in the amphitheater," I say.

"That we are. And my guess is the lobbies have been here all along, artificially created zones, like holograms," Jackson says.

I spin and spin again, watching the walls crumble, watching the Committee's deception fall away.

CHAPTER**TWENTY-NINE**

THE EDGES OF THE CLEARING BLACKEN AND CURL LIKE BURN-ing parchment, revealing more and more of the amphitheater, tiers of seats rising all around us, disappearing into darkness. Every seat is occupied by a humanoid figure cloaked in drapes of cloth, their faces hidden.

Kids from the other teams startle and spin as they become aware of the lobby boundaries failing and the hidden world behind the walls. Most of them are seeing this place for the very first time. This isn't my first exposure to the Committee's abode, but even for me, the sight is chilling.

As I take in the shifting throng of bodies before me, I'm stunned by the sheer size of the amphitheater. It's at least as long as two football fields, end to end, packed with bodies.

Was it always this big, or is the Committee still manipulating my perceptions?

I scan the faces near me, trying to catch sight of the rest of my team. "Can you see Tyrone? Or Lien or Kendra?" Even a glimpse would reassure me.

"No," Jackson says. "I think I saw Tara there"—he points—"a second ago, but there's no sign of her now."

The space around us condenses, bodies packing tighter, and I realize it isn't that space is getting smaller, but that more people are being pulled in.

"It's like the Committee's respawning every team, all at once," I say as Jackson grabs my hand and starts forward, shouldering his way through the crowd, towing me in his wake. I don't put up a fight. Times like this, size and attitude make a great combination.

"Yeah, and I suspect the crowd's only going to get thicker," he says over his shoulder, pitching his voice to carry over the growing din.

I look around, trying to figure out where he's leading me. The walls rising from the floor of the amphitheater are at least twenty feet high—were they always that high?—surrounding us like a cage. A prison. No way to climb out. As the crowd grows thicker, groups melding into one another, the space fills until all around me is a sea of bodies. I can no longer see any hint of the remnants of the lobbies; there's just the amphitheater all around us, and the shadowy figures leaning forward in their seats. Watching. Waiting.

Someone grabs my belt loop. I glance back, yanking Jackson to a stop as I do.

"Tyrone!" He leans in and we give each other awkward one-armed hugs as we're jostled by the crowd. When he pulls back, he searches my face, expression somber. He knows about Luka. I can tell. Still, I try to find the right words to confirm what he clearly already suspects, but he shakes his head and says, "Later. He deserves more than a second of silence in a crowd."

Tears prick my lids, but I blink them back and nod. He's right. What Luka deserves is for us to win, to somehow overcome the Committee, to make certain no more kids die for their amusement.

"Lien?" Tyrone asks.

"We saw her in a lobby with another team, then we lost her, but she's here somewhere," Jackson says.

Tyrone's shoulders relax a little. "So she got pulled to another team? So did I, but I have no clue where they are now. Have you seen Kendra?"

Jackson shakes his head. "Not yet."

"I like the way you added 'yet.'" Tyrone offers a small smile. "Leaning toward the sunny side, Jackson?"

"Eternal optimist. Learning from Miki."

Tyrone snorts. "You know what the hell's going on? Why we're all here?"

I fill him in, telling him about Lizzie, the Drau, the Committee's true motivations, keeping my explanation brief. Tyrone looks like he just took an elbow hard to the gut.

"So . . . Lizzie . . . she's the one who made the lobbies fail? Brought us all here?" he asks.

"She and her team took down the wall," Jackson says. "But I think it's the Committee who are pulling all the teams here."

Why? What's their plan? The unasked questions hang between us.

"So what's *our* plan?" Tyrone asks.

"We're aiming for that end of the amphitheater." Jackson points.

"Why that end?" Tyrone asks.

"It's closer than the other end."

Tyrone shakes his head. "Lead on."

Our progress is slow, Jackson holding tight to my hand, Tyrone keeping his finger hooked in my belt loop.

"Tug any harder and my pants are going to come down," I say over my shoulder.

He waggles his brows. "I wouldn't mind seeing that view."

"Not if you want to keep your eyes in your head," Jackson says, pushing through the crowd.

I roll my eyes. "Even in the midst of all this, you're a cocky ass."

"Ouch," Tyrone says at the same time Jackson says, "Always."

I'm struck by how calm we are. Our world's been shaken, but we're holding up against the quake. We're the buildings that sway, not the ones that collapse.

Tyrone and Jackson are shoulder to shoulder in front of me now, using their size and determination to clear a path. I hang close behind them, fingers knotted in the backs of their shirts. No way I plan on losing them. We're a team. We stay together. The three of us make slow progress through the ever-enlarging crowd.

We're almost at the far end of the amphitheater when I hear a scream coming from behind me. I look back but see nothing through the throng of bodies. An unnatural stillness falls over the crowd, silence hanging thick and heavy until someone cries out again. It's like the cue for pandemonium. Noise erupts and the crowd shifts, becoming restless.

Jackson grabs my wrist and drags me the rest of the way until we stand against the high wall, looking up.

"I need to know what's going on," he says. "Get on my shoulders." He crouches beside me. Catching on, I clamber up and he straightens, giving me a better view above the heads.

I see clumps of kids pushing each other. "There's something going on at the far end. I can't see—"

"Stand," he orders and grabs both my hands.

I push down as he pushes up, giving me leverage to get my feet on his shoulders and get myself upright so I have a clear view. And what I see chills me to the core.

Drau light, darting through the crowd.

"Drau," I call down to Jackson.

"How many?" Tyrone asks.

Groups of kids move to the right, the left, the trajectory of the Drau guiding the direction of the crowd's movements. The Drau aren't all in one place. They're scattered between the teams.

"I can't tell how many. They aren't all in one place." I glance down. "My gut's telling me the Committee brought them here, not Lizzie and her team." Which doesn't bode well for anyone trapped in this place.

Kids edge against the wall, pushing, stumbling, fear etched on their faces. Dark surges of greasy black ooze erupt from a handful of weapon cylinders. Voices rise, people yelling, shoving. Anxiety passes through the crowd like a wave, everyone trying to get away, get to safety.

Jackson stands solid against the surge of bodies, Tyrone bracing him, the wall at their backs.

"We need a better vantage point." Jackson bends and I slide down from his shoulders. He straightens, runs his hands along the smooth surface of the wall and shakes his head.

"There," Tyrone says and shoves his way through a group of kids, following the curve of the wall. I'm not sure what he's seeing, but after a few seconds Jackson says, "Perfect," and picks up the pace, shouldering kids aside as we go.

The temperament of the crowd shifts from restless

to frantic. Someone slams my shoulder as they run past, nearly spinning me clear around. Tyrone steadies me and positions himself as a barrier between me and the shifting throng. Our progress slows as we fight against the growing tide. I figure we're a breath away from chaos.

Jackson stops and gestures at the wall. "Handholds. Let's go."

I squint and see a series of niches in the wall. Decorative? Functional? I guess it doesn't matter.

"Up," Jackson says.

I tip my head back. Twenty feet with only the handholds. No safety net. No rope. No time to hesitate. I shove my toe in the lowest niche, reach up for the highest one I can get to and start to climb. Tyrone starts up behind me, with Jackson climbing last.

We clamber up the wall, legs and arms at awkward angles. My fingers ache and cramp. Panting, I pause at the top, mustering the strength to haul myself over the edge, then I push on, shoulders screaming, toes cramping, until I roll over the upper limit of the wall and fall at the feet of the faceless soundless watchers in the stands.

I freeze, lying on my back, staring up at them. Tentative, I reach out and drag my hand sideways through the hems of their robes.

My hand passes right through them.

"They aren't real," I cry, rage streaking through me as I get to my feet.

"They're real," Jackson says, rolling over the top of the

wall. "They just aren't physically here. They're in a different plane, sitting there, watching." He surges to his feet. His head rocks back and his arms come up to the sides. "Having fun?" he yells. "Enjoying the show?"

There is no answer. I don't think he expected there would be.

Below us, the crowd shifts and flows like an angry ocean. Flashes of light dart between groups of armed kids who fire on them, the oily threat of oblivion belching from their weapons. The Drau fire back, and kids cry out in agony as the light sears them. Did no one down there—Drau or human—get the memo on cooperation?

The cloaked figures behind me just sit there watching.

"So we're here," Tyrone says, raising his voice to be heard. "Now what?"

Jackson looks out over the crowd. There are more Drau out there now. I have a feeling they're going to keep coming, that the Committee will drop in as many teams as they can ram into the space and let us kill each other in a mass frenzy. I feel sick at the thought. I wonder that Lizzie and her team didn't anticipate this. Or maybe they did and they counted it as acceptable loss. Sacrifice a battle to win the war.

"Kendra!" Tyrone says, and points.

I look down, following his direction, and I see her, expression set, weapon cylinder held double fisted. But she isn't shooting. She's . . . guarding. There are two kids cowering behind her. They look like they can't be more than twelve or thirteen, new to the game would be my guess given their wide-eyed expressions of utter terror. Feet planted shoulder-width apart, Kendra stands between them and the panic-driven surge of the crowd, a tiny, brave sentinel.

It's almost like she feels me watching her because for a second, she looks up, sees us, and smiles. I mouth Lien's name and do a double thumb's-up, just in case Kendra hasn't seen her yet. Her smile widens. Then she goes back to guard duty.

"Looks like Kendra grew a pair," Tyrone says, his tone tinged with both pride and affection.

Directly below us, three kids take out a terrified Drau that tries to escape their weapons.

"We need to stop them," Jackson says.

"How?" Tyrone asks. "Yell at them to stop? They won't hear you, never mind listen. I can barely hear you and I'm standing right next to you while you yell at the top of your lungs."

He's right. But we need to do something. We need to make them listen. How? How to get them to listen when beings they've been trained to view as the enemy dart through their midst?

If I could just talk inside their heads—

With a gasp, I whirl to face Jackson. "You've always been able to talk inside my head. Can you do that to them? Can you push your thoughts out there into all their heads?"

One side of his mouth quirks in a smile. "Let's find out." He vaults onto the top of the wall and takes a deep breath, his head tipping back, his arms loose at his side, palms forward.

Miki? I hear him inside my head.

Words pour from Jackson's thoughts into mine, images, ideas, strong and loud. I watch the crowd, willing them to hear. But they don't. Or if they do, it's like the faintest whisper, the buzz of a fly that they swat away.

"Amp it up," I yell at Jackson.

His shoulders sag. I wonder what toll this is taking on him. Then he straightens and rolls his head to the right, the left, before sending out another blast, stronger, wider. A few people stop and look around, a hasty glance over a shoulder, a quick turn to look behind. They hear him, but they don't believe.

It isn't working.

It's one thing to talk inside my head, another to reach out to a thousand people or more.

I move to the edge of the wall and reach up, resting my palm against the side of Jackson's thigh. His muscles are stone solid, like every cord and tendon is tensed to its maximum.

And then I feel it, a massive blast of power, his thoughts, his emotions, rolling from him like a giant tidal wave, crashing through the amphitheater at large, pushing into every living thing out there, telling everyone to freeze where they are.

For a second, it seems to work, the noise dying, all movement stopping.

I look over at Tyrone, watching as his expression shifts, eyes narrowing, head tilting.

Hope unfurls, only to be squashed like a bug.

The battle renews, louder, wilder. I can't tell who's firing, who's falling. It's anarchy. Kids run at the wall, clawing at the surface, trying to get out of the crush.

I whirl to Tyrone. "Did you hear him? Could you hear his thoughts?"

"I didn't exactly hear him, but I felt something. Like a nudge, a push, a feeling."

A feeling. A nudge.

"Make it stronger," I yell at Jackson. "You need to make them listen."

He nods, jaw tense, the muscles of his forearms so tight I can see every ridge and dip. I don't know if it's from pain or exhaustion. Part of me wants to pull him down from where he stands atop the wall, to tell him he doesn't need to do this. But he does. No matter what it costs him, he does. And he wouldn't step away from this even if I begged him, because that's who he is.

I lean over the wall and a boy's eyes lock with mine. My heart hammers as he reaches up to me, his face twisted with terror, his lips forming the words "Help me." On instinct, I reach down, reach for him, but he's so far away, like I'm on the roof of a three-story building and he's on the ground. He jams his fingers into one of the notches we used earlier when we climbed the wall, dragging himself up inch by agonizing inch. Three feet . . . four . . .

His eyes hold mine as the crush pulls him under and I lose sight of him, the crowd tearing him away.

Heart heavy, I straighten and turn back to Jackson. His fists clench. His whole body shakes. He tries to reach the crowd below us, another surge of thought and will pulsing from him. I can feel it, taste it. His command to *stop, just stop* echoes through me, reminiscent of the power of the Committee or the Drau.

Again, the surge freezes for a millisecond, as if everyone down there hears a whisper just beyond their reach. Then the clash resumes, screams and cries carrying up the amphitheater to the night-dark saucer overhead.

I catch sight of a blond head. Kendra. She's surrounded. Where are the kids she was protecting earlier? Safe? Dead?

I look around, sick, horrified. I'm trapped here on the wall, watching, able to do little.

Able to do nothing.

Even if I leap into the fray, what difference will I make?

In the pandemonium, tiny isolated battles erupt, kids firing on the Drau. The Drau firing back. Everyone caught in the crossfire.

The crowd surges to one side as a group of Drau streak through. It's as if they're a plow and the humans are snow, pushed out of their way. Below me a kid falls. Others swerve to try and avoid him. He skitters, crablike, to the side and somehow manages to get back on his feet.

Where's Lizzie? Where are her teammates? We could use some help here. All I can think is that the Committee is blocking them. Because I can't bear to think that the Committee's defeated them.

Below us, I see Kendra again, her bright curls a beacon drawing my eye. Then, directly behind her, I catch a glimpse of the kids she was protecting earlier. She still has them safe, but for how much longer?

With a strangled cry, Tyrone swings a leg over the wall, like he plans to try and climb down the way we came up. I grab his arm and when he turns his head toward me, I see my own torment mirrored on his face.

"You won't make it," I say.

"I have to try," he says. "Right now, while I still have her in my sights."

We stare at each other for a long moment, and then I slowly uncoil my fingers and Tyrone is gone, over the wall, climbing back down into the writhing crowd.

I turn a full circle, searching, searching . . . and then I see it, high, high above us. The floating shelf. The Committee. Looking down on the destruction. Enjoying the show.

My stomach churns. I grab Jackson's arm to get his attention and point. He follows my direction and his whole body tightens, like he's imagining springing up a hundred feet and landing there to face the Committee down, to tear them down, to make them pay.

It's like they're laughing at our efforts, Lizzie's and

ours, like they're saying, "You wanted the Drau and human teams together? Here you go. Enjoy."

"We have to stop this," I yell. "We have to stop them. This is a slaughter." It is.

Kids are falling beneath the Drau weapons, beneath human shots hitting the wrong targets, beneath the crush of bodies. They're dying. And the Drau are dying, too. I hear their screams as the black ooze swallows them whole, or maybe I feel their screams in my heart, in my soul.

Jackson rips off his glasses, and his eyes meet mine. "I need more power. I need to reach them."

Not just the humans. He wants to reach the Drau, too.

He stares at me, his expression tortured. "I need you, Miki. It's all I can think to do."

I know what he's asking. He needs me to trust him, to amp up his signal, to give him my energy to supplement his own. He almost reached them, almost made them listen. With my help . . .

An image forms clear and sharp in my mind: Lizzie, her eyes staring blank and sightless, her con red. He's showing me what he saw the day he killed her. He's showing me the risks.

He doesn't know if he'll be able to stop.

But if I don't help him, all is lost.

He holds his hand out to me. I take it and he pulls me up beside him on the wall, his eyes locked on mine.

He doesn't say it, not out loud or in my thoughts, but I know what he's asking. *Trust me. Trust me. Help me trust myself. I don't see another way.*

I hold his gaze. I feel the jolt of our connection, followed by pain, like my insides are being pulled out through my pupils. I've felt this before, the first time I ever looked in a Drau's eyes. I remember the agony. That memory consolidates with the reality of my right now, the agony ripping me apart.

It wasn't like this in Detroit when I shared my energy with Jackson to keep him alive. It wasn't painful, not like this. Agony wrenches my thoughts from any coherent track. All I know is pain. So much pain. And cold. I'm so cold.

I can't feel my feet, my hands. I can't feel my legs. They collapse from underneath me and I stay upright only thanks to Jackson's arm around my waist. I'm bent back in a bow, and he's hunched over me, like we're a couple on TV doing the tango. And I am fading away, weaker . . . weaker . . .

He jerks his gaze from mine.

The pain recedes.

"Did it work?" I croak.

He bows his head, shoulders slumped.

He failed. We failed.

I'm so weak I can't even turn my head to look. I don't need to. I can hear the screams of the wounded, the dying. I feel the terror hanging in the air like smoke and the gray fog of my depression oozing into my thoughts.

They're dying. They're all dying.

All of them.

MomSofuGramDadCarlyRichelleLuka

I didn't stop it.

I couldn't stop it.

In the end, everything's out of my control.

CHAPTER **THIRTY**

"YOU NEED TO TAKE MORE," I WHISPER, SOUNDLESS, THE words carrying from my thoughts to Jackson's.

"It will kill you."

"It won't. You won't."

Still he hesitates.

"It isn't just about me. You need to be strong enough to reach them. *We* need to reach them, make them stop fighting, make them listen. If we don't, we all die anyway."

"I—"

"Steer the nightmare, Jackson."

I stare into his eyes. Again, the connection jolts between us, like a rope connecting me to him, pulled taut. All I see are his eyes. His mercury eyes. Moving. Dancing. No . . . I'm the one moving. Shaking. Cold, so cold.

He takes my energy and uses it to boost his signal as he broadcasts his demand to *stop, just stop*. To remember what we told them.

I'm floating away. Almost gone.

I remember dreaming about Sofu. About Lizzie, running beside me.

Lizzie, with her green, green eyes. Lizzie, who the Drau saved because they saw the energy exchange between her and Jackson.

I think about that, my brain soft and fuzzy.

Exchange. Exchange.

The Drau can kill by sucking all our energy, leaving us a dried husk.

But they thought Lizzie was worth saving.

I'm missing something here. What am I missing?

Exchange. Two ways.

Give and take.

With a gasp, I focus on Jackson's eyes, his mercury eyes; they swirl with a million shades of gray, so beautiful. I don't fight, I don't struggle. I let energy flow from me to him and then I catch the tide as it ebbs, coming back to me.

Two ways.

My energy flows to him and his to me, and together we are so much stronger than either of us alone. We share and in sharing make it bigger, stronger, and this time when Jackson pulses his thoughts to the crowd, they go loud and wide.

Everything goes dead quiet.

He broadcasts images, thoughts, emotions outward. A powerful signal, like he's the electric guitar and I'm the amplifier, taking the signal in one form and putting it into another. Making it loud and clear enough for everyone to hear.

Drau and human alike see what he sees, know what he knows about the Committee, the battles, Lizzie, the plan.

And below us, they stop, just stop. No one moves. No one speaks.

I feel cold pins at the base of my skull, at my temples. The Committee, trying to get in. Not just into my head—into everyone's.

Together, Jackson and I will them away, will a barrier between the Committee's thoughts and ours, between their thoughts and those of everyone out there.

Slowly, Jackson straightens, pulling me upright with him, his eyes never leaving mine. The energy flows between us still, softer, gentler. And then the connection snaps.

I stare out at the crowd below and see Lien and Kendra and Tyrone. Tyrone scoops Kendra onto his shoulders so she can be seen above the crowd. With a yell, she lifts her weapon cylinder above her head. Eyes turn to her, heads swivel. She throws her weapon down and it clatters on the ground. Lien follows her lead, and then Tyrone.

For a long second, no one says a word. Then a boy next to Tyrone tosses down his weapon, and a girl next to him does the same, and then a girl next to her.

"We won," I say. We won this battle, this small battle in a massive war. Overcome with emotion, I close my eyes and let the enormity of what we've accomplished flow through me.

And when I open my eyes again, we're alone. *Almost* all alone. No humans. No Drau. No tiers of cloaked figures.

Just the Committee of three, floating on their suspended shelf, which sinks from high above until it's level with us. As one, their faces turn to us, and they are the faces of nightmares; what I see is impossible to process, impossible to describe. My brain can't understand what they are.

"We should not have created you. You are flawed. A mistake," they say, their voices raking talons along my nerves, but somehow, I can take it, somehow it doesn't break me, doesn't even bend me, and I realize it's because of Jackson, because of the energy we shared. He's always been able to tolerate this direct mind-to-mind communication better than me. That ability's been transferred now.

"Am I alone a mistake, or all your human progeny?" I ask, but in the back of my mind is what Lizzie told me, that the Committee is omniscient. Or did she say *almost* omniscient? There's a huge difference there. Because omniscient beings don't make mistakes.

Will they kill us now? Can they wipe out our existence with the wave of a hand?

"Where are they? All the kids who were here?" Jackson demands.

"You will tell us." Do I sense frustration in their words? Are they even capable of that emotion? "We did not remove them."

I blink, confused, and then I'm not. They want us to tell them where all those kids went, where the Drau went, because they don't know. They didn't send them off with a wave of their hands.

Lizzie, Jackson says straight into my thoughts.

She saved them. She got them out. And the Committee is anything but pleased.

I guess they are capable of some emotion, because in this moment I can feel their rage.

"You are to blame, Miki Jones. Without you, there would have been no destruction."

I'm not sure why they're singling me out, but that isn't the question that matters right now. "No destruction? What about all the lives you stole? For nothing more than entertainment. What about all the families who lost their children to your stupid game? And not just humans. Other species, all across the universe, for millennia. With your vast resources and knowledge, this is the best you can do? Pitting kids against each other in battles to the death while you watch and cheer?"

"There is honor in playing well. Dying well."

"There's honor in living well," Jackson grates out. "And

yeah, honor in dying well, if you're fighting for something that matters."

"You cannot stop us."

They don't say that as a challenge. They aren't rubbing it in. They're stating a fact. We can't stop them.

"We can try. We can fight," Jackson says. "There's honor in that."

"There is," Lizzie says, materializing beside us, a team of ten Drau with her.

I don't know if the Committee is capable of being startled, but I can definitely sense that they're thrown off by this development.

"You were terminated, Elizabeth Tate. You are out of order. You have no place in this dimension. Return from whence you came."

She shakes her head. "See, that's the thing about killing me off. It kind of negates any hold you have over me. And I may be dead in my world, my dimension, but not in others. We"—she looks at her team of Drau, standing sentinel at her back—"will stand against you. And you know the Drau have technological aptitude that will give you a run for your money."

If I were four, I'd take this opportunity to stick my tongue out, waggle my fingers against my nose, and say, "Nah-nah." But I'm not four, so I gloat silently instead.

A second of silence stretches uncomfortably long. "We have studied human emotion. You will wish your sibling to remain viable. This is a hold we maintain."

I gasp at the threat against Jackson. Lizzie squeezes my fingers but doesn't answer them.

The base of my skull prickles. My temples pound. The sensation of needles prodding at my brain sends shivers crawling down my spine. They're trying to get in, to steal my thoughts and put theirs inside my head. I draw on emotion, choosing hope, building a wall to keep them out, fighting, fighting. They're so strong.

Jackson cries out and clutches his abdomen. I scream as blood gushes between his fingers, hitting the floor in fat red drops. I leap for him, horrified, terrified, and he pulls his hands away, loops of his intestines tumbling out from a gash that splits him from ribs to pubic bone. He lifts his head and stares at me, and as I look at him, I see Jackson, from the corner of my eye, standing off to the side, screaming my name. I see his lips form words but can't hear a sound.

They're tricking me. Playing me. Trying to mess with my mind.

I blink and there's no blood. No intestines. Just Lizzie on one side of me, Jackson on the other, and a phalanx of Drau at our backs. I shut the Committee out and I didn't let depression in. Another victory.

"You have destroyed centuries of work in a millisecond," the Committee says. "We will begin anew."

The implicit threat in those words sickens me. Do they mean to terminate all the kids seeded with their DNA? To start again here on Earth? Or elsewhere? Some other galaxy, some other universe?

"We know how to counter your hold," Lizzie says. "We will fight you. We will win. As long as it takes. I'm not restricted to this dimension. I can move anywhere you move, go anywhere you go. We will follow you to every new version of the game you seed. We will fight you. And even if it takes millennia, we will win."

"You could build, but you choose to destroy," I say. "You could save entire galaxies, do wonderful things for species everywhere."

"We may not interfere. We may not influence the development of any sentient being. These are rules we put in place for the safety of all."

"That makes no sense. You alter our DNA. You create hybrid species. What do you call that if it isn't interfering?" I ask at the same time Lizzie says, "You can't interfere in a positive way, but you can kill kids in a game?"

"We do not kill. They kill. We watch. We are eternal. You are not."

"So you're saying we can't understand what it's like to be you?" Jackson asks. "Poor you, who lives forever."

"It is a difficulty." Clearly they can't understand sarcasm. "And you are mistaken, Elizabeth Tate. You said you will win, if it takes millennia. You do not have time of that nature. Only we, the Committee, are eternal."

"Yeah. Wrong. I do have millennia. I am the collective consciousness of Elizabeth Tate, neither alive nor dead."

Beside me, Jackson tenses at her words. Not that what she's saying is a surprise, but hearing it confirmed has to be tough on him. She's Lizzie, but not. I can't imagine how he feels about that. "I can't go back to my world, my real world, but I can go forward, and I intend to fight you every step of the way."

"You cannot go back, but you can go forward. An interesting point." The Committee fall silent, and that creeps me out. I feel like they're plotting, like what Lizzie said planted the seeds of an idea I know I'm not going to like. I think both she and Jackson are thinking along the same lines, because Lizzie takes my hand at the same time Jackson slides his arm around my waist.

"You cannot go back. But Miki Jones can. She was the catalyst that caused all to fail. We will remove her from the stream of events and all will be as it should be."

My skin tingles and colors grow too bright, sound too loud, the rasp of my own breathing like a saw grating in my brain. The pounding of my heart a jackhammer, dangerously loud, gouging chunks from my limbs, my lungs, my gut.

"Noooooooooo," Jackson yells, from far, far away.

He reaches for me, his face a mask of anguish, and my hazy thoughts coalesce until I understand what he's figured out. They're removing me from the stream of events. They're bending time and taking me out of the equation.

I think they're killing me.

"Jackson," I whisper, reaching for him, trying to

memorize the lines of his lips, the curve of his cheek, the hard angle of his jaw, willing him to remember me even as I don't see how that's possible. If they kill me before he loves me, how can he remember what he felt?

And then he's gone. All gone.

Everyone leaves. Even me.

CHAPTER THIRTY-ONE

I STAND AT THE EDGE OF THE FIELD BEHIND GLENBROOK HIGH, leaning against the chain-link fence that marks the edge of school property. Carly's stretched out on the grass under the giant oak, legs crossed at the ankles, her upper body resting on her bent elbow.

She looks at me and lifts her brows. For some reason, the sight of her makes me feel like sobbing.

"Did you see him?" Deepti asks.

"See who?" I ask, my tone abrupt.

"What bug crawled up your ass?" Dee asks as Carly sits up and says, "New guy."

A creepy sense of déjà vu shimmers and fades. I fall back a step, the links of the fence rattling as they take my weight. I'm barely aware of Kelley saying, "Incredibly hot new guy."

I stare at them, feeling sick. My head jerks up and I see a boy running laps on the track. Dark hair. Lean build. Luka.

My heart lifts.

He's alive. Safe.

Back then.

But is he safe now . . . I mean, months from now?

Why am I thinking this?

Because Luka died—will die—on the bridge.

I shiver and wrap my arms around myself, waiting, waiting . . . but I don't know for what.

For the boy to start talking inside my head.

I freeze, wondering if I've completely lost my grip on reality, if the depression that's weighed me down for two years has pushed me over some invisible edge.

JacksonRichelleLukaTyroneLienKendraDrauCommittee

I take a sharp breath and spin toward the road. The crossing guard's helping the kids across.

Janice Harper's little sister. She isn't there yet, but she will be.

"Lizzie," I whisper.

"What?" Kelley asks.

I just shake my head.

The Committee sent me back to the moments before I got pulled into the game the very first time, the moments before I ran into the road to save Janice's sister,

347

the moments before I got hit by the truck. They sent me back so I wouldn't enter the game, and if they never pull me, events will unfold differently. I won't save Jackson in Detroit. I won't communicate with his dead sister. I won't amp his power the day they face the Committee.

They sent me back to make Lizzie's coup fail.

But somehow, Lizzie worked it that I kept my memories. I remember it all. I know everything I gain and lose in the coming months. I know everything I learned through the game.

Somehow, Lizzie defied the Committee and left me all those memories so I could make a choice: to run out in the road in front of that truck. Or not.

My choice. I'm in control.

And Jackson, where is he? Not talking inside my head. And I think I know why. Because somehow, the Jackson who was there that day is the Jackson who knows how it all ends. He's not luring me into the game. He doesn't want me to choose to be part of it.

He doesn't know that Lizzie's helped me remember.

Does Richelle live if I never get pulled?

Do Dad and Carly get hit by that car if I never get pulled?

Do I run into the road no matter what, but in this reality die rather than get pulled into the game? I shudder, not liking any of these possibilities.

I whirl back to look at Luka, running on the track. Maybe there won't be a mission to the bridge if I'm never pulled. But if there is, does he survive it? Or does he die regardless of the choice I make here today?

Wait . . . It isn't today. It's dozens of yesterdays ago.

My friends are still talking, their words reaching me from far, far away. Aviator shades. Guns ought to be licensed. The conversation is painfully familiar. The tone of Dee's voice as she says, "Oh. My. Gawd." The way she claps her palms together.

Everything is exactly as it was.

Except me.

I close my eyes and wait for Jackson's voice inside my head. But it doesn't come. I check the path, the fields, the corners of the school, hoping to see him there, knowing I won't.

Everything's the same, but different.

Everything's—

I must make a sound, because Carly jumps to her feet and rushes over.

"Hey," she says, rubbing circles on my back. "Panic attack? You okay?"

I lift my head and stare at her eyes, her face, the little lines of concern etched between her brows. I throw my arms around her and hug her tight.

"I love you."

She shakes her head and hugs me back, and I can hear the confusion in her voice when she says, "I love you, too. Always have, always will."

Dee bounds to her feet and yells, "Group hug," then

she's tackling the both of us a second before Kelley tackles the three of us and we all fall over.

I remember the way I felt that day, how desperately I just wanted to be normal.

This is my chance. I could lie here on the ground, let the events unfold as they will. Luka will run for the street in a minute. He'll save Janice's sister. And if he can't make it in time, Jackson will. I know he's here somewhere, watching. Believing that the Committee sent me back with no memories of the game. Believing this is my chance to never be pulled at all.

He wants to give me this. To change events he regrets. But the thing is, it isn't his choice—it's mine.

I can choose to pretend it was all just a nightmare. I can choose to pick up my life where it got interrupted, to be part of the world without the gray fog haunting me or the game tearing me up inside. Maybe in time, I'll start to believe it was all just an ugly dream. Maybe in time I'll be able to convince myself of that.

Will there be a Jackson in this world if I choose not to run into the road? Will I meet him in the cafeteria? In the gym? On the track?

The sun's warm on my face. My friends roll away and sit up and start chattering again, about classes and what to wear to the Halloween dance.

I could chime in.

The lure is overwhelming.

The Committee doesn't want me back in the stream,

but they don't control everything. I don't believe they control the vagaries of fate that put Janice's sister in the path of the truck that day. They can only use events to their advantage.

I push to my feet and smile as my friends talk. I look at Dee and Kelley, thinking how awesome they are. I look at Carly, memorizing the streak in her hair, the sound of her voice, the way she laughs.

Then I turn and run for the little girl hunkered down in the road, directly in the path of the oncoming truck.

I respawn in a place I've been before, white walls, white floor, so bright it burns. After a minute, a dark rectangle appears. I walk through to a curving hallway, more white on white. The air's cold and dry and smells stale, with a hint of air freshener.

Right or left?

I think it doesn't matter. I think whichever way I choose I'll end up exactly where I'm supposed to be. I choose left, following the curve of the corridor until just ahead I see a massive arced bank of what appear to be computers. There's a person there with her hands on the control panel. She's dressed all in white, her back to me, her hair pulled into a high ponytail.

She twists at the waist and turns her head to look over her shoulder. She smiles and says, "There you are."

"Where else would I be?" I ask, smiling back at her.

Strong arms close around me from behind. I close my

eyes and rest my head back against Jackson's shoulder.

"I wanted you to make a different choice," he says. "I wanted you safe."

"What makes you think you get a say?"

"I don't. I know that. And the truth is, the girl I love wouldn't have made any other decision."

"So what now?" I ask. "The game's over, right? At least, human involvement's done."

"It is," Lizzie agrees. "It would take too much effort for the Committee to have to rebuild what we broke. And I'm guessing they might be thinking that human soldiers are too unpredictable, irascible—"

"Uncontrollable," Jackson interjects.

"And cocky," I add. I look at Lizzie. "What happened to all the kids who were in the amphitheater? And the Drau who were there? You said that once we're in the game, we can never go back, not fully? So where are they?"

"Some have joined us," she says. "And some are"—she pauses, like she's searching for the right words—"I guess you could say they're sort of in an in-between place while my team works on a way to send them back. We thought it wasn't possible, but the Committee sent you back, which means it is possible. We just have to figure out how."

I nod. "What do you mean by 'joined us'?"

"There are other places where the game's only beginning and we"—she gestures and I look around to see a group of Drau come along the corridor, and . . . Tyrone . . . Lien . . . Kendra—"we are the ones to follow the Committee wherever they go, to find a way to stop them, permanently."

Jackson holds out a kendo sword like no other I've seen. The blade glows bright white. So white it burns. "Welcome to the rebellion," he says. "Gear up."

EPILOGUE

DAD DROPS ME AT THE HOSPITAL. HE'S DOING BETTER, SO much better. He decided that AA just might be good for him after all, and he goes a couple of times a week. He's been out of the hospital and sober now for just over four weeks. No more bottles on the table or the counter. No more watching him cut himself off from all the things he used to like to do. He even went to his fly-tying group.

"See you later," he says. I lean over and hug him, careful of his ribs. They're still sore if I squeeze him too tight.

I hop out and head for the elevators, then Carly's room. I come see her every day. Weeks ago, they stopped giving her the meds that were keeping her in a coma, but she hasn't woken up. Not yet.

"Hey," I say, dragging the chair closer to her bed. She

doesn't answer. She never answers. But she knows I'm here. She can hear me. I open my chem textbook and start reading out loud. When she comes back to school, I don't want her to be too far behind.

About an hour later, there's a commotion in the hall, someone laughing. I stand up and go to the door to find Carly's mom and dad walking toward me, arm in arm, heads together. Carly's mom's smiling. Laughing. Walking like she's floating on a cloud.

She looks up and sees me standing there and rushes over to envelop me in a hug.

"What is it?" I ask, my heart speeding up.

"Kristin Beck," Carly's mom says.

It takes me a second to catch up, to remember who she's talking about. Then it clicks. Kristin's the girl who was in neuro-ICU when Carly first got hurt. She was in a car accident two weeks before Carly. She's been in a coma ever since, just like Carly.

"She woke up," Mrs. Conner says, her smile a mile wide. "This morning. She asked for ice cream and the book she was reading for English class. She remembers that, but she doesn't remember anything about her accident." She squeezes my arm. "She's going to be okay."

The way she says it, I can tell she isn't just talking about Kristin. She's talking about Carly.

Kristin woke up. After so many weeks. She's going to be okay.

So Carly could be okay. *Will* be okay.

"And," Mrs. Conner continues, her eyes sparkling like she's saved the best for last, "Carly opened her eyes this morning and turned her head toward me when I said her name."

I gasp and press my fingers to my lips. I've done a ton of reading about comas; visual tracking's a major sign of improvement. I throw myself at Carly's mom and we hold each other, hope shining like the hottest sun.

When I get off the elevators a while later, I just stop for a second and take in the view. There's a boy leaning against the far wall, legs crossed at the ankles, arms folded across his chest. Honey gold hair frames his face in messy waves. His eyes are covered by black-on-black Oakleys and his smile's dark and sexy and cocky, and just for me.

I haven't seen him since our last mission, when Lizzie pulled us to the white room for our latest strategy meeting, which was about three minutes or three hours or three years ago. The time-shift thing fighting as one of Lizzie's rebels is just as freaky as it was when I was fighting as a soldier for the Committee.

But whether I see Jackson in this world or the other, whether we're fighting back to back or sitting side by side in the caf at school surrounded by our friends, I trust that he has my back as I have his, that he won't leave, and that together, we're steering this adventure that is our lives.

"Ready?" he asks, snagging my backpack off my shoulder and slinging it over his. "Pizza for dinner?"

I cut him a glance through my lashes. "If we load it with veggies."

He laughs and leans in to kiss me, his lips warm and firm and wonderful. Then he hooks his arm through mine and together we walk out the doors into the cold night.

So what's the game now?

No game.

This is my life.

ACKNOWLEDGMENTS

A BOOK'S JOURNEY FROM THE TINY SPARK OF AN IDEA IN THE writer's mind to the finished product cradled in the reader's hands is long and, at times, tortuous. I've made this journey many times, through rewrites and revisions, tight deadlines and turnarounds, days where the words flow like water and days where they ooze onto the page like a sloth, and I have been lucky to have a group of wonderful people holding my hand every step of the way.

Thank you, Robin Rue (for having my back and loving my work, for talking me down from the ledge and telling it to me straight), Beth Miller (for being all-around awesome), and the amazing team at Writers House.

Thank you, Maria Barbo, for stepping in and taking the editorial reins for the final book in the trilogy, for being excited about this story, and for being a pleasure to work with. And thank you to the team at Katherine Tegen Books, who work hard on my behalf.

Thank you to the usual suspects: Nancy Frost, Michelle Rowen/Morgan Rhodes, Ann Christopher, Kristi Cook, Lori Devoti, Laura Drewry, Caroline Linden, and Sally MacKenzie. We started this journey together and I am so grateful to have you as my traveling companions along the way.

Special shout-out to my beta reader, Elly Takaki, for asking a ton of questions and watching out for loose ends.

Thank you to my family and friends who have been so incredibly supportive and excited about each book I have written.

To Henning, Sheridan, and Dylan, who have supported me every step forward and every three steps back, who sit patiently while I read the same chapter aloud to them again and again, who cheer the small victories and cheer me up through the setbacks. I love you beyond words, beyond dreams, beyond the infinite stars.

And a special, supersized thank-you to my readers, for opening the door and inviting my stories in. This book, all my books, are for you.